Happy Birthday and All That

BY THE SAME AUTHOR

The Bluebird Café

Happy Birthday and All That

REBECCA SMITH

BLOOMSBURY

First published in Great Britain 2003

Copyright © 2003 by Rebecca Smith

The moral right of the author has been asserted

Bloomsbury Publishing Plc,
38 Soho Square, London W1D 3HB

A CIP catalogue record for this book is
available from the British Library

ISBN 0 7475 6566 X

10 9 8 7 6 5 4 3 2 1

Typeset by Hewer Text Ltd, Edinburgh
Printed in Great Britain by Clays Ltd, St Ives plc

To Sarah and Cecily

ACKNOWLEDGEMENTS

I am very grateful to Southern and South East Arts and The K Blundell Trust for their assistance.

I would also like to thank Alexandra Pringle, Sarah Lutyens, Victoria Millar Chiki Sarkar and Susannah Godman.

Thanks also to Matthew Smith who inadvertently gave me the title.

AUGUST

HERE WAS FRANK WITH a trolley that was empty but for Tom and the flowers that James had said he wanted to buy for Mummy, and there was Melody, standing on a podium next to the Take-Away-Style Curry counter. She was looking pretty cute in her green uniform and some inappropriate shoes. Every so often she interrupted the music to tell people about special offers. Frank hadn't realised that it was a Superstore Party Nite.

'There'll be 30 per cent off for the next twenty customers at the pizza counter . . . and 20 per cent off all purchases of savoury bakery items tonight . . . And now a spot prize for safe trolley steering. My manager, Mike, is touring the store right now with a big box of Celebrations for someone with a wheely fantastic way with their trolley!' Melody told the chilled air.

'Go away Frank' she hissed away from the microphone. He took the bunch of flowers and poked her leg. James and Tom laughed.

'Piss off, Frank!' she said, perilously close to the microphone. 'And now a prize,' (she kicked at him with her spiky toes) 'for our oldest and youngest customers. If you think that might be you then come on up to the stage by the curries. We're looking for our oldest and youngest in store right now . . . piss off, Frank.'

He was standing in front of her in mock-adoration, now strewing the stage with chrysanthemums. They'd been on special offer. The music started again.

'Look. I'm going to the toilet until you're gone. Now piss off or the manager's going to be on to me.' She jumped neatly off the stage and disappeared through a 'Staff Only' door.

Those who fancied themselves the oldest customers were making their slow way towards the empty stand. People with babies just days old were starting to queue. Free nappies might be on offer. Frank picked up the microphone just as Melody reappeared.

'Get down! I'll lose my job!' she laughed.

'And our next prize,' Frank said, 'is for the couple who most resemble each other. Matching trainers? Similar girths? Same tattoes and haircuts? Get up here. We've a year's free shopping to give away!'

'Frank!'

'Get down Dad!'

'What else are we looking for?' he continued, 'We've got prizes in these categories: most obnoxious toddler, heaviest and lightest pensioner, most ridiculous hairstyle – but our star prize of a lifetime's supply of frozen food will go to the person who, in the judge's opinion, least needs the contents of their trolley! So get yourselves up here.'

Melody's manager was back. He seized the mike and two security guards got Frank in an armlock and marched him out of the store. James, close to tears, pushed Tom in the empty trolley behind them.

'Looks like we're going to Tesco's, kids' Frank said. 'We can get Mum some nicer flowers and have chips in the café. What do you think?'

'I saw Mrs Fleance in there, and another teacher watching you,' said James.

'It was just a joke,' said Frank 'Mum will never know.'

* * *

Mum was at home, sorting out the washing.

Her name was Posy, unfortunate but true. She had spent her life failing to live up to her namesake, Posy Fossil in *Ballet Shoes*. She tried her best, and wore scoop-necked T-shirts that were described as 'ballerina-style' in catalogues, swirly skirts, flat shoes, and now there was even a fashion for wrap-around tops, just like the pink ones her aunts had knitted for her. She'd given up ballet at twelve, concentrated on jazz dance and then nothing. Not dancing anyway.

Posy had tried to give her own children (at least the boys) more sensible names. She had James, Poppy, Tom and Isobel, but then their surname was Parouselli.

Parouselli. The name had seemed like a present. She heard carousel music, and saw candy canes and pink and yellow parasols. The merry-go-round ponies whinnied for joy at it; they pawed the ground and leapt up and down their poles. Dick van Dyke did a little dance. She had tried it out – Posy Parouselli – before she'd even met its owner. She'd been like her thirteen-year-old self, trying out her name with that of whichever boy she currently liked. Perhaps it was the name she'd fallen for. She saw it on lists for lectures and tutorials. Frank Parouselli. She was smitten.

What a disappointment it would have been if Frank hadn't been like himself: tall and dark with eyes the colour of a Cornish summer sky, the blue you see in August when you are swimming far out from the shore, and look back to where the sky meets the gorse-covered, pineapple-scented cliffs. Frank Parouselli. It was lounging in a stripy deckchair, licking an ice cream, reading something funny. Ah, first impressions.

Frank played stand-up bass. His band 'The Wild Years' were slowly greying and balding. The New Year's Eve gig seemed to come round more and more often. The twice-weekly practice sessions had become a weekly night down the pub with Melody, the pretty 22-year-old who sometimes sang with them. They still had their spot at The Oak Tree and a number of other regular gigs too.

Frank had sold his motorbike. The Parousellis had a green Volvo estate.

'It's a prep school car,' the man at Ringwood Motors had told Posy, and she'd smiled; as if they'd ever be able to afford prep school. She entertained vague and silent hopes that the children might win scholarships, perhaps the boys might even go to Winchester College where their grandfather had been, but only as day boys of course.

'Better drowned than duffers. If not duffers, won't drown.' Frank said, quoting the absent father in *Swallows and Amazons*, which James was ploughing through. Frank didn't believe in private education, and nor did Posy, apart from for her own children.

Frank knew that he was more or less the man in that Talking Heads song 'Once in A Lifetime'. He and Posy had loved it when they were students, but now here he was waking up every day thinking 'Well, how did I get here?'

He was almost that man, but not quite. He loved Posy, he loved the children. It was all the trappings he could do without; the Jolly Good School, the importance of Start-rite shoes at thirty-seven quid a go (and he was going round in holey old deck shoes, not that he cared, or damp beige desert boots, £12.99 from Portswood Shoefayre.) He hated the chit-chat in the playground that was oxygen to Posy, all the committees that she was on.

'I don't know why you bother. Why don't you all just decree that every family has to give £50 a year instead of all this endless fundraising? Think of the time and effort you'd all save! Or just let somebody else do it.'

'But what if everyone thought that? There'd be no pre-schools if nobody volunteered. I feel compelled . . .'

So she spent long evenings at the Chair's house making things out of saltdough, and stuffing felt Teletubbies and

Tweenies for the St Peter's Pre-School Autumn Fayre.

The only time Frank felt like himself now was when he was playing; but even with The Wild Years he sometimes felt out of it. He was the only one who was married. Al was divorced, with one child, Finn, whom he didn't see often enough; Rich and Ron were still single. They drove from pub to pub in Rich's van, which was really the band's as they'd all put £300 in for it. They hung out in student pubs and looked at girls. When Frank went out with them he felt about eighty-years old.

Posy folded the clean towels and jammed them into the airing cupboard. The slumbering volcano of quilts and blankets and swimming towels looked so inviting that she was tempted to throw herself in, to find oblivion in James's leaping dolphins duvet cover. She must pull herself together, wake herself up, hit the Diet Coke. She didn't have long before they'd be back from the supermarket, and Isobel might wake up at any moment.

There were many things that Posy wasn't allowed to do. These included being depressed. If ever Frank noticed her being sad or melancholy or miserable (it had to be quite extreme for him to notice, and involve audible sobbing) he would say things like:

'Everyone feels like that Pose, you've just got to carry on,' or,

'But don't you think that depression is the ultimate self-indulgence?'

It was a different matter if Frank was depressed. His depressions were existential crises, intellectual matters. They'd last for weeks, usually around Christmas and New Year, or family holidays, the arrival of their babies, or other people's birthdays. They involved him getting very drunk each night and watching action thrillers, aeroplane hostage movies, and made-for-TV dramas on Channel 5. The next day his breath was such that Posy declined any offers he made to do the morning school run. He would usually not be up in time anyway, having fallen asleep on the sofa, then woken up to find something else unmissable: 'The Properties of Rope' on the BBC Learning Zone, something like that. He would tell Posy all about it. It was lucky his work never involved early starts.

That was the clean stuff put away. Now for the hip-high heaps of the dirty. She knelt on the landing and started to sort it into colours.

Those whom the gods wish to damn they first call promising. Frank Parouselli, BA Hons (First Class) English Literature, was a BettaKleen distributor. This was one of the day jobs that he couldn't give up. Posy kept her eyes down as she worked so as to not see into the spare room with its stacks of the BettaKleen catalogues (most of the customers and the other distributors called them 'books') and the array of products awaiting delivery. Frank had to make up the orders, sorting the microwave cooksets, the sink tidies, the plate stackers, the ceramic teddy scouring-pad holders, the swing-bin fresheners, into the mean little bags that the company supplied. Frank was amazed that anyone could want any of it.

'Hey!' he nearly told his customers, 'Don't buy it. Won't it just highlight the emptiness of your life, the futility of your existence? A viscose carrier-bag dispenser with cheeky chick motif won't bring you happiness. Whatever need it is you are trying to meet, whatever void in your life you are trying to fill, the tartan trollymate isn't the answer.'

'I am a Pedlar of Pointlessness,' he would tell people at dinner parties who asked what he did.

'He's really a musician,' Posy would quickly add. They found that they were rarely invited back. Frank so often seemed to do something that Posy thought was inappropriate. There had been the time when he had eaten a huge platter of cherries that Posy said had been clearly for decorative purposes only. Not only had he wolfed down handfuls of them, implying that the huge five-course dinner he'd just eaten wasn't enough, he'd put the stones back in the bowl.

'You must have realised that they weren't intended for consumption. There would have been a small empty bowl for the stones if anyone was meant to eat them,' Posy told him later. She was also mortified because she thought that he had been much drunker than everyone else, sitting there like a grinning gnome, laughing when nobody else did.

'Cherries for display purposes. So they live in a department store window. That's obscene, 'Frank replied, and left for his shed at the bottom of their garden where he went to smoke and practise.

Posy didn't allow smoking in the house, so Frank was always walking out on the family, leaving for his shed. Posy insisted on it, but it made her feel as though he always had somewhere better to go, and that she was being dumped in the kitchen like someone boring at a party.

Posy's kitchen was sunny and yellow with a long farmhouse table where the children did painting. It was the kitchen she'd always wanted. She found herself smiling as she wiped crumbs and jam from the oilcloth.

She and Frank had been together for years now. They'd first shared the upstairs of a Victorian house with a turret and slates and a pointy roof that made Frank think of the Dragonmobile in Whacky Races. The weekend that Posy found out that she was pregnant was the week end after her father had died of liver failure. Her mother had died two years earlier of cancer, caused, Posy and her sister Flora were certain, by years of walking around with internally clenched fists, years of biting her lip and swallowing her feelings and anger in case she invoked the wrath of their father. Posy and Flora were left the Surrey Tudorbethan house they so hated. They sold it, and at twenty-five Posy had tens of thousands of pounds. She was glad that her father hadn't known about her baby. She was planning to break the cycle, to be with someone not like Daddy. She married Frank.

Frank advocated throwing Posy's inheritance in the river, or giving it anonymously to a centre for alcoholics or the homeless or battered women. Posy thought he was probably right. She had hated that house. Every room had held some horrible tableau. The dining room was probably the worst, all the farcical family dinners, and the time he'd smashed their Easter eggs. Biff, biff, biff, His slow hand like a cartoon fist. He'd been jealous of the pretty eggs, even though he'd said he didn't want one, that he hated chocolate.

'Bloody great idea for a religion' he'd growled. 'Glorification of a Roman torture method!'

The real reason was that he felt excluded from something the 'girls' had. They'd watched open-mouthed, three empty eggshapes, and then Flora and Posy had fled to their friends round the corner, leaving their mother to face the music, again. The friends had been out, on the sort of Easter Sunday walk on Tadworth Common that other people's families went on. They'd walked down to the garage and bought each other and their mother the only eggs left. Caramac.

Posy decided to buy the biggest, most beautiful house she could afford. It was Edwardian with five bedrooms, sash windows, fireplaces and stained glass, and overlooked Southampton Common. She had fallen in love before she'd even crossed the doormat. The hall had black and white tiles. There were so many rooms that she and Frank joked that they could spend the whole day there and never meet. They could sleep in different postcodes. There was a lot to be done, but she thought that they would slowly do it all.

When Posy chose her house she had no idea about the wildlife that would come with it. There were foxes and badgers and squirrels on The Common across the road from them, a hedgehog in their garden. A grey squirrel liked to sit on their fence and eat from Plested Pie bags and Ginsters pasty wrappers. Their garden was visited by woodpeckers and wood pigeons, chaffinches, treecreepers, wagtails, goldfinches and bullfinches. She wondered if it was the proximity to The Common that gave them such huge spiders, spiders whose steps across the ceiling at night were audible, spiders that terrified Poppy.

Until she had her house Posy hadn't known that slugs came so big, or in such an array of colours: horrible oranges, deathly greys and colourless ones like creatures from the deepest, coldest oceans. Perhaps that came from living under the Parousellis' bath and in the cupboard under their sink. She never knew when she was going to come across some fresh horror. And having children made it much worse. Today there had been a curled-up, dessicated caterpillar in James's pocket. School-trouser fluff had clogged its little boots. She had taken it into the garden and tried to revive it in a puddle. She left it beside some tasty-looking leaves. When she checked later it had disappeared, but she feared the worst. She decided that she would have to talk to James about it, explain that caterpillars had a right to freedom. He would probably cry, even though she'd tell him that it had probably survived and crawled away. Oh remorse, remorse.

There was ivy growing on the front of the house. Posy chopped it back and tried to drag it down when it managed to penetrate the windows. It forced its way in overnight, coming through the gaps between the upper and lower casements. If ever they went away, Posy imagined that it would have taken over the house by the time they came back. They'd return to find it sleeping in their bed; it would finish the jam and let dirty mugs pile up in the sink.

The house had leaks and missing tiles, and rattling, rotting windows. The outlines of the floorboards were visible through some of the carpets.

'Don't pay someone to do it. I'll fix it,' Frank said for the first few years, but he never did. Eventually all the money was gone, and paying someone was no longer a possibility. Posy looked longingly at the ads for builders and roofers and handymen in the back of the *Advertiser*. She knew that there was an underground stream nearby. She thought that it was flowing away with her chi, as well as causing the damp stripes along the walls. Frank had no time for any of it.

'Hey! I thought I married a Bohemian, someone with values, so why are you always spluttering about guttering? Did you ever see a house fall down? Well, did you?' he asked.

'Re-pointing is necessary!' Posy said. 'I keep having bad dreams about falling through rotten floorboards. Other people's windows aren't like this.'

'Oh Pose, you don't want to fall for any of that replacement windows crap. It's all a scam. A capitalist plot.'

'I didn't say *replacement* windows. Perhaps when Isobel's a bit older I could do some of them myself.' Perhaps she would sit happily in her pram whilst Posy rubbed down, filled and re-painted some of the windows.

'Why don't you get Flora to sort the windows out for you?'

'Because we haven't got any money.'

Flora was the ideal person to solve the Parouselli's damp and window problems, to re-point everything. She was the proprietor of 'Perfect Solutions', a company dedicated to sorting things out. 'If it's legal we'll do it!' the leaflet boasted. Flora organised parties, anniversary celebrations, sometimes whole weddings. She cleared out cupboards, streamlined houses (feng shui an optional extra), imposed filing systems, hired and fired cleaners and gardeners, obtained quotes and engaged plumbers, builders, roofers and handypeople of all descriptions. She easily tackled the simpler repairs herself. She did other people's Christmas shopping. The floor plan of John Lewis was behind her eyes like a circuit board. Her clients received complimentary Christmas presents fro Perfect Solutions: L'Occitane lavender bath milk for the women, a delicious-smelling, soothing shaving gel for the men. Perfect Solutions knew how busy and stressed they were, that they needed a treat. Flora had even written people's thank-you letters for them. She assembled self-assembly furniture. The coming of Ikea to Southampton would see her profits soar.

Flora managed all of this without ever getting her cuffs dirty. She always wore very clean, very crisp, linen shirts, often with matching trousers that gave her a stern Maoist look and impressed her clients.

Even as a child Flora had been unnaturally neat. As an eight-year-old she had chided Posy for not closing cupboards or shutting her drawers properly. On the last day of each term she'd look as neat and shiny as on the first. Her possessions endured forever. At thirty-six she still had a mauve-plastic folding brush and comb set that she'd bought at Superdrug when she was fourteen. She had the world's tidiest make-up bag (no clogged mascara, or stubby lipsticks, or damp, cracked compact). Her bars of soap stayed immaculate even to the last sliver. The only thing that threatened to slip out of her control was her bright yellow hair, which was curly and tended towards the frizzy. It had to be restrained in a very tight plait. Posy's hair was similar, but she let it do what it wanted, and it made a wild brown halo around her face.

It had been seeing Posy struggle at Christmas when James and Poppy were small that gave Flora the idea for Perfect Solutions.

'I hate Christmas. It's a route-march of consumerism with slave labour by women!' Posy had raged just out of earshot of her children. 'I was up till midnight making a sheep's outfit, and tonight I've got to make a page's outfit. And tomorrow night I'll have to do all the cards. I have to home-make everything because you can't buy any Christmas food that won't possibly contain traces of nuts. And then James will probably reject it all anyway, and just want soft-scoop rasp-berry-ripple ice cream instead.'

'Make Frank do more then,' Flora said.

'Oh he's hopeless. He acts as though all the present-buying and wrapping, and cards and shopping and decorations were some folly of mine, some private hobby that he shouldn't interfere with. And nobody except you will get me any good presents, even though I'll have spent hundreds of hours on everybody else. What I really need is a wife.'

Posy wanted someone kind and unflappable, a sort of human Renault Espace. Someone who would remember to buy kitchen roll, who would empty the bin without being asked, who would always have plasters and antiseptic wipes in her bag. Someone with a smooth, gentle face, and soft, strong arms.

'I need someone like you full-time,' she told Flora. She wasn't really thinking of Flora. She was thinking of her friend Kate. She had once dreamt that she'd been browsing the stalls at the Pre-School Christmas Fayre hand-in-hand with Kate. They knew how many jelly beans there were in the jar, and had correctly guessed the weight of the cake. They had watched the clown show together. The children were off, safely engaged elsewhere.

The reality was that Kate would be running the raffle and Posy would be doing one of the less popular stalls; shelling-out endless 20ps, whilst trying to restrain (at least a little bit) James and Poppy's acquisitiveness and passion for gambling on the Beany Baby tombola. Her youngest would be thrashing in her arms, desperate to be crawling around on the hall's dirty floor, to get under the stalls and to be scalded by cups of tea.

The grass on the Common was studded with cigarette butts and turning to yellow dust, but the Parousellis still went there nearly every day. They hadn't been away this year. (Izzie was too young for a holiday to be a holiday.)

Oh August, low season for fêtes, bazaars and jumbles. Posy was getting withdrawal symptoms. Her love of them was genetic. Her mother had always been on their school's P.T.A., and would do the book stall or the white elephant – something that didn't require her to make anything. Aunt Is was a queen of fêtes. Every weekend there seemed to be one. Her friend Beatrice (known to the girls as Aunt Bea) made felt animals, and they donated honey for sale. If they weren't manning a stall, then they would take their young visitors to somebody else's Open Garden or at the very least to the W.I. market far a haul of Jam and Cakes.

'Tuck in! Tuck in, girls!' they'd say; words to gladden any heart.

The girls often stayed with Aunt Is in the holidays. The time dragged. Aunt Is lived in St Cross, in a house overlooking the Water meadows. Sometimes the girls would walk along Kingsgate Road and into Winchester. If they were by them-selves they could go into Bluebells, their favourite shop, and buy the sort of things that their aunt thought utterly pointless – smelly rubbers, magnetic cats, mini dried – flower paper-weights, Flower Fairy notebooks and pens – and they thought necessary to their happiness.

'Utter junk,' Aunt Is said. 'Lot of nonsense, no use to anyone.' These opinious didn't stop her from decamping to Cornwall to help Aunt Bea run The North Cornwall Bee Centre with its own gift shop and café, just a few years later.

Posy and Flora tried to make the walks as long as they could, visiting any museum that was free, looking in the charity shops, stopping to listen to any busker or street entertainer who didn't look liable to involve them or embarass them. They patted the bronze boar near the Courts, they browsed (pointless! pointless!) the Tourist Information Bu-reau. They would even look at whatever exhibition the Guildhall was sporting: The Guild of Embroiderers, Rotary

Regalia . . . The citizens of Winchester seemed oblivious to the prison looking on the hill, and went about their Hunter-booted business as though it wasn't there, about to slide down on a lava flow and engulf them all. Flora and Posy sat on the steps of The Buttercross and drank Coke. They sat on benches in the Cathedral Close and read and read. Sometimes there was a film crew working on an adaptation. They hoped that they might be spotted.

'We'd be great as Elizabeth and Jane Bennet,' Flora said, even though Posy hadn't done *Pride and Prejudice* yet, and was doomed to get *Mansfield Park* for O'level. 'But I bet we'd end up as Mary and Kitty.'

Aunt Is always took them on a tour of the Cathedral. She was an official guide and on duty at least twice a month. The highpoint of their visit would be a trip to the Theatre Royal where they would eat ice cream in the interval and never, ever, go to the bar.

Much of the time was spent taking the dogs to the Water meadows. They liked to walk past a house where a parrot called Persephone lived. The girls stopped and peered. Persephone's owner waved, but never invited them in.

Aunt Is knew every dog that they met. Flora and Posy were introduced. There were long conversations about swans. If they went by themselves one of the dogs always ran away, meaning the girls yelled and searched and worried, and finally trailed the useless lead home to find that the dog had beaten them there, and was tucking in to a dinner of biscuits mixed with raw cabbage and carrot and pilchards.

'Demon Hound!' Aunt Is barked, handing round pieces of crumbly fudge, that might have been toffee or perhaps Kendal Mint Cake. Often Posy and Flora couldn't imagine how the time until the next meal could possibly be filled. Fortunately there were many meals each day, most of them involving jam. There was a whole cupboard devoted to it.

Every summer Flora rearranged the jars, putting the newest at the back, and explained the system to Aunt Is who laughed and said 'Thank you, Flora.' But still five-year-old jars rubbed shoulders on the table with the only just bought. The Aunts spooned the green layers off the top ('Penicillin. Can only do you good.') Posy chose honey, mostly because she had a crush on Rupert Brooke. Aunt Is had a 1915 edition of '1914'. Posy propped it up on the bedside table so that she could look at it as she fell asleep.

Aunt Is reserved some special recipes for her vegetarian nieces. The things the girls most dreaded were Cheesy Rice (a blackened pyrex dish of rice poached in milk with strings of melted cheese and chunks of boiled celery, cut to resemble caterpillars), and on their last day, High Tea. Posy, of course, always pictured them sitting on wooden thrones, a version of the Mad Hatter's Tea Party. The reality was cold discs of very soft carrot, and hardly cooked shop-bought quiche. Aunt Is considered a whole one each appropriate.

'Mushroom for you, Flora? Posy? Leek and broccoli? I remembered that those were your favourites last time.'

'Mmm. Yes please,' they would say politely. She heaped cauliflower onto their plates.

'Tuck in! You've a long journey.' And then there would be delicious cakes and meringues from the W. I. and strawberries and plums or gooseberry fool. Mummy collected them (Aunt Is was her aunt really) and drove them home over the Hog's Back.

Fifteen years later when Aunt Is moved to Cornwall, Flora decided to buy her house. Flora's inheritance had been prudently invested, and was sitting there, a big fatty lump, force-fed corn. She had the house valued and paid her Aunt the asking price.

'It will all come back to the two of you eventually,' Aunt Is said.

It was lucky that Aunt Is took almost everything with her: nothing could have survived Flora's plans for the perfectly stream-lined, beautiful home. The old mangle and some enamel basins planted with Californian poppies that were left sitting by the back-door step were sent to live at Posy's.

SEPTEMBER

WHEN JAMES PAROUSELLI gave his teacher the note, she expected it to be about 'The Asda Incident' as she'd come to think of it. But it wasn't. Mrs Parouselli seemed unaware that her husband was deranged.

'Dear Mrs Fleance,' (Posy had written in her neatest writing.)

'You might think that I am this flaky kind of person, but I am not. You have the wrong idea of me. I am very organised really. Very together.

James's lack of plimsolls is really a sign of how organised I am. His feet, as you probably have noticed, are so narrow and so flat that I have to get special Start-rite plimsolls with velcro flaps, not just elastic, and even then he requires special insoles or they would still fall off. These have had to be ordered by Frenches' and take two weeks to come. I did order them well in advance of the new term, only to find that his feet had grown one and a half sizes in a fortnight. He's gone from 11 ½ to 1. And they were professionally measured beforehand. Incidentally these plimsolls cost £12.40 with the insoles as extra, not £2.50 as the Ladybird ones do, and we have tried Clarks ones too. They never fit.

Anyway, what I wanted to say is please excuse James's lack of plimsolls. It isn't his fault, and it isn't really mine. I am a standard solid Mum, even though my children's feet are not of standard width. Not flaky or unreliable.

Yours sincerely,

Posy Parouselli.'

'Flaky? Flaky?' Mrs Fleance thought of the cream crackers, and the cheese straws and the Cornish wafers that James Parouselli brought in for snack time. He did always seem to be the child with the most crumbs down his front, to come in after lunch with the biggest blobs of yoghurt on his sweatshirt.

Flaky. Was Mrs. Parouselli flaky? She remembered the home-school visit she'd made to them just before James had started in Reception. She *had* noticed that the windows were in need of attention, the paint peeling, dry and damp wood exposed. Or perhaps she meant chocolate flakey. Mrs Parouselli could certainly once have looked like a Flake advert girl, that poppy field one, but not any more. She imagined all the Parousellis on The Common opposite their house, eating double 99s.

How should she respond?

'There's a lot worse than being flaky,' she felt like saying. At least Mrs Parouselli wasn't one of those pushy critical parents, always on about the reading scheme, and trying to prise other people's children's baseline assessment scores out of her. She marked the letter to go in James's file, and gave Mrs Parouselli a special smile at hometime.

When she opened the door a dinosaur fell on her head, then a tunnel, and then a bucket of Popoids.

'This cupboard!' said Posy, trying to sound jolly, not tearful, annoyed, murderous or despairing, even though there was nobody there to hear her scream.

'This cupboard is driving me mad!' It merited its own item on the agenda at every St Peter's Pre-school and Toddler group meeting. Each group blamed the group who'd been in the hall the day before them, and everybody could blame the Sea Scouts, who had lots of irregular meetings and had once been seen mucking about on the mini-trikes and hiding things in the sand tray.

It was Posy's turn to set up the hall for Toddlers. Isobel was asleep on the stage in her car seat, her mouth an isosceles triangle. Minute particles of dust from the dusky pink curtains, the memories of a thousand amateur dramatics, pantomimes, and ballet shows, and words of thanks from the vicar drifted down on to her as she slept. Tom was trundling up and down on a new green tractor with a trailer. He'd been the first one there and he was staying on it. The committee should have bought six of them. The Barbie bike and the ride-on Thomas had nothing on it.

Posy dragged out the water tray and the dough table, the 'home-corner' stuff – a wooden washing machine, cupboards, sink, oven, microwave, plastic fruit and veg, pizza, birthday cake and ice creams, and some scratched red chairs and a table.

'Now they can sit around and moan about how tired they are and be disappointed' said someone behind her. 'Want a hand?'

It was Caroline, Al's wife. Al's ex, Posy corrected herself. Caroline in her Boden gingham capris, looking like a sad Doris Day sans ponytail, a rare voice of dissent at Toddlers where 'Mustn't grumble' was the order of the day. If only Caroline's life had turned out more like the Boden catalogue, an endless series of perfect days on the beach with X (architect) and their three children (wearing a selection of Mini Boden).

There were plastic pieces of toast and slices of some pink stuff, possibly salami or luncheon meat from The Early Learning Centre of a bygone age.

' "Have a reality sandwich" is what Frank would say,' Posy said. She liked Caroline, and was unfazed by the rumour that Caroline didn't pay her Access bill off in full each month. Even so, she thought that Caroline could be a bit of a loose cannon at Toddlers.

Caroline kept Posy up to date on the current state of hostilities with Al, often telling her things that she didn't want to know.

'I think I'll get the Duplo zoo out. We haven't had that out for a while,' said Posy.

'I'll help,' said Caroline.

There was a landscaped board, various bits of fence, and a gang of bland-faced zookeepers to keep it all under control. Caroline dropped a handful of assorted animals on to the lake.

'This one's Al,' she said, picking up a hippo. She built it a very small pen and laughed as she trapped it inside.

'Sometimes I almost start to forget what he was like. God. It was just like sleeping underwater with a hippo – all that farting and grunting like he'd eaten too many lily roots – and the great damp, sweaty bulk of him when he was drunk. And he was always at his most amorous when he was at his most smelly. What's Frank like when he comes home after practices?'

'Oh, I'm usually asleep by the time he gets it,' Posy lied. She was too loyal to spill any beans about Frank; even though she often wanted to, she wouldn't be drawn. Posy was determined that her children wouldn't have a broken home. She and Frank lived by the maxim 'No Raised Voices'. Meanwhile her true thoughts and resentments were punched out by a teleprinter in her head and reams and reams of them piled up unread.

'We practically live in different time zones. He often doesn't come to bed till after two, and I'm up at six or something every day with Isobel. But it does drive me mad when he comes in and sets the smoke alarm off with a bacon butty or by burning toast. He sometimes likes to grill things when he's been playing. He says lighting the grill with a match is life-affirming . . . and possessing a toaster would be bourgeois, an affectation, and as for tumble driers, or dishwashers . . .'

'Just like Al!' Caroline laughed.

'Shall I get the paints out, or glue? Both I suppose,' Posy wondered.

'How about just crayons?'

'I know: chalks and black paper. Janie's down for clearing up and her baby's due in a few weeks. I want to make it easy for her,' said Posy.

'Takes you back, doesn't it? Al was so dreadful at those Active Birth evenings. Talk about hostile! I should have known then.'

'Well I ended up with Hunter S. Thompson as my birthing partner,' said Posy. 'When Poppy's looking for a mate, I'm going to say "Forget Romance. What you want are DIY skills." '

'And earning power,' said Caroline.

'But she won't listen.' They shook their heads.

'It was when I found I was seriously contemplating killing him,' said Caroline, 'that I realised that divorce was better for Finn than his Daddy being dead and his Mummy being sent to jail. That's if they'd caught me. I'd come up with the perfect murder based on a movie I saw on Channel 5. Want to know it? Might come in handy, like a spare packet of tissues in your bag.

'I do quite like Frank most of the time' objected Posy, but Caroline told her anyway.

'I was going to put so much neat alcohol into one of his drinks that he would definitely die. I think that would have been undetectable, well, unnoticeable in someone who drinks like Al, don't you? Foolproof, huh? And he'd have had a killer hangover if he didn't die.'

By the end of their marriage, but just before the final split, Caroline had been consumed by hatred. She had spent her time perfecting tiny acts designed to express her contempt. Al liked his tea weak and milky with plenty of sugar. Each time she made him a mug (and she was too determined not to put herself in the wrong to not make him one if she was making one for herself) she made it a little stronger with a few grains less sugar. She stirred in extra bitterness. The last few times that they had made love (oh what a misnomer that was) she had mentally worked her way through the Lakeland Catalogue, listing the things she would buy if she had unlimited funds (completely plain white matching mugs, plate stackers, machine washable doormats, a patio heater, a juicer . . . it was a long list). Then she thought about how she would like to replace the worktops and cupboard doors in their kitchen, if only she could afford it. Then she thought that if she stayed with Al she would never have a new kitchen. Realising this made making the decision easier. She knew that she was like a cold, hard, winter tomato. If they cut into me, she thought, they will see that all the pips have turned black.

After Caroline booted him out, Al really went to seed, like a big old onion left on an allotment. The booze and takeaways had taken their toll.

Posy wondered why almost nobody else at Toddlers was divorced. How come the figures were one in three, or was it half of all marriages now? At St Peter's it seemed more like one in twenty. Subsidence seemed to be the thing that these couples lived in fear of. She thought that there must be a lot of divorces yet to come, or perhaps this wasn't a representative group.

The car park began to fill with BMWs and MPVs. All-terrain buggies made light work of the gravel. The person whose turn it had been for the tray-bake piled slabs of chocolate cake, lemon drizzle cake and gingerbread onto the unbreakable, pale green, unique-to-church-halls crockery. It was spawned by the damp cupboards, made to appear magically by the conjunction of the 'How To Use This Water Heater' notice, with the never-quite-dry tea towels and the 'Please Leave This Kitchen As You Would Like To Find It. Thank you – Parish Office' sign.

There were healthy snacks for the children, curved slices of apple that the Parousellis called Apple Rainbows, saltless breadsticks and mini rice-cakes. Posy couldn't help thinking that the children could do with something that had a few calories, but most of the mums gave them their cake anyway.

She sat behind the table with the register and the empty Flora Light tub for people's pound coins. She couldn't remember the names of all the children, let alone their parents who were mostly known only as Ashleigh's Mum, Dylan's Mum, Darcey's Mum ... If you flicked back through the years of the toddler group register you saw the rise and fall of children's names. In the early nineties there had been twenty-eight Hannahs and seventeen Jacks. Then there was the year when people had thought they were being so original with Callum, and now they names fought on the page in a competition for the most unlikely. Welcome Jerome, Jessamy, Bradley and Bramley (these were apple-cheeked twins) and Cain, who fortunately wasn't a twin, but had a baby sister called Scarlett (Scarletts were now two a penny). There were surnames for girls' first names and very many jewels. Sapphire was still a rarity, but Rubies and even Diamonds were now common. There was a child whom Posy had thought was called Leah (relatively sensible) until he took down his trousers and peed on the slide, and Posy realised that he must be called Lear. At a nearby toddler group was a Chloe who was, for reasons best known to her parents, a 'Khloey', and babies with apostrophes in their names (a Clay'd and a Hayd'n had been the trailblazers).

Posy always sniggered when she read Cnut – they must have been joking – surely, and then she remembered that she was called Posy.

She glanced up to see that Tom was still driving the tractor up and down, up and down, and Isobel was still asleep on the stage. She could see steam from the urn rising in the kitchen. The chairs around the walls of the hall were taken up by coats and changing bags, mums and child-minders, two dads all alone. She could only hear snatches of other people's conversations through the swimming pool echoes of sound.

'But she does say the silliest things. At that party she said "Deeko is my favourite brand of napkins." I mean who has a favourite brand of paper serviettes?' Were they talking about her? Deeko was her favourite brand of napkins, but she couldn't remember telling anyone, least of all those two.

'I don't think she's very practical. She always looks a bit, well, faraway.'

'Off with the fairies my Mum used to say.'

Wish I was, thought Posy, wish I was. She fingered the small disc of the Flower Fairy mirror in her pocket; it was the Poppy Fairy. She'd meant to put on some mascara and lipstick and had, as usual, forgotten. There had been a time when she'd not felt dressed if she went out without earrings and make-up. Now she didn't even wear her own watch. Its battery had run out and she carried Frank's in her pocket. It had some sort of cheap metal on the back that brought her out in a rash.

'Want some coffee?' It was Caroline to the rescue. 'I think you can desert your post.' Posy hadn't really been signing people in, they'd signed themselves in.

'So how's life at the Parousellis?' Caroline asked.

'Oh you know, same . . .' said Posy. 'Isobel slept through the night twice last week and James joined the Cubs but this week he wants to leave. Franks gained two pupils and lost one. If you hear of anyone who might be interested . . .'

Posy knew that Caroline probably wanted to know if there was any gossip about Al, anything that Frank might have told her.

Now that the worst of the divorce was over, Posy sometimes envied Caroline. Imagine being able to live on toast and jam and Diet Coke if you wanted, and not having to make proper dinners. Men always seemed to want to eat something proper and fattening. Caroline had lost piles of weight. Al was meant to have Finn on Saturdays or Sundays, so Caroline could have a whole day to herself, but it usually ended up being just an afternoon. Al was always oversleeping, or the van broke down and he was stuck somewhere with the battery in his mobile running low.

'Fancy coming round for some coffee?' Caroline asked.

'Just a minute . . .' Posy could see Tom on the other side of the room. He was trying to drive the tractor up the slide, whilst two girls in sparkly pink- and purple-striped velour leggings pelted him with pieces of the vanilla-scented playdough. She knew that Kate must have made it. She could smell that it was real extract, not cheap artificial essence. She picked some lumps of it out of Tom's hair, and a big clod out of the hood of his fleece. What a good shot one of the girls was. Then she heard Isobel crying and retrieved her from her car seat on the stage. She stopped crying straight away, but Posy could feel the unmistakable bulge in her nappy. She took her off to a freezing side-room, the store of Sunday school collages in balls of tissue paper, dangerously tall stacks of chairs and damp floor cushions that belonged to nobody.

'At least you can't crawl ye,' she told her as she wiped and dried and packaged her up again, dismissing as usual thoughts of the possibly carcinogenic gel in the nappies.

She gave Isobel to Caroline and went to wash her hands. The light in the Ladies seemed impossibly bright. She caught her reflection in the mirror in the instant before she had adopted her usual expression, a resigned, things-could-be-much-worse smile. So that was what she was really like. Her eyes looked as though they had been punched out, her chinline was undefined, her lips were like a pair of dead worms.

'I am turning into a playdough woman,' she thought.

Back in the hall she said 'Coffee next week would be great.' She would have to pull herself together, knock herself back into shape. 'What day suits you? Any day's good for me really.'

'Tuesday morning?' Caroline offered.

'Or afternoon? Tom's at pre-school in the morning, say about one-thirty, that would give me time to do his lunch . . . I'll just check.' She found her DoDo diary under a box of breadsticks and some tissues in her bag. There was a column for each member of the family. Week after week, page by page, the same things came around – ballet, toddlers, pre-school, Frank's guitar pupils, music club, Tumble Tots – sometimes it calmed her to see it. Her days were prescribed, stretching out in front of her and behind her. Had they really managed to do all of those things? It should have been like a metronome, keeping them all to time, but so often colds and tummy bugs and mysterious viruses interrupted the flow that she sometimes wondered if she'd ever pick up the beat again. The whole world would go marching on without her, leaving her stuck for ever at 3.47 a.m. looking out of a bedroom window with a sticky bottle of Calpol in her hand.

'Oh no. The health visitor's coming. I don't know why. I expect Isobel's on the At Risk register or something.'

'Probably she fancies Frank,' said Caroline. 'Or she wants to see how the experts do it.'

'Monday afternoon?'

'Fine.'

'Oh, that's my birthday. I hadn't even written it in. Well you come to me then. Come after school for tea.'

Posy had no idea why she'd said that. Politeness she supposed. She'd invite Flora and Kate round too; that would make things all right.

Posy hated being a Virgo. It was so dull and brown and sensible. If only she'd been an interesting Gemini, or a beautiful Aquarius, or anything else. Not that she took any notice of any of it, of course. Also, how come, she thought, she'd been called Posy, not Flora? Well Flora had already been used up as Flora was older. But why Posy? If only she'd been called something a bit less ditsy and diminutive she might have amounted to something, she could have been somebody.

She'd been up in the night with Isobel, but only twice. Now it was 7.14 and the children were awake, but Frank wasn't. She had woken from a lovely dream that seemed like a birthday present in itself. She had found a whole set of orange Le Creuset saucepans, still boxed, in the Oxfam shop for £6.99. The shop had been about to close, and when she had offered a ten-pound note for them, the woman behind the counter had fiddled about, trying to find the right change. Posy had immediately said 'Oh, keep the change,' and the woman had given her a Gift Aid form to fill out. Posy had woken delighted with her purchase, her beneficence, and the thought that the woman had taken her to be a tax payer. She lay there smiling and pretending to be asleep.

'Dad,' whispered James in a stage whisper loud enough to wake the neighbours, 'Dad, wake up. It's Mum's birthday and we have to get her presents.' Tom was doing his usual heavy breathing close to her ear.

Posy made some impressive cartoony snoring noises. Per-haps, she thought, we could tour the world, and play in all the capital cities: 'The Family Parouselli — Mouth-Breathing and Snoring Entertainers of Kings'. She kicked Frank to wake him up. He would sleep through anything — Isobel crying, the cat being sick on the floor on his side of the bed, a child having a coughing fit, the strange and sinister noises that came from The Common.

'Dad! We have to make her a cup of tea . . . Dad come on . . . I'm not allowed to do the kettle yet' James said. Poppy and Tom started to thump Frank on the legs, but still he slept on. Posy tried some more kicks, and then rolled over, deftly pulling the quilt off him and wrapping herself in it.

'Hell!'

'Come on, Dad. We've got to get Mum's presents, and Mrs Fleance said that if you shout "Hell", and you aren't a vicar, then that's swearing.'

At last he was up; they'd be late for school at this rate. She could hear Isobel snuffling and kicking the bars of her cot. Frank pulled on the heavy, mustardy, velour dressing gown she'd given him for Christmas. It was meant to be luxurious, old gold, like a smoking jacket perhaps, but cat fur, Isobel's Ready Brek and Frank's morning aromas of Old Holborn and bacon samies had given it the character and appearance of an old yellow Labrador.

Posy loved birthdays, especially the children's, and doing all the stuff for them. She had a slight fear of her own birthday though, not a fear of getting old, but of what she might get.

She hardly ever bought things for herself. She only ever had one or two lipsticks at a time. Even a £2.79 nail polish from Superdrug constituted self-indulgence. In her mind that equalled a pack of Ladybird socks for Isobel, around two days' dinner money for James or Poppy, or a session of Tumble Tots for Tom. It was a pity that she didn't reckon her allocation of treats in terms of the number of pints of beer consumed by Frank each week.

If someone gave Posy a scarf, that would be her scarf until it fell into holes. She would use whatever the present was for ever even if she didn't much like it. She was baffled by some of the things she saw in the shops – the plasticy flowers that danced, radios with lips that synched in time to the music, slippers and mobile phone covers with Groovy Chicks on, Bagpusses that stuck to the insides of car windows, fibre optic feng shui fountain lights – things that would all soon be so last year. If anyone gave them to Posy she would be compelled to wear them out, or to keep them for good. She knew that there must be people who simply threw them away once the craze for Shaun the Sheep rucksacks or whatever had passed.

She was horrified by the toys that the children got with Happy Meals, or rather the vegetarian version consumed by the young Parousellis, which consisted of the sour chips and a flaccid, almost empty roll. She pretended that Flora hadn't told her that the shakes were made not with milk, but beef fat. When, after an hour, the toys were discarded she was compelled to give them a permanent home in the square Ikea basketdevoted to action figures, even if the children didn't really know who the things represented, and would never see the film they were designed to promote.

But here they came with the tray, the tea, and the presents.

'Happy Birthday Mummy!' 'Happy Birthday Mummy!' 'Happy Birthday Mummy!' Hugs and kisses all round. Frank perched on the end of the bed, holding Isobel, whilst Posy opened her presents. He could hardly bring himself to mouth these clichés.

'Happy Birthday and all that' he muttered, hardly looking at her.

'Badedas. My favourite!'

'That's from me,' said Poppy. 'It was my idea to get you bubble bath. Can I have some tonight then?'

'Maybe a tiny bit. I don't think it's very good for children's skin.'

'Please Mummy. I am a girl. I did get it for you.'

'We'll see. Now what's in this one?'

'We'll see means no,' said James in his most smart alecy voice.

'It's got shampoo in it,' Tom said.

'You aren't meant to tell her, Tom' Frank said.

'Well, she did ask,' said James.

'How lovely. My favourite shampoo.' It was a bottle of Superdrug Coconut Oil Shampoo for Dry Hair, the brand Posy chose because it combined not having been tested on animals with being very cheap.

'We knew you must like it as it's the one you use,' said Poppy.

'Very clever,' said Posy. 'Very, very clever.'

'They were doing three for the price of two, but Dad said one was plenty,' said James.

'James. You don't have to tell her that,' said Frank.

'I'm glad you didn't waste any money,' said Posy. 'My hair might not be dry any more once I've used the whole bottle. Very wise.'

'These are from me,' said James.

It was a pale-blue nylon scrubby puff with some Dove soap and body wash.

'Another one of my favourites. Aren't you clever to get all of my favourites?'

'We got it all at Superdrug,' James explained.

'Even cleverer,' said Posy.

'Don't forget your cards.'

'Cards are my favourite bit, specially home-made ones,' said Posy.

'I think cards are boring. Unless they have money or toucans in,' said James.

'Grown-ups like cards. I didn't know you were so keen on toucans.' She must remember this, perhaps find him a rain-forest-themed birthday card with a pop-up toucan.

'Not boring clothes toucans like Aunt Bea once sent us.'

'What is he on about?' asked Frank.

'Clothes toucans?' asked Posy.

'You know, Mum. When you swop them for pyjamas or something. Toys R Us toucans and Smith's ones are what I like.'

'Oh those toucans,' said Posy. 'I'll remember that.' And she would. When James's next birthday came round she found herself searching every shop in Southampton until she found a rainforest card.

'Come on you lot. You'll be late for school,' said Frank in a rare burst of parental zeal. They made it to school on time. Posy opened her cards whilst the rest of them ate breakfast. Frank didn't send cards. She had four from James, all on a Robot Wars theme, five from Poppy, hearts, flowers and rabbits, and a picture that Tom said was of a tiger. It was orange, black and angst-ridden. She had a card from Aunt Is and Aunt Bea, something floral from the Bee Centre shop with, oh joy, a twenty-pound note. That was it for now.

Just an hour later she was slumped outside the pre-school. It was 9.15. James and Poppy were in school, Tom and his cronies were banging on the hall door.

'Open now! Open now!' the little gang shouted. Posy wondered whether the pre-school ladies found the children menacing, but they were locked safely inside the building, putting the finishing touches to the day's activities which included string paintings and a Chinese takeaway set up in the Home Corner with real (cold, cooked) noodles to ladle into foil dishes. They were oblivious to the mini-siegers at their gates.

Isobel had fallen asleep in her pushchair and so would be awake and needy when they got home. No time to do anything, again, or anything ever again.

Looking back towards the school Posy could see a group of mums in Lycra cycling shorts, all laughing and stretching their hamstrings prior to their run. They went running straight from school, or went to their gym, or to play badminton. Probably, Posy thought, to return to sparkling homes and notes from their cleaners saying

MORE FLASH AND POLISH PLEASE.

More flash and much more polished than me, thought Posy. How did they get time for this gratuitous self-indulgence? she wondered, wishing that she was one of them. She thought of them as the Thin Legs Club, and feared that it was a club of which she would now never be a member.

She decided to spend her twenty pounds from the Aunts on something for herself, a fitness video or yoga classes or something. Perhaps she would start going swimming, she used to love swimming; if she took Isobel to a parent and toddler session she might be able to do it, or maybe they should all go more often. She pictured the children shivering, somebody would be crying, and they would all get ear infections and veruccas. Maybe not. Perhaps if she found lessons for the children then she and Frank wouldn't need to go in with them. She realised that she had lost the thread.

Eventually the pre-school door was opened and Tom marched in. She saw him find the card with his name and photo and hang it up on the board to show that he was there, then sit obediently down on the mat to wait for everything to start. He didn't even notice her kissing the top of his head and saying 'Bye bye darling, I'll pick you up at lunchtime.' Of course she would. She was pleased that he was taking her so much for granted. She would have to remember not to eat whatever he brought home today. The week before Tom had been really upset when she had absent-mindedly eaten the model snake that she'd found in her pocket. It was saltdough, she'd thought it was pastry, had been really hungry, and hadn't even noticed what it tasted like. They had been meant to take it back to paint that week.

In Safeways she bought things that the children would like to eat at her birthday tea. Jammy Dodgers were Poppy and James's favourites. Tom liked Iced Gems. Doughnuts, Jaffa Cakes and Hula Hoops were essential too. Circles of French bread and some grapes and plums would slave her conscience. She saw that the Iced Gems were now made with added vitamins. Well that was all right then. Flora could be relied upon to bring a cake.

She had forgotten the fruit. She went back to start again, and caught sight of her big moony face reflected above the pumpkins. She quickly looked away, down into her basket. No wonder I am so fat, Posy thought, if this is what I buy. She decided that she herself would stick to the bread and fruit.

Teatime. Caroline and Finn were waiting on the doorstep when they got home from school. Caroline had a big bunch of earwiggy but gorgeous yellow roses from her garden, some ginger body lotion, and a glass jar of sea-salt scrub with sweet almond and evening primrose oils. (It would also have been lovely if the next morning Tom hadn't accidentally knocked it into the bath, causing chips and a crack and a salty, slippery slick.) Kate and her children brought slices of mango dipped in chocolate and a pair of mugs with oranges on. (Oxfam Traidcraft without a doubt.)

Flora arrived with a fat sponge cake with pink icing, decorated with crystallised violets and rose petals. It was the nicest thing of the day so far.

Posy went to the back door and yelled out into the garden 'Come on Frank, it's teatime.' She was never sure whether or not Frank could hear her yelling at him when he was in his shed. If he was playing, then he definitely couldn't. It was maddening.

'Poppy, go out and bang on Daddy's door and tell him that it's teatime and we want him to come in.'

'But I haven't got my shoes on Mum.' Poppy was worried that everything would be eaten before she got back.

'Put your wellies on then.' Yet more hesitation. 'Come on. It is my birthday. Please be helpful.'

'Yes, hurry up Poppy, it is Mum's birthday,' James said, surreptitiously counting the doughnuts.

'OK. This is a birthday treat for you, Mum,' Poppy said.

'Well, thank you. I'll remember this.'

'I have to do everything,' Poppy muttered as she stomped towards the back door, then a terrible scream.

'Muuuum! Help! There's a slug on my welly!'

Aunty Flora to the rescue. She picked the slug up using some kitchen roll and hurled it into the outer darkness of the mahonia bushes near the back door. Then she and Poppy went to fetch Frank. They could see him through the shed window.

He was smoking and staring into space. Well honestly, thought Flora, he might at least make the tea on his wife's birthday. Frank had actually forgotten that it was Posy's birthday. He was trying to catch at the hem of a song that he had heard in a dream, a new song; but it was eluding him. He could just feel some of the notes. He'd had the whole thing off perfect when he was asleep. Flora & Poppy banged on the window. The song was gone.

'Daddy it's time for tea.'

'I'm not hungry, honey.'

'But Daddy, everybody's waiting for you and there's birthday cake!'

Flora gave him a very stern look.

'Birthday cake? Then I'm starving!'

He chucked the almost-out end of his roll-up into the bushes to join the slug.

'It's pink with real flowers on.' Poppy told him. 'And there are Jammy Dodgers.'

Whenever Frank saw Flora he was mightily relieved that he had married the right sister. He infinitely preferred Posy's dark curls to Flora's fair ones. Strange, he thought, that the features that were so appealing in the one, when slightly altered, could seem almost unpleasant in the other. That must be it, seeing the one you loved slightly changed. There was something surreal and sinister about it, as though a deception was being perpetrated. Or perhaps, he realised, it was just that he sensed Flora's constant disapproval of him. She might as well be wearing a T-shirt emblazoned with 'You Should Pull Yourself Together. Get A Proper Job. Start Winning Bread.' Perhaps he should get one made for her for *her* birthday.

It was like that baffling story in Genesis where Jacob is palmed off with the wrong sister. 'And lo, it was Leah!' Frank was jolly glad that he had managed to marry the Rachel of the pair at first go.

But Posy didn't look that pleased to see him when they all walked into the kitchen. All she said was 'Oh. You're here now.'

Everybody else was sitting around the table. Posy was holding the baby and trying to make tea at the same time.

'Bit dangerous, that,' he told her. 'Watch out with that kettle.'

She thrust the baby at him and continued, adding extra milk to his mug. He liked it with just the tiniest dash.

'Tuck in, everyone,' said Posy. 'Don't wait for me.'

'No. You're only the birthday girl,' said Flora, but they all started anyway.

'How's the band then, Frank?' Caroline asked. 'Still getting the gigs? Still pulling in the crowds? Making megabucks?'

'You bet,' said Frank, his mouth full of Pringles.

'The big mistake people make with Pringles, Wotsits, Hula Hoops, all of those things,' said Flora, 'Is ever having one.'

Her own plate was a neat arrangement of thin circles of French bread with Flora Light and marmite, grapes, plums and cherry tomatoes.

'Don't you like Wotsits, Aunty Flora?' Poppy asked. She was sitting between Flora and Frank resting her head on Frank's shoulder whilst trying to hold hands, when both hands weren't needed for eating, with Flora.

(At least Poppy still likes me, Frank thought. Flora and I are united by loving these children.)

'It's not a matter of liking, or not liking them, sweetie,' Flora said. 'It's a matter of making a choice not to eat them, feeling happier if you choose not to eat them.'

Poppy looked baffled.

'But I like choosing them *and* eating them,' said James. 'We all do.'

'Not Flora,' Frank heard himself saying. 'Flora Poppins. Practically perfect in every way.' Flora chose to ignore him. Even though it was meant as an insult, she took it as a compliment.

Posy got up from the table, even though she had only just sat down. She put on a CD. The Quintet of the Hot Club de France.

'This is partyish,' she said. She felt as though everyone was forgetting that it was her birthday. Shouldn't they all be being very nice to her? This was just another step into the fog of Mummy Invisibility. Your birthday no longer matters.

'I should have got a magician to come,' she said. 'Pass the Skips.'

'Skips really do have the worst smell in the world,' Flora said, shaking her head as she offered her sister the bowl. How could Posy possibly be going to eat some?

'No, no. That's Pickled Onion Monster Munches' said Posy. 'Skips are lovely. A real delicacy. They remind me of being a sixth former.'

'Your Madeleine,' said Kate.

'No, she's Posy,' said Frank.

'Ha ha. I think macaroons would be nicer, or florentines, but it's Skips that really take me back,' Posy said. She let one melt on her tongue and assumed a wistful expression. 'Sometimes I would eat two bags for lunch and an apple, and that would be all. Very successful if you're dieting. They're only about 97 calories a bag.' It was only later that she'd come to think about 'empty calories' and 'nutrients' and 'fat content'. As a teenager her aim had been simply to eat as few calories a day as possible. At that time when deciding to eat anything at all was a wrong decision.

'My favourite sixth-form lunch was a peach and a flake.

Hardly any calories. Or a cuppa soup and two ryvita,' Flora said.

'*Pas devant les enfants*,' said Posy, remembering that one of her main ambitions for Poppy was that she wouldn't have an eating disorder.

'You started it,' said Flora. 'Anyway, I remember you getting hot cheese and onion pasties from the bakers.'

'That's my girl!' said Frank.

'I may have, once or twice. Or bought them for other people. Oh, do you remember that lovely floppy hot chocolate in brown plastic cups in the canteen?'

'I do remember some awful girl spilling vending-machine chicken soup all over my beautiful woven wicker pencil case. It was dreadful. I could never get the smell out.'

Posy had often been paralysed by shyness or embarrassment, and ordering anything from the dinner ladies had been beyond her. How were you supposed to know which one to ask for beans or peas or lasagne or jacket potatoes? So she missed the hot dinners and choose the things that you helped yourself to: apples, plates of cream crackers with yellow bendy cheese, or, if it was a day when she was feeling brave and could justify eating, she might have just the hot pudding. This was easy enough because it came from a separate hatch with just one lady. Chocolate sponge with chocolate sauce. Comfort in a cruel, cruel world.

'Time for cake!' Flora announced. She cleared a space in front of Posy and lit the candles. Everybody sang. Posy blew the candles out in one go. Then they had to be relit seven times so that James, Poppy and Tom, Finn and Kate's three children could each have a go

'Wish, Mummy, wish!' James shouted, as Flora passed Posy the bread knife.

'I don't need to wish for anything. I have everything that I could possibly need because I have all of you,' Posy said.

'Oh you have to wish for something.'

'I wish I could have a magician at my next birthday,' Posy
said.

'Silly Mummy. It won't come true because you told us,' said
Poppy.

'Wish again Mummy, but keep it a secret.'

She closed her eyes and made another slice in silence, and
then cut pieces for everyone. Frank was given his last of all.
'Here you are Carpenter,' she said.

'Makes you the Walrus,' he said.

'I am the Walrus,' she said, looking down at her stomach.
'Cut us another slice.'

Posy smiled at him. He thought, 'that is the first time she has
really looked at me all day.' He was profoundly grateful for
Poppy's continued devotion. He felt her slip her little paw,
sticky with cake and party food, into his.

The band was red hot that night. Against all odds for Frank as
his had been a really crap day. It started just after seven which
was unheard of for him. Posy had lain there groaning that she
had been up all night, and couldn't he get them up, just this
once? So he had. He wasn't made to get up early, and of course
Isobel's nappy had leaked something foul and yellow right up
her back and on to her vest and Babygro. Posy couldn't have
put it on properly in the night, or maybe she'd known. He
supposed that somehow she had known, she always knew
everything like this, and that was why she had refused to get
cut of bed, had made him do it. He dipped Isobel in the sink to
get her clean, dumped the disgusting baby clothes in the bath
for Posy to sort out, and then took Isobel in to Posy for the
morning feed. He plonked her down on the bed and went off
to make the tea. All this before 7.30 and he still hadn't had a
cigarette.

He wasn't cut out for this sort of thing. He thought that he
was doing everything right until Posy came storming down,
thrust Isobel back at him and snarled something about having

already done that feed an hour ago. And then she was furious about the baby clothes – as if that was his fault. She said that he was leaving a trail of destruction and detritus for her to clear up. Talk about unreasonable. She had burst into tears so Frank thought that the best thing he could do in the circumstances was to get himself out of her way. He had gone back to bed.

He heard James, Poppy and Tom going downstairs laughing. At least someone in the house was happy. Then he heard Isobel start her usual 'Our, uur' moan in her highchair. It could really bore through your skull. It meant that she had finished her breakfast and wanted to get down. Posy must be too distracted to attend to her. Then he heard an argument breaking out, and Posy yelling at him, pretending to be polite.

'Could you please come down here and help me!' When he arrived in the kitchen she said 'Thank you,' in her meanest voice. 'I've been calling you for five minutes.'

What a lie!

'Any tea in the pot, Pose,?' he said to wind her up further. 'Come on. Give us a kiss, darlin'.'

'Uur. Uur. Uur,' from Isobel.

'I haven't had the luxury of enough time to make tea,' she told him.

'Mummy's cross with me today,' he told the children, but they'd started arguing over the toy from the cereal packet. He saw that it was actually very desirable, a little credit card type thing with some real stardust under the plastic, lots of information, and a pretty, Hubble-ish picture about where it was from.

'Wow. That is cool,' he told them. 'I know, I'll have it.' He did feel a sudden need for it.

'Aw Dad.'

' 'Snot fair.'

'I was the one who found it.'

'I need it for something.

'So do I,' said Frank. 'OK. First one to be completely ready for school or pre-school can have it. The one who comes second can have the next one.' He put it into his back pocket. Isobel was still going 'Uur, uur.' He lifted her down from her highchair. Posy swiped at her with a flannel, rather roughly, Frank thought. He didn't see the point of endlessly cleaning them up. You were fighting a losing battle. Why not ignore the build-up of snot, yoghurt, crumbs and ickiness during the day and just give them a good hose down at bath time? Posy really could save herself a lot of time if she cut out all the unnecessary stuff. He decided not to say anything though.

It was foggy. Once Isobel stopped moaning he could hear that tune coming at him again. It had been going on all week. He thought it might just be in his head. They often heard the ship's foghorns. He and Posy loved it on New Year's Eve: they would rush outside after midnight to hear them all honking away. This was different though. The notes seemed to have merged and were playing a tune

'Du da der du doo da da,' again and again. Nobody else seemed to be hearing it.

'Hear that Posy?'

'What?'

But it was gone.

When they had all slammed out of the house for school and pre-school and Music Time he went out into the garden for a smoke. He heard the tune again.

'Du da der du doo da da . . .'

Once back inside he saw that the answering machine was flashing. Bound to be some long complicated message to do with some committee, or Flora's merry barking. He listened anyway.

'Hello Frank, this is your Grandad. Hello Posy. Hello children. I wonder if you could pop in today Frank. I just need a little bit of help with something. I'll expect you this morning, shall I? And could you go to the hardware shop on the way and get me a new sink-catcher? You know what I mean. Your mother has decided to throw mine away. Thanks. Grandpa.'

Frank liked the way that old people signed off their messages on answering machines, as though they were reading from little slips of paper. They probably were. But Hell's flaming teeth! Sometimes he wished he had a proper job so that he could disappear for hours on end. Perhaps he should invent one. Coming up with the salary to fool Posy might be a problem though.

He knew what else Grandpa wanted. Another two months had gone by. Time for another BettaKleen campaign. Grandpa's legs might not be quite up to it this time. If they could just take the books round, and go back in a few days to collect the orders . . . perhaps Grandpa would feel up to helping him (helping him – get that!) to do the deliveries too when they came in.

Dear God. He hadn't been put on the earth for this.

Grandpa dwelt alone in the flat above 'Fancy Ways'. His flat was used by the family as an overflow stockroom, and his views of Portswood High Street were sometimes partially obscured by boxes of ornaments, out-of-use display units, stacks of wrapping paper and out-of-season cards. This wasn't enough to spoil his enjoyment though, there was always something going on, some drama unfolding for him to watch – a pedestrian pensioner vs. student riding on the pavement road rage incident, a delivery at Peacocks, a shop having a new awning fitted, the endless roadworks, the semi-derelicts on the bench near the library, the traffic wardens hard at work with their ticket books – always something to cheer him up.

Frank left a note for Posy, 'Gone to help Grandpa with something.' Perhaps that would make her appreciate him a bit more. He could, unfortunately, be down at the shop in less than fifteen minutes.

He managed to delay himself a little by going into Portswood Hardware, one of his favourite shops. He knew that they needed lots of things – there were endless projects and fixings of things that Posy wanted him to do – but now that he was here his mind went blank.

'Looking for something?' the kindly man in grey overalls asked him.

'This and that', Frank said. And a length of hosepipe long enough to reach from the exhaust of an E-reg Volvo estate through the driver's window, and if there are any special clips for attaching it securely, and if you have any maps of the New Forest showing pretty but deserted parking places . . . What was it that Grandpa had wanted? Frank supposed that he should be grateful that they didn't have a garage. Imagine the constant temptation to top oneself in there. To park inside and let it fill up with fumes, or to hang oneself from the up and over door . . .

'Have you got one of those stupid metal things that old people have in their sinks to catch disgusting gunk?'

'Sinkmate? Just to your left. Eighty-three pence.'

'Thanks mate.'

Frank smiled as he remembered a joke that he'd read in James's *Best Joke Book in The World Ever*. 'Did you hear about the ice-cream man found dead in his van, covered in nuts and strawberry sauce? The police think he topped himself.' Posy had said that she thought it was very unsuitable.

'Fancy Ways' was just along the road.

'Francis!' His Mum looked really pleased to see him. 'How are you all? We haven't seen you for ages.'

'Mum, you saw us all last week!'

'Last week is ages when you only live a few minutes away,' she told him.

'Well, I'm here now.' She could manage to make him feel guilty within seconds of walking through the door, it got him every time. 'How's Dad?'

'Oh not so bad. He was out of breath badly from moving all the new glass pierrots. They are much heavier than they look.'

'You should have waited for me. I'd have done it for you,' Frank told her, thinking, 'Send in the clowns, there ought to be clowns. Don't bother, they're here.'

'How can I wait for you if I never know when you might be coming?' He couldn't think of an answer to this.

'Grandpa phoned me,' he told her. 'He wants some help with something.' He hoped that this might win him a few more points, get him off the hook a bit. Luckily a customer came towards the counter with a paperweight and a gift box. 'I'll just go up and see how he is.' Frank skedaddled for the stairs behind the 'Staff Only' door.

He knocked on his Grandfather's flat door and went straight in. He could hear the TV. Grandpa was watching *Trisha*.

'She's pretty, this one,' he told Frank.

'Hi Grandpa, you OK?' Frank didn't bend down to kiss the grizzled, unshaven cheek, or to shake his grandfather's very cold, stiff hand. His grandfather's shoulders looked bony through the layers of vest, shirt, pullover and cardigan. His thin knees were pointy and painful-looking through his trousers. Frank was always reminded of the skeletons of some of the smaller beaky dinosaurs, Ornithomimus or Compsognathus, the one that was no bigger than a hen. He and James knew all the names of them from *The Big Book of Dinosaurs*, and his other favourite *If Dinosaurs Came To Town*. Don't bother, they're here, Frank thought to himself.

'Cup of tea, Grandpa?'

'If you're making one.' Frank would certainly never choose to make a cup of tea in Grandpa's kitchen, which was cluttered beyond even Frank's disorder threshold. Doing the simplest thing involved negotiating a path through trailing flexes, past the Calor gas heater (always on, even on the hottest days), moving piles of dishes (clean and dirty were hard to differentiate), as well as the boxes of tissues, Scholl ointments, empty glasses cases, letters, Christmas cards and pictures by the children dating back years, and the foot file which was perpetually clogged with pieces of grey debris that always made Frank think 'Dust you are, and to dust you shall return.' Frank knew that his mother was up here, several times a day, trying to impose some order on things, but that Grandpa undid it all within minutes, scattering dirty tissues around his feet, filling the bath with cold water and then hurling his bedding in because he thought it needed a good soak balancing the two-bar electric fire on the draining board to try to keep his hands warm while he failed to wash up. The possibilities for creating chaos and squalor, and for setting up accidents waiting to happen, were endless. Frank thought that even Flora would be unable to keep Grandpa in check. Eventually Frank returned to the sitting room with two mugs of tea and half a packet of fig rolls that he had found beside the washing-up liquid.

'No point getting the best china out, eh?' Grandpa said, taking a big slurp from the chipped Garfield mug Frank handed him. Frank's was a Farside Christmas-theme mug, also damaged stock from the shop downstairs.

'Good for you to have a mugful, Grandpa. Posy told me she heard something on the radio saying that old people don't drink enough.'

'What's that? What are you saying?'

Frank ignored the question. How could he explain that what he had said was as so often the case with Grandpa, too banal to merit repeating.

'So what did you want some help with?' he asked, loud, clear and slow.

'Them books. In the bedroom. Arrived yesterday.'

Frank found his way back across the room and into the bedroom. The BettaKleen catalogues were piled high on Grandpa's unmade bed, next to a Kleenex Mansize box stuffed with apple cores, satsuma peel, an empty Digestive's packet, the filmy wrappings of processed cheese slices, and the papers of several packets of Halls Extra Strong Mentholyptus throat sweets: the detritus of Grandpa's most recent midnight feast, which, Frank surmised, must have ended in a coughing fit. Or perhaps he just ate packets and packets of Halls for the taste alone. Frank saw that there weren't just the Bettakleen catalogues to get rid of, but two supplements, a health and diet one (a particular favourite of his) and something new, 'Your Lucky Magic'. They would weigh a ton. Grandpa would never be able to shift them. Frank cursed the man who had talked Grandpa into this whole network selling thing in the first place. It was despicable. Grandpa had lapped up all the stories about 'part-time job – full-time money', about people building pyramids of sellers and then retiring in splendour, of people whose sales won them holidays with spending money. As if Grandpa was ever going to attain those dizzy heights. The only person he'd ever managed to persuade to join him in the enterprise was Frank, and was only because Frank felt so sorry for him and worried about him going up and down the stairs in the blocks that were part of Grandpa's round. It wasn't even a local round. Portswood would probably have been much more lucrative, but that was already somebody else's territory. Somehow Grandpa had agreed to do Weston, bloody miles away on the other side of the city, the most easterly part of Southampton, a huge estate washed up on a green no-man's-land that dissolved into a pebbly shore.

Frank was often tempted to suggest to Grandpa that they swap Bettakleen for a paper round. It would be less onerous and more lucrative. Grandpa wouldn't even discuss giving up BettaKleen though; he said that he would soon be fit enough to do it by himself again, and if Frank didn't want to help, well, then he'd manage somehow. And of course Grandpa didn't want anyone else to get his round, BettaKleen or a rival company. Oh no, not after he had spent all that time building it up.

It seemed that there was nothing to be done apart from doing it. Frank began to load the catalogues into the tartan trolley that was their trusty Bettakleen companion. And here's a few kilos of disappointment, pointlessness and futility, Frank muttered as he put the last few bundles in.

'What's that? What's that?' Grandpa asked.

'Nothing Grandpa, just checking we had enough.' If only the world, and especially Posy, could have seen that there was something heroic about lugging that trolley down the steps and into the boot of the car, and then going back to get Grandpa and his carrier bag of things he'd need for the journey, the spare glasses, Spaldings catalogue, packet of tunes and a half-empty box of tissues in case of emergencies, and the little black vinyl purse which contained Grandpa's money as he insisted on paying for the toll bridge and then on giving Frank a pound coin, towards, he said, petrol and tobacco. If only this work was rewarded the way being a hospital consultant was, or an accountant, or a systems analyst. If only 'Being Frank' was considered to be proper job in itself.

'Going well is she?' Grandpa asked.

'What?' Did he mean Posy?

'The car. Going well is she?'

'Like a dream.' said Frank. He always forgot that he and Grandpa had to have these manly conversations about how the Parousellis' car was running. Each time Frank took Grandpa out he resolved to clean the car so that it resembled a more fitting topic of conversation, but every time he forgot. Fortunately Grandpa was too shortsighted to see how dusty and crisp-crumbed the car was, or to notice the Sunmaid raisins (preferred snack of modern middle-class toddlers) that studded the floor and back seats. Frank had no idea why anyone ever bought them. Sure, children liked the cute little boxes, but they never actually seemed to eat the raisins, just to scatter them in trails wherever they went. Perhaps in some sort of private toddler raisin morse code, they were all leaving messages for each other: 'Why can't she just be done with it and give me Wotsits and chocolate buttons on car journeys?' 'Wibbly is a fat pig', things like that.

They drove off down Portswood High Street, past Safeway, past Wickes, down into the badlands of Bevois Valley, over the level crossing, past the Saints Stadium, finally onto the Itchen bridge. Off peak fifty pence. To the Parousellis the elegant concrete arch, surely the biggest bridge in the South, with its views up and down the river and out past Ocean Village towards the sea was worth much more than that. Frank always wondered why the sides hadn't been made even higher; a suicide would be able to jump quite easily. Could it be that the bridge made people feel so cheerful that they changed their minds?

Woolston, on the other side of the bridge, really did seem like the sticks to Frank.

'I remember when all there was was the floating bridge,' Grandpa told him, just as he always did. 'They said then it would take till past the year 2000 for the bridge to pay for itself. I wonder if it has yet.'

'Doubt it,' said Frank, as he always did.

Soon they were driving along the road beside Weston Shore. This wasn't necessary, but Frank always made this minor detour so that Grandpa could have a quick look at the sea. The shingle and mud had once been thought of as a beach, and families had spent whole days there, now it was usually deserted. The water had a caustic look and nobody paddled any more. There were dog-walkers and people digging for lugworms, but no picnickers and rarely any children. Just yards from this was Weston estate, six towering blocks that looked like the last of England, innumerable flats, a precinct, some houses, and when she was in, Melody.

Weston had been the subject of every government and local authority improvement scheme ever. There was a long, impressive roll call of them – Local Projects, Estate Action, Housing Renewal, Community Safety Initiatives, Community Action, Single Regeneration Budget – but these might never have happened. It still needed more. Now it was a Sure Start Area. The vortices between the blocks capsized prams and blew over buggies. It was a struggle for the young mums to get to the bus stop for the number 17 that would take them away past the Vospers yard, over the Itchen Bridge and into town. Melody didn't have a baby though. She lived with her parents. To be still at home at twenty-two! Frank and The Wild Years found it astonishing, but to Melody the pros were obvious – wide screen TV, DVD player, another TV in her own room, everything comfy, Mum doing all the cooking and washing, all for £20 a week. She did have to put up with her little brother, Mark, who at nineteen was not that little and worked at Q Tyres earning more than she did. Just the dog would have been enough to drive Frank away. It was a spiteful little Jack Russell cross, a really pointless dog. It always seemed to have a special sneer for Frank.

The music teacher at Melody's school had said that she would go far. Melody had a future as Southampton's answer to Celine Dion, but without the nose. So far though, she had only made it to the box office of The Mayflower, where she had landed a job as an assistant after Frank cost her the job at Asda. It had been a blessing in disguise, really. The Mayflower was much classier than Asda. In quiet moments she would read the programmes and daydream about being in one of the shows herself. She would undo her ponytail and let her silky blonde hair fall over her face. She had the ideal hair for a contemporary young person, dead straight, longish, fair, very manageable. She could have been mistaken for one of Atomic Kitten.

Frank knew that Melody would be at work. There was no chance of meeting her. He had only ever seen her house in the evenings when he'd been dropping her off. Her mum had placed an order oncethough. Frank had got Grandpa to knock on the door with that one. It had been for a stupid white plastic shelf-thing that was designed to stand on a corner of a bath. Frank could imagine Melody's mum thinking that it would be very handy. He wondered if she had been disappointed or if it had changed her life after all.

Taking the catalogues round wasn't really that bads all they had to do was shove them through people's letter boxes. It was going back and trying to retrieve them or, if they were lucky, some orders that Frank dreaded. People out here went for bulky, awkward things, buckets, brooms, bins, wipeable self-assembly bedside cabinets, the sort of things that they wouldn't want to carryhome themselves. Frank was hoping that Asda.-com home delivery delivering, Argos Homedirect, and all that crew would put paid to the whole BettaKleen empire. Surely it could only be a matter of time.

In the tower blocks they rode to the top in the lifts that were all, thankfully, working that day and then slowly made their way down, floor by floor, using the stairs. Grandpa waited and looked out of the landing windows while Frank went along the corridors shoving catalogues through people's letter boxes. They broke for lunch and got fish and chips, eating in, both paying for their own and having second cups of tea to put off returning to their deliveries. There were still many more blocks to do.

'If Posy could see this she wouldn't always be bloody moaning, Frank constantly told himself. They met almost no one, but he could hear the sounds of life coming from behind the doors – hoovering and washing machines and Tweenies, all merging. Frank had the feeling that he was visiting the back doors of a cliff-top gull colony. On the other side would be the young in their nests squawking for more food, while their parents were off fishing and flying.

Posy would still have been moaning if she had seen him. He

should be doing a proper job. She should have married a GP or a solicitor or someone who worked for IBM. He wasn't even any good at DIY.

A couple of hours later they were done. He took Grandpa home, dropping him outside to avoid going into the shop again. Frank thought that just as there is a theory that each heart has a prescribed number of beats, so there was a limit to the number of times he could set foot in Fancy Ways without dropping dead. He thought that he must be somewhere near the maximum already. He parked the car just as Posy and the children were arriving home from school. Isobel was fretting in the pram.

'Daddy!'

'Daddy!'

'Daddy!'

'That was good timing,' he said to Posy. He loved how pleased the children were to see him.

'Would have been better if you'd been in time to collect them,' Posy grumbled. 'I had to break Izzie's feed.'

'Sorry,' he said. 'Sorry. I was just helping Grandpa.'

'Why do those stupid leftover catalogues have to live at our house?' Posy demanded, as she always did.

'You know how cramped his flat is . . .'

'Huh.' She turned away from him. He saw that Grandpa's trolley was still in the boot of the car. It would doubtless be needed. He would have to take it back. Dear God, hadn't he already paid his debt to society?

'Could you make the kids some toast? I just want to go and finish this feed.' Well, he could manage that.

An hour later Posy still hadn't come down. He went up to see her. She was lying on their bed, Isobel blissed out with sucking; they were both asleep. Radio Four would keep them that way.

When CBBC finished the children realised that they were still hungry.

'Let's go and get some chips,' Frank told them. 'A nice surprise for Mummy.' He could take back Grandpa's trolley at the same time. With the kids waiting in the car and some chips cooling in their paper, he would have a good excuse not to go in.

'Oh no! Not chips! You know I'm trying to lose this weight.' Posy said when they returned. 'Well I'll just have a few.' She piled a side plate with them. Lashings of Waistline salad cream meant that it wasn't really that fattening. Brown bread and Flora Light for the butties made it positively healthy. 'Do you mind doing the baths before you go out? I'm just really tired . . .' No he didn't mind, not much.

Frank felt as though Posy really made him pay for his nights out with the band. Of course he enjoyed them, but conveniently she seemed to forget that the band was his work, and their main source of income. It was a long time since she'd brought in any money, and all she did was complain.

Frank always played on Wednesdays. It was Posy's favourite night of the week. When the children were in bed she remembered that she hadn't shut up the rabbit for the night. Lettice received constant death threats from local foxes. Posy and Frank found pigeons' wings, scatterings of feathers, chewed shoes, disembowelled and slashed balls on the so-called lawn, and had to dispose of them appropriately. Posy put on her bendy M&S sandals and went out into the garden. Lettice was calmy nibbling dandelions.

'All organic,' Posy told her. 'Guaranteed 100 per cent pesticide free, the rabbit equivalent of eating the finest fresh rocket salad.' She gave Lettice a brief cuddle, kissed her silky ears, and shut her securely in the hutch. The first stars were coming out. Posy sat down on the steps, hugging her knees under her soft cotton skirt, the way she had when she was a girl. Django the cat came and joined her. The flower bed beside them was over-run by evening primroses. She watched as they started opening. 'One enchanted evening . . .' she thought, and made her breathing slow and calm. She no longer heard the hum of the traffic on The Avenue. Her ears were tuned into the soft whispers and creaks that came from The Common, overlaid by Lettice's rustlings. Through the dusk came the opening bars of a song 'Da da du du du da da . . .' She smiled. 'When You Wish Upon a Star'. She would sit there all evening and drink in the beauty and tranquillity. Then she heard the sound of crying coming from upstairs. Ho hum, Isobel. She heaved herself up and went inside. By the time she reached Isobel's room the noise had stopped. Just a bad dream. She turned off the children's lights, lifting a Beano off James's face, returning a monkey to Poppy's pillow, putting the quilt back on Tom. Back downstairs everything was dark. The garden seemed uninviting and cold now. She might as well watch *ER* and *Sex in the City*, neither of which Frank would tolerate. She really ought to do her fitness video. She drank two glasses of water instead. There was a family-size bag of Rolos in the cupboard, perhaps she would just have one.

During the ads she muted the TV. The noises of her home at rest, the boiler flaming and relaxing, water in the pipes, the sighs of the fridge, the rattles of the sashes when a train went past, all served to comfort her as she sat on the floor and ate the chocolates one by one. She created a Rolo-shaped mass from the gold papers, scrunching and destroying the evidence of how many she had eaten, even though there was nobody but herself to deceive, and nobody who might censure her pigginess.

Meanwhile at the pub Frank was making his second pint last as long as possible. It was his turn to drive Melody home, so unfortunately he couldn't get wasted. But The Wild years had been red hot that night.

It was often the way: he went out with no expectations and everything just clicked. It was some sort of special electricity, something in the air, in their blood temperatures. It was all perfect, complex and beautiful. As he played he thought of the beautiful Indian brass wire ball that Father Christmas had given to James. It was called a mandala, something like that. It had beads on the wire and could be made into different shapes, but it always came back to being a sphere.

Last orders came and went. Eventually they were loading up the equipment. Melody remained aloof to this bit. She had an impressive policy of never, ever helping. She would sit at the bar and smoke and sip her last drink. Or lounge around making comments as they staggered past her with the PA. From the way her T-shirts clung Frank speculated that she must wear the sort of bras that he only ever got to see on billboards. She blew smoke in great clouds as he passed her. He inhaled deeply. How sweet it was. She had pale, slender wrists, and wore silver and aquamarine bangles that jangled each time she moved. She would never ask for a lift home. It was her divine right. One of The Wild Years would take her home. She always hoped that it would be Frank.

She could have had any of the others, and they had all tried their luck at some time or other, but Frank, the one who wasn't available, was the only one that she would have had. It wasn't that she was desperate or anything. She just thought he was pretty good-looking, and funny, and kind, and talented. And married. Actually she quite liked the idea that he was married. His wife obviously didn't know how lucky she was. Melody remembered seeing them all together in town. Posy had been wearing a hippy skirt that was bunched up around her waist and made her hips look enormous. Posy hadn't taken much notice of Melody when Frank introduced them. She seemed to be hunting in her bag for something. When James piped up

'Daddy, is this the lady you were throwing flowers to in Asda?' Frank had quickly ushered them all away. It looked as though Posy hadn't heard anyway. Pity. Melody would have liked to see him get out of that one.

'Ready Melody?' Frank said. She drained her glass and nodded. 'Haven't you got a coat?'

'You are such a Dad!' she said.

'I'm not,' he said. 'Really I'm not.' But she was lighting another cigarette, not listening.

He drove slowly because there were so many students about. You never knew when one of them was going to come lurching into the road in front of you. The lights were all for them, and soon they were through the city and heading over the Itchen Bridge. The warm, salty air streamed through the open windows.

When they were almost at Weston he heard that tune again.
'Do Da Do Da Do Da Da . . .

'What is that?' he said. It had been bugging him all day.

'When you wish upon a star . . .' sang Melody.

Of course, of course. It was playing again and again, getting louder. Jimminy Cricket was sending him a message from across the Solent.

'Mind if we go and see where it's coming from?' he asked.

'Don't you know?'

Instead of turning inland towards the estate he took the coast road, down past The Seaweed Pub, and soon they were parked on Weston Shore.

'When you wish upon a star . . .' The tune came again, louder.

'When you park on Weston Shore . . .' Frank sang.

'Look! There it is!' said Melody. 'I'd love to go on that.'

Suspended in the darkness in front of them, strung with pink and yellow beads of light, was a ship.

'Off to Neverland,' said Frank.

It was the Disney cruise liner.

'When you wish upon A star . . .'

'I don't suppose I'll ever get to go on that ship,' Melody said.

She sounded so mournful and little and sad. He leant over and kissed her.

There was something oblong digging into his leg. He pulled it out of his pocket and chucked it out of the window.

When you wish upon a star . . .

It was like being young, doing it uncomfortably, desperately, with half your clothes still on.

Posy had no passion any more. He wondered if she had ever had any. He suspected that it had become a wifely duty for her, listed somewhere between unloading the washing machine and making the packed lunches. He almost started to tell Melody 'My wife doesn't understand me.'

'Undo your hair' he said. She shook it out of its ponytail and it fell across her shoulders and her pale little breasts. They were like shells. He had a mermaid in the van with him.

'You are so, so beautiful,' he said. When Melody took off her jeans he found that her stomach was smooth and taut. He couldn't help notice the contrast with Posy's, which had become, as she put it, like a used teabag, and as stripy as a tiger from stretch marks. Dear God, he was lost, lost.

Melody was making all these little noises that were making him crazy. Posy (oh why was he thinking of Posy?) seemed to have taken a Vow of Silence in bed soon after Jimmy arrived.

He couldn't stop himself now. This was what his life was meant to be like. The pink and yellow lights and the notes were all around them.

Afterwards they smoked (oh the intense pleasure of being with someone who smoked afterwards,) and watched as the Disney ship disappeared into the night.

'Melody,' he said. 'Melody.' The name was music to him. 'I should never have done that. You know my situation. It was beautiful. You are beautiful. The most beautiful thing to happen to me in a long time. But I shouldn't have. I'm sorry.'

It was a lie. He was not sorry, not yet anyway. He wanted to kiss her again.

'Hey Frank,' she said. 'No big deal.'

He dropped her off and drove home very slowly. Back home, seeing the children's shoes lined up in the hall, ready for the morning, he realised what that thing digging into him had been. Shit. The stardust card. He knew without a doubt that one of them would ask him for it in the morning.

OCTOBER

Tom's was the next birthday. It involved a Batman theme party with black, grey and yellow balloons, bats in the party boxes, and a bat symbol cake with four candles, made by Flora. There were six small batmen, a Spiderman, Bob the Builder, two princesses who were ostracised, and two children whose mummies or daddies hadn't realised that it was fancy dress. The present from Aunty Flora was swimming lessons, not just for Tom, but for James and Poppy too. She had gone ahead and booked them at a pool within walking distance and on an afternoon that she knew would suit Posy. She said that she would take the children herself when she could.

'Wow!' said all of the Parousellis. Frank tried to appear suitably grateful too. 'If I wanted my kids to have swimming lessons, don't you think I'd arrange and pay for them myself?' was what he felt like saying.

Amongst Posy's favourite sounds was the squeak and rustle of balloons tied to the gate for a child's party and, even better, the sound it made if it rained on them the night after the party.

She had always wanted to live in Paris, in an attic apartment, to be a Françoise Sagan character, and see the Parisian sky 'cut into pathetic triangles' by the rooftops, to lie on her bed reading a new novel whilst the rain drummed on the sky light.

Hearing rain on the balloons in the dark was the next best thing.

She'd bought a one-way ticket and no returns were issued on the Eurostar that had taken her from aspiring Sagan heroine to Mummy. It made her think of her own mother listening to a Dr Hook record, 'The Ballad of Lucy Jordan'. Now Posy, like her mother and the woman in the song, realised that she'd never ride to Paris, in a sports car, with the warm wind in her hair.

She listened to the rain on the balloons and finished the last of the supper dishes.

'Want some help?' Frank appeared in the kitchen just as she took off her rubber gloves.

'No thanks. I'm all washed up already.'

She would untie the balloons from the gate the next day and throw them away when the children weren't looking. She hated it if they started to look deflated and sad. Rather than noisily burst them she made little snips at their necks so that they would silently perish. She knew from experience that this could only be done to balloons that had already started to wither.

'If you don't mind,' Frank said, 'I might just go out for a bit, if everything is done . . .'

'I thought you'd be staying in seeing as it is Tom's birthday. But if you want to . . .'

She had imagined them sitting in companionable silence, exhausted but happy after the day. After all it was a special day. 'It doesn't matter.'

'Ok then. See you later.' He kissed the top of her head and was gone. It seemed to Posy that Frank could only take so much of the happy family stuff. When they'd had a lovely day he seemed to need to do something to neutralise it, obliterate it from his mind. He seemed to have two separate existences. She wondered which was his real life.

Frank thought that Posy looked a bit miffed but that she

wouldn't really mind. She could probably do with a bit of time to herself; he certainly could. Soon he was sitting in the pub with The Wild Years.

'Here's to a kid-free zone!' he said. Then Melody arrived with one of her friends. She plonked herself down on the bench beside Al, even though Frank had moved up to make room for her.

'What would you like?' Frank asked.

'My round,' said Al.

'I can give you a lift home,' Frank said, as soon as Al disappeared to the bar.

'No thanks,' said Melody, and she shook her head.

Posy was in bed when he got in, but she heard the TV and smelt his kebab. There was bound to be something unmissable on. Frank was more tired than he realised. It had been a very long day. He fell asleep with the kebab half-eaten on his knees. When he woke, just after four, he was freezing. The heating had gone off hours ago. He had a sort of cramp (or could it possibly be gout?) in one of his feet. He tried a few more of the chips, but they had become floppy and sour, the remains of the kebab were stone cold too. He realised with pleasure that he had eaten the two big green chillies. Their hats and stalks were on the side of his plate. He was impressed. He couldn't have been that drunk if he'd bothered to get a plate. The bin was too full for him to cram it all into, so he left it beside the sink. It could be dealt with in the morning.

When Posy came down the next day she thought that he had deliberately left it for her to clear up. It looked obscene. The vile, green, bitten-off chilli tops were the final insult. She scraped it all into the overflowing liner, tied up the sack, and hefted it out to the wheelie bin All this before she'd even had a cup of tea.

A few hours and many cups of tea later she was outside dealing with the shrivelling balloons. Flora arrived.

'I'm just on my way to a storage solution. I thought you'd like these. I've already picked over them. They aren't wormy.'

It was a bag of apples from what Posy and Flora still thought of as Aunt Is's apple tree. The tree had been Flora's for years now, but they couldn't forget how much they had enjoyed picking the apples, and how much they had hated cutting up the windfalls. Their Aunt had a very thrifty attitude towards them. ('There's plenty of good in that one. Musn't let them go to waste' she'd say even though there were hundreds of perfect ones still to be gathered in.) The tree had once been espaliered but Aunt is had eventually let it do what it liked. Flora now kept it well-pruned. Aunt Bea had told her that a pigeon should be able to fly through the branches.

Posy took the bag of apples and picked up her scissors.

'Thanks.' Now she would have to do something with them. Unfortunately they weren't eaters. 'I was just deflating these balloons.'

'Well thank goodness you're doing that outside!'

Posy looked blankly back at her

'Haven't you ever thought about the germs inside balloons? That warm exhaled air kept enclosed. Everything allowed to grow, to breed, and then people just blithely pop them or let them down in the house, in enclosed spaces. I suppose after a day it wouldn't be too bad, but you've had balloons lasting in centrally heated conditions for weeks before, haven't you?'

'I hadn't really thought about it. I don't think many people have ever suffered from balloon-bred diseases.'

'How can you be sure? There probably just isn't the research yet. Don't your children always seem to get ill after a birthday?'

'They always seem to get ill, full stop,' said Posy. 'I really don't think I can start worrying about balloon germs.'

They went inside. Tom was lounging on the sofa watching Teletubbies, Isobel was strapped into her car seat with an activity frame in front of her. Posy slumped down beside Tom.

Flora thought it odd that she made no move to switch the Teletubbies off, or even turn them down. They seemed to be having some terrible misunderstanding which involved Tinky Winky endlessly saying 'pardon?'.

'Oh, how utterly like the Teletubbies to say "pardon",' said Flora.

'Pardon?' said Po, joining the fun.

'Oh Posy, how on earth do you stand it?' Flora asked.

'I just don't hear or see it anymore,' Posy said. 'Sorry. I really should switch it off,' but she didn't, not wanting to have to amuse Tom.

'I've just become immune to it. It all washes over you. You operate above or below the din. It really is possible to think of two things at the same time, to have two separate trains of thought running together. I try not to look at the Teletubbies anyway . . . their fat, padded, bottoms . . . they always look as though their nappies need changing . . . oh great, it's the tapdancing teddy. I love this one.'

Flora sighed.

'Do you know, the day before yesterday,' she said, changing the subject, 'I was doing a clear out for a woman who had a box with several hundred old rubber gloves in it. The ones at the bottom were perished and stuck together, but she still didn't want to throw them away. She said that when one of her current pair got a hole in it she didn't want to waste the other one, so she started a new pair but kept the old survivor. I have no idea what for.'

'Cat sick?' suggested Posy 'Cleaning the loo?' She had a lot of sympathy for Flora's clients.

'But she never actually used any of them, just added to the heap.'

'Oh.'

'I advised her that she had to think of rubber gloves as disposable, like kitchen paper, that she should never have more than one pair out and a spare pair in the cupboard.'

'Or she could buy a box of those transparent throw-away gloves.'

'Well . . .' said Flora. 'I don't think she would actually use them.'

'But she'd know they were there,' said Posy.

Flora gave a muffled howl of exasperation.

'Actually,' she said 'There was something I wanted to run by you, as a stressed parent'

'Oh yes?'

'I had an idea in the night, a way of expanding the business. "Model Role Models." What do you think?'

'Er,' said Posy.

'Model Role Models. I would supply people on an hourly basis to do things like help with homework, teach children to read, play football, make cakes, do craft activities and clear up afterwards, go on walks and identify flowers, teach children to ride bikes. All the things that modern parents know they should be doing but either have no time or inclination for.'

'Hmm. But where would you recruit these Model Role Models?'

'Childless people? Grandparents who live too far from their own grandchildren? Aspiring grandparents? Poor but efficient parents?'

'I don't know,' said Posy. 'You'd have to get them all police-checked. People might not want someone in the house who was better at baking and football than they were.'

'Maybe it needs some more thought.' Flora was slightly disappointed by Posy's response.

'Maybe.'

Just when Posy thought that she was doing everything right she'd overhear someone saying, 'See you at Football!' or 'How's Tabitha's German going?' She knew that Tabitha was seven. She was in James's class. Or 'I wondered if you might be able to lend us your spare toddler-sized wetsuit.'

'I thought that we had all the bases covered by starting swimming lessons. I thought that wrapped it up,' she told Frank. 'And now I find out that there's some Saturday football club we aren't members of. What's next? Pre-school squash? And tennis lessons! They are all doing tennis lessons! We haven't even got a tennis racquet between us.'

'But would James want to do any of this?' Frank sighed.

'Or Poppy or Tom,' said Posy. 'Tom's age go too.' She pulled a desperate face.

'Look,' said Frank. 'They don't need or want tennis lessons. They should be out climbing trees and poking around in ditches with sticks by themselves. What's important here Posy?'

But she wouldn't let it drop. 'And some of them are Beavers, I found that out last week. And Badgers.'

'Well ask James then. Ask him if he wants to do any of this stuff. As long as it's less than one pound a week.'

When she asked him James said: 'Mum, I would go to the football, even though I'm not as good as Duncan. But what I really want is for us all to go skiing.'

'Ah, skiing. You'll have to ask your Dad about that one.'

'George's been five times and he wants to know when we're going. He said we could go in half-term like he is.'

It had been the same after September 11. After the initial horror, people's concerns seemed to turn to family-preservation. She imagined that this was yet another thing that she wasn't up to speed with. The families with wetsuits were certain to have chemical and biological warfare protection suits stashed in the back of their MPVs. This she didn't discuss with Frank.

She'd bought a six pack of Evian and put it in the cupboard under the stairs with a carrier bag full of plasters, tins of beans, nappies, baby wipes, a torch and some biscuits. That would have to do. She had wondered about keeping a can of petrol for emergency escapes by car (Frank was always driving around with the tank practically empty) but decided it was too much of a fire risk.

But the suits. What could she do about the suits? Was there a local stockist? How would she manage to breastfeed? Did they come in little sizes? She thought of them coming in little sizes and then had to stop herself thinking about it. This way lies madness. Better to hope for a nuclear strike and all perish in the initial blast.

Flora came round on her way back from sorting out somebody's computer.

Poppy let her in.

'Hello Aunty Flora. It's Friday. Sweets Day.' Poppy hugged her. Flora held on to her for a long time, stroking her hair.

'Hello best niece.'

'Would you like some liquorice Aunty Flora? It's quite a required taste.' Poppy politely offered her bag of mini Liquorice Allsorts.

'Yes please. Mmm. Yum yum.' Flora chose a small black chimney. She calculated that this would have the lowest sugar and awful things content.

'Mum's in the kitchen.'

'Thanks sweetie, and for the sweetie.' Poppy returned to CBBC. Flora found Posy scrubbing potatoes.

'Hi. Finished that installation thingy already?' Posy asked. She was constantly amazed at how much Flora managed to fit into her days. All Posy managed to do was to get through each day and make a stab at preparing for the next one.

'Honestly,' she said. 'I don't know why people buy these things if they don't know how to use them. She didn't even know how to use e-mail.'

'I expect that's why she bought it,' Posy said.

'What? And the companies that sell them should install them free of charge. They tell people that it is simple. But that's only if you're confident and competent.'

'Stay for tea?' Posy asked.

'Just a cup. No cakes. I'm on my way to the gym. I missed it yesterday.' This was very unlike Flora.

'Oh?'

'Rush job on a house move. Emergency help with packing. This poor woman, eight-and-a-half months pregnant and about to move house. Her skinflint husband had insisted that he and "this mate" would do it all. Of course the mate's van is suddenly "unavailable", and the husband does his back in. He was lying on the floor watching Sky Sport whilst this poor woman and I worked. Very fishy. I found her some movers but it was too late for any packers.'

'That sounds like harder work than going to the gym.'

'I know, but I have to cover all the muscle groups.'

'Well you must be right, and you know what Madame would say, said Posy, quoting *Ballet Shoes*, 'Miss your practice for one day, and you'll know it. Miss it for two days, and your teacher will know it. Miss it for three days and the whole world will know it!'

'Too true,' said Flora, looking critically at her long, lean legs in their cropped blue jersey sweatpants.

'I wish I could come with you. I'd love a swim and a steam.'

'Then do.'

'Oh I can't.' This was what Posy always seemed to say. With a wave of her hand she indicated the chaos of the kitchen 'I've got to make their supper.'

'Can't Frank?'

'Oh he's off somewhere with AI. I think they were meant to be helping someone move actually, in the van.'

Flora, like Posy, thought that she might never measure up, or that if she did now then she mustn't let things slip. She felt as though they were always upping the stakes. She was naturally slim, always at the gym, she swam fifty lengths three times a week, but still it wasn't enough. There was always room for improvement. The mid-thirties was no time for sliding. She had her nails done sometimes; did them herself most of the time, not quite to New York standards, but still. She had pedicures and tried to stay on top of her feet. But she remembered how when she was younger, nobody had even thought about upper arms. Now there were endless articles devoted to them. Upper arms just hadn't existed. Now new standards had been introduced. And the latest thing was shoulders. She was astonished. New guidelines were on the way. It was thanks to the dresses at award ceremonies. How could you tell if your shoulders passed muster? And now she had read, it was beyond contemplation, that people were having plastic surgery, cosmetic enhancement Down There. What would Aunt Is say if she read about it? Flora thought that there really ought to be limits.

Posy didn't tell her, couldn't tell anyone, that the reason she wanted a swim and especially a steam was that she was now permanently unclean. That morning she had woken early. The house was quiet. She was wide awake, full of energy, happy. Isobel might sleep for another hour yet, they all might. She tiptoed downstairs. If she used the downstairs bathroom there was no danger of waking anyone. She made herself a cup of Lapsang Souchong and sipped it standing by the open back door whilst her bath ran. This was what her life was meant to be like. It was going to be a warm, beautiful day, Indian summer. She had a magazine to read (thank you Flora). She slid down into the lavender foam (thank you Flora). She could stay there for forty minutes at least, and wash her hair, and maybe paint her toenails before they all got up. Oh bliss, oh silence, oh joy. She quite liked her body when all she could see of it was her hands holding the magazine and her knees sticking out of the foam. She might just drift off for a while.

Eventually after two extra blasts of hot water, the magazine exhausted, her skin shrivelled but very soft and scented, she got out. She thought she could hear voices upstairs. Seven-forty.

She'd had hours to herself. Dry, relaxed, restored, the last of the water drained away, she stooped to clean the bath and put her shampoo where the children couldn't reach it. Then she saw it. A huge, bloated, orange, very dead slug. She was too horrified even to scream. She picked it up in a wad of loo paper and threw it out the window. Someone was banging on the door.

'Mum. I have to go to the loo.'

'Just a minute.' she said in a cracked voice.

'No I have to go NOW.'

'Go upstairs.'

'I can't. There's no loo paper left. Muuuum.'

'OK. OK.'

She had to have a shower. She seized her packet of cleansing wipes (they said that they would remove waterproof mascara, but slug contamination?) and fled upstairs. Isobel was screaming. Poppy and Tom were arguing. Frank was still asleep. She locked herself in the upstairs bathroom and tried to wipe everywhere. She used the whole packet. She had saved so many tokens from Special K Red Berries for them, and now they were all gone. She couldn't get that slug out of her mind. Had it been there for her whole bath? Had it been lurking there before she ran the water and been scalded, drowned or bubble-bathed to death? Might it have been on her, gone on to her foot when she looked out the back door, and she herself had carried it into the bath? Where had it been all the time? Might it have been on her? Under her? Ugh. Maybe it had been lurking under one of the children's flannels and had fallen in, perhaps quite near the end of her bath. Maybe, oh maybe, it had been under the plug, and so hadn't been in with her at all, had only come up into the bath when she pulled the plug out. She could hope, but she would never know. Now she would always be The Woman Who Bathes With Slugs.

Frank was amazed at the way that Posy could blend with the crowd in the school playground. She could really pull the wool over their eyes and look like one of the Mums. Then he realised that she was one of the Mums, and that was clearly how she intended to look. He wondered if they had all been kitted out at some secret nearly new sale, perhaps run by the NCT. Invitations were given out on the maternity wards, with special shopping privileges for people who had home births. There were regulation sandals, special bendy ones from M & S. There must be forty pairs of them (navy, black or ill-considered white) in the school playground on any morning from May to October. They were indestructible.

And boy had she changed! One minute she was dancing around the kitchen in a slinky black dress, smoking Camels and drinking huge goblets of white wine on ice; and the next she had stopped completely, just like that. No gum, no nothing: no turning back. And she'd expected him to as well, just because it was something she was doing. The black dresses had disappeared, and instead all these shapeless things arrived in the post.

'Since when did you wear pale pink sweatshirts?' he'd asked, and she had burst into tears. He hadn't added that they were pig colour. Perhaps he didn't need to. He supposed that she could see for herself, and she was getting pretty enormous. And the stripy tops! It was as though she had gone undercover. Secret Agent Pregnant Posy. He was still waiting for the real one, if there was a real one, to come back to him.

Once he had found her reading *Junior* magazine. He'd said, 'Isn't it bad enough having children without having to read about them too?'

'Oh Kate gave it to me. There's an article about nut allergies,' she'd replied, looking up, hurt; but he had already left the room.

He knew that she worried, but he had no idea how anxious she really was, that she couldn't cross the road with the pram without thinking 'I hope there isn't an invisible car coming . . .'

Frank had never really thought about the long-term, or

about long-term compatibility. 'It'll all pan out' could have been his motto, or perhaps his epitaph. He had just drifted into the whole thing with Posy because she was so damn pretty. He'd never really wanted a relationship. How he hated that word. Relationship. And people saying that they couldn't relate to things and people going to the gym and stage one and two car seats . . . It was all a load of shit as far as he was concerned.

It had all just happened, her money and the house, which had once been a place for parties and band practice. Not anymore. She couldn't be doing with all of those trailing wires. He had once been allowed to store the PA. in one of the bedrooms. The Seaside Bunnies had put paid to that. She was still on at him because he hadn't ever finished putting up the border. As if a baby cared how its room was decorated. The border was so high up that it would just be a blur to it anyway. It wasn't his fault that it had cost £20.75 a roll from Designers Guild. It co-ordinated with the musical mobile that Posy had hung above the cot. a boy and a girl rabbit danced forever around an apple tree. Round and round they went in their perfect world, but they would never meet.

She was trying to turn him into someone with a Brita water filter, someone who used Domestos anti-bacterial lemon-scented wipes. He knew that there was one piece missing from her 'Perfect Family – Perfect Lives' jigsaw puzzle: a high-earning Daddy. Well he couldn't measure up to that.

But he did love her, whatever that meant. He figured that it was just a phase, just her latest incarnation. Existentialist to Mummy. He would stick with it and hope that she'd get more reasonable once the prolactin wore off again.

Things hadn't turned out like this for Al. When he'd quit his teaching job, Caroline had quit him. Frank and Al agreed that she was a hard, hard woman. Al had been really struggling. Teaching English to fifteen-year-olds was no picnic. A few months after Finn was born he suddenly just couldn't take any more. He decided to leave before the stress destroyed him. Caroline had known he was unhappy at the school, but even so, she went ballistic. Where did it all leave her? That was what she wanted to know. OK, so he could walk into a supply job the very next day (although he chose not to) but he hadn't even consulted her, just upped and done it. The ice entered her heart.

Al eventually got a part-time job with the scrapStore, driving their van, picking up junk from companies to be used by adventure playgrounds and playgroups and so on. The pay was pretty crap, but he was bringing in a bit with the band, and he thought he would be happier, have more time with Finn. Caroline thought differently. In her plan he was soon to be a Departmental, then a Deputy, and then a Head. The pay in teaching really wasn't bad once you got out of the sergeants' mess. She was going to have to go back to work part-time now. Until Al had decided to backslide, back pedal, whatever, things had been looking rosy for them.

Al said that he was writing a comic thriller called *'Filed Away'*, about an evil pensioner who attacks people with his incredibly long and sharp poisonous toenails. The police are baffled until one day a bright young cop goes back over some unsolved cases that are languishing in the files . . . Caroline didn't find any of this funny.

'The thing you have to watch out for,' Al told Frank, over their fourth pint, 'is when they start talking in all this made-up emotional language, as though they've secretly been reading *'Men are from Mars,'*

'They probably have,' said Frank.

'All this daytime TV crap about "meeting needs".'

'They do watch daytime TV, when they aren't reading magazines and self-help books.'

'But there was nothing I could do. I was doomed. Once she switched into that mode I was done for,' Al went on.

'I'll be all right,' Frank told him. 'Posy would do anything before she would appear on *Trisha*. She's too buttoned up. Not a "spill the beans" kind of a girl. She just wants everything to appear perfect and calm.'

'You wanna watch out, mate,' Al said. Frank didn't appreciate what he still had. 'It's contagious. Divorce and discontent. There was this study in Sweden . . .'

What Al didn't tell Frank was what Caroline had really said.

'The thing is Al, I just don't love you anymore.'

There was no answer to that.

One thing that had interested him throughout the proceedings was how colloquial the breaking of hearts turned out to be, how mundane.

'It's like, gone beyond the point of no return,' she had said. He'd thought 'Shit, shouldn't the language be, like, like Shakespeare, for something like this?' If this was a 'life event' then he could do without them.

He swirled the last of his beer around and around in his glass, first one way, then the other: rough seas.

Frank had drained his own glass.

'Fancy another?'

Now each Thursday, thanks to Aunty Flora, James, Poppy and Tom had a swimming lesson at an ancient pool, a swimming baths really, just south of The Common. The pool belonged to a college that had once been run by runs. Posy liked to think of the nuns taking a swim. Nuns and Swimmers – good title for a book or a painting. It was the Parousells' kind of pool, all cracked blue tiles, keyless lockers, no flumes or jets or even a tea machine. The water was bath hot, but the college had problems with its heating and when the oil didn't arrive the parents who sat at the poolside watching their offspring were in a thick fog. Condensation dripped onto their heads. 'If only we were at Kew Gardens,' Posy thought. Tom had to sit through his older siblings lessons, half an hour each, once his own had finished. She and Frank bribed him with Wotsits or Teddy crisps to make him sit still. It was also the occasion of his weekly carton of Toothkind Strawberry Ribena. If things got desperate they gave him white chocolate buttons.

Posy liked watching the children swimming, liked knowing that they would be able to do it in an emergency, that they were enjoying it, that they were getting some exercise. Frank found it depressing.

'Oh can't you take them Pose? You know I hate it.' he begged.

'How can you hate it? It's lovely seeing them make progress.'

'No it's not that. 'Course I like them swimming. But don't you just find it a bit bleak, all those children struggling, getting told off if they put their feet on the bottom?'

'Can't you try to see it differently?'

'And so many of the children are fat. Here's all the evidence they need that we're becoming obese as a nation.'

'They aren't that fat,' said Posy.

'Open you eyes, Pose! Remember when you were at school? Only one or two kids in a whole school would be overweight. Now it looks like half of them.'

'Well, I never noticed,' said Posy. Actually she had noticed but she would never have said anything; she had much too big a complex about her own body to comment on other people's. Frank had no such complex and no qualms about stating what he saw as harsh truths.

'Well, I hope none of the other parents ever hear you say anything like this.'

'Do them good if they did. It's all their fault. They're the ones loading up the trolleys.'

'Maybe swimming's not typical,' said Posy, trying to excuse the nation's children and their parents.

'Yeah, you're right,' said Frank. 'Swimming probably is the exercise of choice of the urban fatty. You can imagine the parents saying "Well, he won't be any good at football, he won't be a runner, I know . . . swimming!" '

'Please could you just take them,' Posy pleaded. 'Just take them without it being an issue.'

'OK. OK.'

'I'll go and pack the swimming things,' said Posy. 'And you can get some chips on the way home.'

'I said OK,' said Frank. Honestly, he was only saying what he thought.

'Or you could even take them to McDonald's . . .'

She had to be out of her mind. Did she think he could stand swimming and McDonald's in one day? He saw hell in a Happy Meal, desolation in the accompanying toy. The marriage of Disney and McDonald's. A marriage made in heaven, so perfect that it made his head spin.

'Posy,' he yelled after her 'I forgot to tell you I have a gig tonight.'

'OK,' she called down the stairs.

It seemed to make no difference to her whether he was in or out.

He was wrong about this. She was glad he was going out because she could have cereal for dinner.

NOVEMBER

A S SHE TRUDGED THROUGH the brown slippery muck of autumn leaves on the pavement (and who knew what it concealed) she could feel the dampness seeping into her boots. They needed polishing. She kept her head down. She had reached that stage of motherhood where any adornment was superfluous. Rings had been the first to go when James was newborn because she feared scratching him or catching his hair on them. She had seen how the hospital midwives turned their rings around when they were bathing the babies. But it all seemed so precarious. What if she forgot and scratched him? Only her plain gold wedding band remained.

Earrings and necklaces were next to go, when James got to the reaching and grasping stage. She remembered the rumours about girls at school who had their earlobes torn in fights. Soon she jettisoned scarves and bracelets, anything that wasn't needed for decency. (No time! No time!) Long ago getting ready to go out had been such a big deal, and took at least two hours. Things had happened after a Badedas bath. Now, in the unlikely event of her and Frank going out together in the evening, the only thing she was concerned about was whether the babysitting plans would work, and whether any of the children would be ill so that they couldn't (or perhaps didn't have to) go. She wondered if the harried mothers of the future would feel incomplete and sad when they started going out

without their navel ornaments. At least that was one loss that
she wouldn't feel. She had forgotten what going out could be
like, the excitement and the streets smelling of popcorn, even
when there was no popcorn.

And so Posy was transformed and things were left behind.
But she was aware that somewhere carousels were turning,
there were people laughing in swing boats, dancing in white
dresses, stepping out of limousines. That there were hotels
with golden mirrors, reflecting golden mirrors to infinity. Her
gloveless hands were chapped, the nails unpolished, her
fingertips had become so scaly that she could have snipped
bits of dead dry skin off them. Somewhere people were trying
on sequinned, embroidered shoes. Posy had her pram-pushing
hat on. You couldn't carry an umbrella and manage a pushchair at the same time. She'd had it for years. It pulled down a
long way, was made of some kind of artificial velvet stuff and
was brown. She was very fond of it. When Flora had given it to
her she had said, 'Does it make me look like Ingrid Bergman,
you know, with this mac on? It has a certain stylishness . . .'

'Oh exactly,' Flora had smiled.

So here was Posy, a dumpy Ingrid Bergman, plodding
through Portswood in her hat.

When she was little she had loved watching old musicals.
She had hoped that when she grew up life would be like that, a
long romance where everybody suddenly burst out singing: a
glorious cycle of song. There would be neat little dances, and
somehow everyone would know all the words.

Huh! though Posy, 'And I am Marie of Ronmania.' She was
on one of her endless circuits, school – pre-school – shops –
home – preschool – home – shops for whatever she had
forgotten – school – home, punctuated by the endless making
of, and clearing up after, meals. She was dragging herself
along, it was like wading through mud. She looked down to
see if perhaps her boots were on the wrong feet. 'Some
marched asleep,' she thought. How was it that everyone else

managed? Was it only her that made such heavy weather of it all? Or perhaps everyone else was the same: only just managing to muster the fifteen minutes of cheerfulness required in the playground twice each day.

A wax-jacketed figure loomed up beside her and then skidded on the leaves, pushchair wheels coming dangerously close to Isobel's. They could get stuck like that for ever, a pair of stags, antlers locked. It was Fraser and Lizzie's mum, also known as Jan, in an expensive hat that matched her jacket. Posy thought it made her look like a stuffed olive. It amazed Posy that she had friends with hats like this. What had they all come to? Now we are all pillocks in stupid hats, endlessly going to the cashpoint and posting letters, she thought. She would often see someone from a distance and think, 'What a stupid hat. Imagine going around in a stupid hat like that', then up close she would realise that it was one of her friends, and that the hat was just like her own. How the mighty are fallen, she thought. Look upon my fleece ye mighty and despair. If she tried hard she could remember a time before fleece had taken over the world; a time when a fleece had been golden, or on a sheep, or at a stretch, the brown bobbly acrylic lining of old ladies' zip-up boots. Come to think of it, a pair of those boots would be jolly useful.

'Horrible leaves,' said Jan.

'Are you all right?' Posy asked.

'Fine, thanks. Just slipped. They should clear all this muck up.'

'I read somewhere that our autumns are getting as good as New England's. Climate change. More rain or something.'

Jan wasn't really listening. Posy saw her surreptitiously look at her watch. I am this boring, boring even to Jan, she thought.

'I think we're in good time. Three minutes in hand.'

Time to slip and fall over and not cry, unless you were a toddler, and then you could howl as loud as you wanted, or time to buy something at the newsagents, or just to be early and stand cold and damp in the playground.

'Didn't see you at the school fireworks,' said Jan. The Parousellis never usually missed a School Association event.

'Oh we bought tickets,' said Posy, feeling guilty. 'But everybody had such bad colds, and Izzie started a temperature, so we had to miss it this year.'

'Always next year,' said Jan with a smile that was intended to offer comfort and encouragement.

(Posy didn't tell her that Frank had said 'Thank God we don't have to go to something for once.'

'But Frank, it's Bonfire Night!' she'd said, looking astonished

'Oh why do you have to celebrate everything?')

Ahead of them two young men were getting out of a jeep, laughing and unloading golf clubs.

'They look too young to play golf,' said Posy.

'Even the golfers are getting younger these days.' This was pretty funny for Jan. The young men looked very pleased with themselves, full of bonhomie. As the mums drew close one of them took off his baseball cap and tossed it into the boot of the jeep.

'Good,' thought Posy. It left him with a dreadful line between the hat-flattened hair and the hair below it, what the Parousellis called 'horrible-hat-head'. Posy wished that Frank and the children were there to see such a fine example. She snorted.

'Horrible-hat-head,' she explained to Jan who looked blankly at her. The golfers were oblivious to them. Posy knew that pushing a pram had rendered her invisible to at least half of the human race. Often this pleased her. She could pass by unseen.

She had to stop for a moment to wipe Izzie's nose, then her own, on the same sodden tissue. Can't even have a cold to myself now, she thought.

Up ahead of them they could see the signature pale blue-baseball cap, ancient brown bomber jacket, khaki canvas trousers tucked into socks, and van Gogh boots of another of the playground regulars. Nobody knew his name, he was known only as Karim's grandfather. His outfit would have looked cool on a student or a DJ. Posy wondered at the shopping trips, perhaps to Help the Aged, that had resulted in his attire.

He did nearly all of the dropping off and picking up of his two grandsons and his little granddaughter who was at the pre-school. He always smiled at Posy and her children, held the school gate open for them with exaggerated gestures of gallantry, and commented on whether or not Isobel was asleep.

'The more they sleep, the more they grow,' he told her, and she constantly wondered the extent to which this was true. He carried an umbrella for each of the children, two *Bug's Life* ones and a *Fetch The Vet* one, but didn't have one of his own, so would use one of the children's if they weren't with him. The diameter of these kiddies' umbrellas was barely larger than that of his head. He ran errands and did most of the shopping for the family too. Posy often saw him heading back from Somerfield or the greengrocer's with a pushchair loaded up with shopping. The family lived in the same street as the Parousellis, but up the other end. She saw him so often that she had come to rely on it, and think that if she saw him then all would be well, and all would be well, and all manner of things would be well.

He waited at the gate to the playground and held it open for them and the pushchairs, giving a little bow as they went through.

'Thank you,' said Posy. Jan just smiled and nodded.

'She awake today,' he said, pointing at Isobel with his chin.

'Yes, she's already had her nap.'

'And where is little one? He asleep?'

'Just at home with his Dad.'

'Another day off for Dad?'

'He's a musician. It's always his day off,' Posy explained.

'Ah.'

'He plays the double bass, you know.' She mimed it.

'I see, I see,' he said, as though this was of special significance. Then the children started to come out and all adults' conversation ceased.

It was Wednesday which meant ballet. They went straight from school. The classes were held in the pavilion of some private gardens. Poppy had just been promoted to the second class. She would be ready to take Grade 1 that year.

Posy desperately hoped that Isobel wasn't going to want a feed. The idea of doing it on one of the benches where the mums waited during the class . . . She had brought a beaker of water. Perhaps that would fob her off.

When the weather was fine taking Poppy to ballet was a treat. Children played in the gardens whilst the parents vaguely kept an eye on them. Isobel would often sit happily in her pushchair or on Posy's knee, watching what was going on. If it rained they would be cowering on the veranda. They couldn't hear the music from outside, but Posy liked to watch the class through the window; seeing Poppy who was quite good, but often a beat behind the others, was like seeing a ghost of her former self. Young, hopeful Posy, pretty in pink. The teacher, Miss Miranda, was in her early twenties and was Poppy's heroine. She had married in the spring and was now pregnant. She had a very small, neat bump and still looked elegant and graceful in her jazz dance trousers and black T-shirt. Posy couldn't imagine her with swelling ankles and a moon face.

'She'll end up like us,' said Jan beside her.

'Oh!' said Posy. It was like a blow to the stomach. She felt her eyes fill with tears but Jan didn't notice. Stupid, stupid, sentimental, disappointed Posy.

'I brought you that catalogue,' said Jan, and she found it in her shiny brown leather bag. That bag must have cost more the Posy's whole outfit. ' "Dance Direct",' said Jan. 'Really good value.'

'Thanks,' said Posy. 'Hours of amusement.' She could read it while she fed Isobel or in the bath.

'I do love going to the ballet shops, but this will save some time.' Actually it wouldn't she would spend ages looking longingly at the outfits, the crossover cardigans, 'practice' tops, trousers that were 'also suitable for streetwear'. Perhaps a pair of the dance sneakers would have her springing the plod to and from school. Perhaps 'Premier Dancewear's bi-coloured knitted stripy boot-leg pants' would make her lithe and energetic and young again. There were posters and videos, scrunchies and rolls of ribbon, bags of resin and shellac for hardening pointe shoes. She even found the packets of kirby grips alluring.

She gazed and sighed, looking at the dancers modelling special socks 'ideal for moving from class to class'. Socks over tights, now that was a great look. These dancers were all that she hadn't been, and now would never be. If only, she thought, if only I could be one of those jolly mums who make jokes about stretch marks and tucking their tummies into their knickers.

She could order tap shoes for herself and Poppy, and they could take lessons together. It appeared that they came in canvas for only £7.95 a pair. She wondered if any of the practice things would fit her, they looked really fluid and comfy . . . She flicked the pages backwards and forwards, her eyes round and greedy for the images of the beautiful, young, unspoilt bodies. Oh to be like that . . . ah, here was something for her. Plume's 'full body sack'. It had 'tank straps which tie at the front' and was 'oversized for better comfort'. She might as well flap the catalogue shut and throw it across the room. She knew that she would look fat and ridiculous in everything.

Oh just give up Posy, she told herself. She would order the regulation RADA leotard, gauzy skirt and and poignant little ballet socks for Poppy. Aunt is and Aunt Bea provided the cardigans. The only thing Posy would really benefit from buying herself was a pair of leg warmers as she suffered badly from cramp in the winter; but she probably had a pair of them from the eighties, stashed away in some binbag in the loft. In her early teens she had longed to be one of the 'Kids From Fame'. She stuffed 'Dance Direct' into her bag she would order the stuff for Poppy later.

She gave it one last glance, the outside back cover, she hadn't studied that yet. Books. 'Diet For Dancers' by Robin D. Chmelar and Sally S. Fitt. The 'S' must stand for 'Super'. It promised 'A Complete Guide to Nutrition and Weight Control', as well as 'How to Lose Fat, What to Eat and When to Eat, Fads and Frauds, Menus and Meal Planning, and Eating Disorders.' That was the thing for her.

It was Stir Up Sunday. Posy had heard it on the radio.

'Stir up, we beseech thee, O Lord, the wills of thy faithful people' it had said.

'This is what life is meant to be like' she told Frank.

Isobel was asleep. The dishes were done, Poppy and Tom were helping her to make Christmas puddings. James had sloped off to watch a video and she had let him go.

'You have to come and stir it, and make a wish when I call you,' she had said.

'All right Mum, I do want to help you, it's just that I've made enough bread and stuff in my life.'

'Go, go! Pudding-making isn't compulsory, but wishing is.'

'Can I watch *Power Rangers?*'

'No. Something nicer. *Iron Giant* or something.'

It was a Delia recipe, and Posy had made it many times before. This year she was making four puddings, one for Frank's family, one for her Aunts, one for Kate and one for themselves. It was really very easy, just a lot of stirring and endless steaming. One by one the children made their wishes.

'I'm not going to put it in the basins till Isobel is up, so she can have a go,' she explained. 'I'm not sure what she'll wish for.'

'Some bananas maybe,' said Poppy.

'We'll have to get Daddy for his wish' said James.

'Oh yes, I almost forgot him.' Frank had disappeared to his shed. 'Go and get him, please Honey.'

A few minutes later Frank and James came into the kitchen.

'So I have to make a wish, do I?' he said, as though he hadn't done this every year since James was a baby. Posy passed him the spoon.

'Smells good.' It smelt of mostly beer. 'Right, what shall I wish for?' he asked. Then the phone started ringing.

'I'll get it,' said Posy. 'You make your wish.'

A few moments later she was calling him 'Frank, for you.' She came back into the kitchen. 'Sounds like one of your pupils. Somebody young. I hope it's not someone giving up.'

'Frank. It's Melody.'

'Oh, how are you?'

'I can't stop throwing up.'

'Something you ate?'

'Not really. I have to see you.'

'We're out at The Oak tonight, why don't you come along? We haven't seen you for ages.' Frank's 'we' meant The Wild Years, not him and Posy.

'I have something to tell you. I'm pregnant.'

Silence from Frank.

'Frank, I said "I'm pregnant." '

'Don't tell me that. Not now. Not on the phone. No way. Oh God. No way.'

'I have to see you. We have to talk.'

'You know my situation here.'

'Frank . . .'

'I can't talk to you now. Sorry. I have to go.' Poppy was standing in front of him with a wooden spoon. 'Sorry. I have to go. I'll call you back.' He hung up before he heard what she called him.

'Just one of them wanting to change times,' he told Posy. 'Don't forget to put it on the calendar.'

The gig at The Oak that night wasn't a great success. Melody came but refused to sing. She told The Wild Years that she wasn't feeling well. She certainly looked what Frank's mum would have called 'peeky'. Her eyes were sticky with tiredness and mascara. Frank had been through this so many times, the signs were unmistakable. During the first set she sat by herself, folding and refolding beer mats or staring deliberately at nothing. When their break came the other Wild Year's headed for the bar. Frank sat down beside her.

'I haven't had a cigarette in two weeks,' Melody told him. 'I just feel too sick.'

'Good. I mean not that you feel sick, although everyone always says that's a good sign. I mean good, well done.'

'Whaddya mean, "Good. Well done." What's it to you?'

'I don't know,' said Frank. 'Melody, I have no idea what I am meant to say or do. I want you to be all right.'

'But what are you going to do?' she demanded.

'I don't know. What am I meant to do?'

'Are you going to be with me, tell your wife? Huh?'

'I don't know. I just don't know. Are you sure you want to have this?' He couldn't bring himself to say 'baby'. He was desperately hoping that she wouldn't want it, that she would decide not to have it, that it would be her decision not to. He wondered if it might be possible to persuade her not to go ahead with it, but no. He knew that would be reprehensible. But whatever he did or didn't do now, he was damned.

'Well that would be bloody convenient for you, wouldn't it?' she snapped back.

'Melody. I'm sorry. I should never have . . . Oh God, I'm

sorry. I don't know what to do. I'll help you in any way I can. You know I'm broke, but I'll help however I can.'

'So are you going to tell your wife?'

'You used to call her "Posy",' said Frank.

'I didn't used to be the other woman.'

'Look, what can I do? And the kids. I can't tell them yet, anyway. Izzie's not even one . . .'

'My mum says that everything comes out some time,' said Melody. Frank bet that she did. Melody's mum would make sure that Melody got what she was owed. He realised that he was now going to have a whole extra set of relatives to deal with. There was no justice in the world. He would have to leave the country.

'Look Melody. I'll do what I can. I want you to be happy. I'll help where I can. It's so hard to say how it'll all pan out yet. We'll just have to take it a day at a time, won't we?' He placed his hand over hers and gave it a pat. The table was wet and sticky from spilt beer. He realised straight away that his gesture would be interpreted as patronising. It was nearly time for the second set. He could see Al and rich and Ron standing at the bar, draining their pints, laughing at something. He rolled a cigarette. 'Hope you don't mind . . .' The whole pub was full of smoke, one more wouldn't make much difference.

'Nice of you to ask.'

'Fancy another?' said Frank. 'An orange juice or something?' He remembered with a pang how Posy had developed a passion for tomato juice with too much Worcestershire sauce.

'I'll bloody drink what I like,' said Melody. 'Why should I listen to you?' The other Wild Years had now joined them. 'Don't expect me to keep singing with you for ever. You're just a bunch of old losers pretending to be young. You should just grow up. And I don't need a lift home. My brother's picking me up. You might as well tell them Frank.'

'Tell them what?' said Al, as Melody left.

'She's in a foul mood,' said Rich.

'Not like Melody.' said Ron.

'Tell them what?' said AI. Frank saw the landlord giving them a nod. He'd like them to start again. The place was filling up with students.

'That she's pregnant. And it's mine.'

DECEMBER

THE PAROUSELLIS WERE ON their way to a Christmas lunch party at Kate's. Posy had a trifle on her knees. She had always liked it in movies and in episodes of *thirtysomething* when people drove to parties, the woman (usually a mum) balancing a pudding on her lap. What Posy only now realised was that in real life that character would be desperately trying not to let it slop all over her skirt.

Key Lime Pie. That was what it should be. She had made a raspberry trifle. She was hoping that there would be a bit left, and that she'd be instructed to bring it home. Yesterday's trifle for breakfast was her favourite food in the whole world.

'Hope there's lots of grub,' said Frank. Posy wondered if she could manoeuvre a cough sweet or a few Smints for him out of her bag. His breath was quite something, last night having been Saturday night. Ah well, soon everybody would be drinking, or at least having a chaste glass of wine or a small beer.

'Hope it's not bloody mulled wine. Hope I don't have to talk to anybody,' he continued.

They stopped at a pedestrian crossing so that a family of four could zoom across on gleaming silver scooters. The sunshine flashed off the shiny metal. Four golden heads bowed in similar attitudes of concentrated enjoyment.

'You could get me one of those for Christmas, Frank,' said

Posy. She could see herself whizzing back from dropping the children off somewhere. (Quite how she'd manage with Isobel on a scooter she hadn't thought.)

'What those?' Frank was incredulous 'Those sneaky little self-indulgent, pleased with themselves . . . those symbols of freewheeling consumption?'

'I just thought that they look fun and zippy, light and free . . .' Posy trailed on

'Three quarters of the world's starving, and you want a fold-up scooter! What is wrong with this society?' He thumped the steering wheel in a futile gesture of road rage against himself. 'Everything that is wrong with this world is encapsulated by those scooters. Fold it up and put it in your briefcase! Capitalism is fun!'

'Can things be encapsulated by a scooter?' she asked, trying to calm him down and throw him off the scent. 'It could be encapsulated by a small spacecraft, or a hamster exercise ball, but a scooter? Don't you think that things have to have some roundness if they are going to encapsulate other things? Anyway, I only thought . . . I only thought that it would be fun to have a go . . .' ('And you wouldn't see me for dust if I had one of those scooters,' she felt like adding.)

She supposed that she would just get more large bags for Christmas. Why was it that everyone always gave her big, practical bags? They must all think that she had too much huge, heavy stuff to lug around.

'Huh' said Frank. He was dreading the party. He hated chit-chat, and he supposed that he wouldn't be able to smoke.

'Anyway,' Posy said, 'You've got a bike so what's the difference?'

'There's a bloody big difference and you know it,' Frank snarled.

'Don't swear in front of us, Daddy,' said James.

Isobel started to cry.

'Don't make Isobel cry,' said Poppy.

'Or Mummy and us,' said James.

They pulled up outside Kate's house. The Parousellis were all set for the party. Posy saw that she hadn't managed to keep the trifle from spilling. She had noticed quite an interesting wave action inside the pretty glass bowl. The raspberry-soaked sponges were a similar shade to her skirt, which was having its first outing since she'd ordered it from last summer's Boden sale catalogue. It had been 75 per cent off. It was unfortunate about the cream and custard. Dry clean only, thought Posy, dry clean only.

Kate opened the door with hugs for Posy and the children. Frank managed to dodge his by offering up Izzie for a kiss instead.

'Mmm,' he said, 'Something smells good. I hope its mulled wine.'

Posy headed straight for the kitchen so that she could read as many labels as possible and work out which foods James, with his nut allergy, might and might not eat. Again and again she spotted the tiny warning 'May contain traces of nuts and or seeds.' Why can't they just put a stroke, she thought. One of the main things that she and Frank had in common nowadays was a shared dislike of sloppy punctuation.

'There are no actual nuts out in bowls,' Kate told her, 'but some of the things you just can't avoid . . .'

'I know,' said Posy, 'Mince pies, anything Christmassy. Don't worry. I'll choose some stuff for him. It's lucky he's so naturally sensible.' She piled a plate with cubes of cheddar, Pringles, cherry tomatoes, sticks of cucumber, carrot and celery, Wotsits and Hula Hoops. James didn't like quiche. She put on a few home-made cheese straws and some bread-sticks. Those, surely, would be all right.

She went in search of James and found Frank sitting on the stairs holding Isobel.

'I think it's a bit noisy for her in there,' he said. 'I think I'll just keep her out here for a bit.' And then I might not have to speak to anyone, he could have added. James was watching a video of *The Muppets' Christmas Carol* with a gang of children who were all grinning, showing their big, white, middle-class teeth.

'This looks jolly scary,' she told the assembled children. They ignored her. 'Here you are, James. Don't eat anything unless Daddy or I give it to you. Lots of the stuff isn't OK. You can have some of the pudding we made later.'

'OK Mum,' he said, managing to take the plate from her without looking away from the screen. His expert hand passed over the cheese, carrot, celery, cucumber and tomatoes and brought a handful of Pringles to his mouth in one smooth movement.

Back in the hall she saw that Frank was talking to Jan, her friend from the playground. She left them to it.

'So then, er, Jean, um, where did you get the boots?' Frank asked.

'These?' Jan said, looking down at her plum suede ankle boots.

'They give you a real principal boy look. Nice. Very Christmassy. And the leggings, and the what do you call that? A tunic? Very pantomimey. Very festive,' he went on. 'I remember lots of girls used to wear leggings and those boots with the turn-overs. Didn't know you could still get them. Or did you buy a lifetime's supply in your teens? I know, eighties revival, read an article about it. And the glasses. Really ironic. Nice touch. Posy used to wear leggings like that. I liked them on her. Never wears them now though. You have to be careful with those. If you had skinny legs you could look like Max Wall. You wouldn't have to worry about that though, would you Jean . . .' He looked down into his plastic glass of lager. When he looked up again she had gone.

'Something I said?' he asked Isobel who smiled back at him.

In the kitchen Posy was helping Kate pour diluted apple and orange juice into paper cups. There were clever little anti-spill plastic lids with holes for straws.

'All ready for Christmas then?' Posy joked.

Kate just grimaced. 'Well, nearly. Just another few hundred presents to buy. At least I finally posted my abroad ones, they might just get there in time . . .'

'I bet they do.' Posy said. Everything that Kate did always worked. 'The party's lovely. I don't know how you do it, and still look so calm.'

'Oh but it's fun!'

'Fun!' Posy was incredulous. She hoped that she hadn't sounded rude. 'And you make it all look so easy.'

'In a way it is easy,' Kate said. 'Just a matter of getting the right combination of Paracodal and black coffee. Really I'm like a swan. Gliding on the surface, paddling away like crazy underneath. I think that's enough drinks.'

Posy snapped on the last lid, managing to spill juice or to her already ruined skirt. 'Oh I'm hopeless,' she said.

'No you're not, just hassled.'

'I'm exhausted. Call centre workers have better conditions than we do. I feel like a failed member of the synchronised swimming team, desperately smiling, waving and drowning.'

'Posy, it looks to everyone else as though you're doing a great job.'

'I almost can't wait for Christmas to be over. I'm longing for the empty days of February. I hate the way Christmas is all up to me; I'm responsible for making everyone happy. And we're broke.'

'Everyone's broke,' Kate said, wiping some splashed juice off the white wall of her breadmaker.

'But we're *really* broke,' said Posy, realising that she was stepping out of line with her outburst by discussing financial problems. 'James has an Argos catalogue fixation. Sometimes I wish he hadn't learnt to read. I don't know how I let one into the house. He reads it in bed and then brings it to breakfast. His product knowledge is amazing. And everything is *only* £16.99, *only* £24.99, *only* £49.99. He knows we don't approve of gameboys, but he thinks Father Christmas might bring one anyway. I keep telling him that Father Christmas only brings little things like parachute men and popguns. But it's all *only* £29.99, *only* £34.99. Oh I despair.'

'Here,' said Kate. 'Have some mulled wine.'

'Thanks. Sorry to moan. I'm all right really.'

Aunty Flora was almost late for the school carol service. She was full of apologies. She had two last-minute-catering for-a-funeral jobs to do.

'A green December, you know . . .' she explained. She was amazed at how little people thought about planning funerals. Nowadays they never seemed to get beyond buying some Pringles and coleslaw. Really, things could be done so much better.

'Stop all the clocks and rush out and buy some nasty quiches and dips. That's all it seems to be for some people,' she told Posy as she folded her black mac and stowed it under the pew.

Poppy was an angel. James's class were singing a song, the sort of modern carol that is best forgotten, and soon will be. Posy remembered fondly the year when he had been a donkey. Tom was relatively good, sat relatively still, eating a plate of the cold mice pies that had kindly been provided by the Parents Association. Flora, Posy and Frank were deeply grateful for the polystyrene cups of tea. Isobel slept in the pushchair, her mouth open, hair sticking straight up, looking crazy.

'Father Jack's asleep,' Frank hissed.

'Oh how can you say that?' Posy asked. He just would spoil the magic, but when she glanced at him later she saw that his eyes were full of tears. Christmas was, she realised, all about babies. The miracle of babies, the redeeming power of babies. She remembered a poster from way back, 'A New Baby is a Sign That God Wants The World To Carry On'. She dabbed away the tears when she saw Poppy take her place beside the manger. She blinked away thoughts of The Massacre of the Innocents.

Behind her a granny, soon to be locked away with Alzheimer's, said loudly during the prayers, 'But I don't like mince pies when they are cold. I don't like them unless the fat has melted. I can't eat them if the fat hasn't melted.'

Christmas Day. Frank managed to ring Melody after lunch whilst Posy, Flora and the children were wishing Lettice a Merry Christmas and giving her a treat of sprouts. He pulled the phone to the end of its tether to position himself where he'd be able to see the back door opening when they came back in. All this sneaking around, he thought, it was like having all the work of an affair with none of the fun.

'Melody, it's Frank.'

'Oh, hello.'

'I was just ringing up to say, er, you know, and see how you were.'

'Happy Christmas to you too. I'm fine. Mum made us a great dinner. I haven't thrown up for two days now.'

Frank could hear the sounds of a good time in the background, and what was probably the dog barking along to some music.

'Sounds like you're all having fun,' said Frank, morosely.

'Yeah. It's all the cousins. Where's your lot then?'

'In the garden, feeding the rabbit some sprouts.'

'Ha. Oh yeah, Mum wants you to come over some time so we can talk about things.'

'Oh,' said Frank. 'OK.' That sounded a bit ominous. 'But maybe we could talk at the New Year Gig.'

'Mum won't be there, will she? And I might not. I might go to a party with some of Mark's friends.'

'OK' said Frank. 'See you soon. Got to go. Sorry.' He could see movement around the back door, approaching shadows, he hung up before Melody had a chance to say anything else.

Frank had been terrified by the prospect of seeing the New Year in with Melody, even in the pub. Oh the future, the possible questions, the expectations ... Perhaps, he had mused, none of this was that big a deal to her. Perhaps, being of the generation that was even younger than Generation X, she would take all of this in her stride, water off a duck's back. Many of Melody's friends had progressed from the highchairs in McDonald's to working behind the tills without batting an eyelid at the artificial lights. Perhaps she was so at home in the world that she would be able to cope with everything with no trouble at all.

JANUARY

IT WAS A RELIEF TO have Christmas over. There was a part of Posy that loved it when the decorations had been taken down, and the house looked stark and austere without them. It was a huge relief to Frank: being so tall, he hated Christmas decorations. During the festive period he had a constant feeling that he was about to be poked in the eye or bopped on the head. Taking the decorations down and stowing them back in the loft was one chore he was always keen to get on with. Posy insisted that they stay up until Twelfth Night. He'd have ripped them all down on Boxing Day if she'd let him. Boxing Day had been spent in Pilchard Avenue with his Mum, Dad and Grandpa. The kiddies had a great time. Posy had managed to be stressed out because Grandpa kept trying to give Quality Street to the children, oh the nut peril for James and the choking peril for Izzie! How could a baby be expected to eat Quality Street? And now it was January and the children would be going back to school.

'And we still haven't done the thank you letters' said Posy. 'Oh how could we have got to January 4th and still not done the thank you letters?' This year she had meant to get James and Poppy to do them instead of just writing them all herself, but somehow each day of the holidays had slipped by on its toboggan of new toys, trips to the swings and boxes of Marks and Spencer's biscuits, presents from Flora's grateful clients offloaded on to them; and still the thank you letters were not done.

'Well I'll do them,' said Frank, 'if it fills you with despair. Tom can draw pictures and James and Poppy can write on the backs of them.'

'Would you? Oh would you?' She was pathetically grateful. 'I'll make you a list.' Posy wrote out the names and addresses of all the people who needed thanking along with what the present had been. This took her as long as writing the actual letters would have done.

'We'll do it upstairs. You won't even have to listen.'

'Thank you. Oh thank you.'

'You can write me a thank you letter. Then I'll take Izzie and we'll go and post them. It will all be done in less than two hours. Come on kids. Put the TV off. If you do this quickly I'll get you some sweets at the Post Office.'

Posy closed her ears to this last bit. Frank marched the children upstairs. When Tom had scribbled a few pictures he started to dictate.

'Right Jimmy, you can do the first one. "Thank you for the swimming towels. Mum says that these cheap scratchy ones are the best for getting you dry. Love from the Parousellis." We don't want to waste time by writing all of our names. Right, next one. "Thank you for sending Izzie *The Very Hungry Caterpillar*. It is a particular favourite. Mum says that another copy will be very useful in case we lose the three copies we already have." Got that? Right, next one. "Thank you for the talking Shrek toys. They were a lovely surprise as they aren't something we would ever have chosen for ourselves. Love from the Parousellis." Right, next one. "Thank you for the videos. Do you still have the receipt?" Well done, Jimmy. We'll soon be done. Don't know why Mum makes such a fuss about it, do you?'

The New Year meant, of course, Posy making fresh attempts at losing weight. If it was a night when Frank was out, playing or practising, or just with the band somewhere, she could escape the tyranny of dinner – all that unnecessary proper food and extra washing up – and have just what she really wanted. This would be three bowls of Special K Red Berries, or a bagel with low-fat spread and jam, a big chunk of French stick with low-fat spread and jam, or if she was being healthy, just lots of salt and pepper. She ate the opposite of the diet currently being advocated by so many celebrities. What she really wanted to do was live on nothing but carbohydrates and sweet things: buns, toast, mashed potatoes, muffins. She had to stop herself from giving the children this diet. They had plenty of vegetables, well, plenty of fruit. She tried to give them proper dinners, pasta and so on, or at least oven chips. Posy's idea of 'health foods' was quite a broad one. Jaffa Cakes were included (complex carbohydrate), chocolate Nutrigrain bars (high in calcium), Milky Bars and White Chocolate Buttons (ditto). Today's menu went like this.

7 a.m. Pot of orange Actimel (good intentions).
10.30 a.m. Two chocolate Nutrigrain bars.
11.30 a.m. Bagel with jam, an apple, two satsumas (healthy, see).
2.30 p.m. Two bowls of Special K Red Berries with sugar (the sugar kept secret from the children. They didn't know that people had sugar on cereal).
4.30 p.m. Another bagel with jam.
4.45 p.m. Chocolate Nutrigrain bar.
6 p.m. Yoghurt.
8.30 p.m. Dinner with Frank or, if he was out, toast and marmite or toast and jam, apple, satsuma and yoghurt. Or more Special K Red berries.

In summer she would swop the satsumas for nectarines and change the chocolate Nutrigrain bars for blueberry or yoghurt and forest fruits ones. She would also have at least fifteen cups of tea, some herbal, some Earl Grey, most of them left to go cold and never drunk. Frank couldn't believe the number of boxes of cereal she got through. She often had to hide empty boxes in the bin and sneak new packets into the house. She wasn't ready to admit she had a problem. She wouldn't discuss it, especially not since he'd made that crack at about getting her a nosebag and keeping it topped up.

Frank's menu went like this:

9 a.m. or anytime up until 3 p.m. whole French stick with packet of bacon (i.e. anytime between when the children left for school & when they returned)
or
All Day Breakfast (extra mushrooms) at The Jackpot Café
8.30 p.m. ish Dinner with Posy
or
11.45 p.m. Chicken kebab and chips
or
Large doner and chips
or
Chicken Buna/Vindaloo/Masala with rice and naan.

He would also have at least five mugs of tea (always drunk) and either a litre or so of red wine if he was staying in, or seven pints or so of bitter if he was out. He snacked on the smelliest type of crisps he could find.

Posy was trying to re-establish her fitness regime. She knew that she would probably never make it to the skinny heights of the playground mums who were training for a half-marathon, but she was trying. She had a copy of 'Back to Me' a post-pregnancy exercise video which she did every so often. How wise and kind the Mummy Exercise Guru looked. If only Posy could enlist her help, or perhaps, she thought, just miraculously turn into her. The instructions often seemed to include special messages.

'Keep your arms soft, but your lower body hard like steel.'

'I will try, I will try,' Posy puffed along. Frank would appear in the doorway, usually with a can of beer or a bag of bacon-flavour wheatcrunchies and put her off by making unhelpful comments.

'What a hideous, emaciated, prancing pixie,' or 'Come on Pose, your legs are meant to be straighter than that,' or 'You could buy some weights if you were really serious about this, you don't have to use cans of beans.'

She knew that she was never going to measure up.

The next morning Kate was looking utterly serene in the school playground. Posy felt fat and tired and haggard and poor. Also close to tears.

'Oh I wish I was you,' she blurted out. Kate noticed the extra sniffing.

'Are you all right?'

'Of course, of course,' Posy said, rooting in her bag for a tissue that wasn't too disgusting.

'No you aren't, you're tired and miserable.'

'Don't be nice to me or I'll cry.'

'Come back for a cup of tea.'

'Thanks.'

'Excuse the mess,' Kate said as she put on the kettle and began to load the cereal bowls and plates into the dishwasher. Posy noticed two crumbs on the granite work tops, and five rice krispies on the table.

'You should see ours.'

'I'm making you some toast and jam.'

'Thanks. I really shouldn't.'

'Shouldn't what? Eat? Have breakfast?'

'I do wish I was you. You are so sensible, and so slim.'

'Have you tried this?' Kate held up a packet of St John's Wort tea. 'Three cups a day. You'll be a different person. Practically everyone's on it.'

'Practically everyone else has a perfect life.'

'Don't be stupid. You sound like a teenager.'

'I know.'

'You have what everybody in the world wants. Good-looking, kind husband, lovely healthy children, big house with a garden. Nobody's life is glossy. Everybody's broke. You're just imagining it all. If things aren't perfect, it doesn't mean that they aren't right.' She passed Posy a blue-and-white plate with eight little triangles of golden toast with raspberry jam, and then went on, 'Did you know that Jan works in Asda on Friday and Saturday nights? Sue might work at the university, but her partner's lost his job and he was just turned down for a hospital cleaner position. Nobody has a perfect life.'

'OK. Sorry. I know I've got to stop whining. Frank says that anyone with two bathrooms has no right to moan about anything ever.'

'Hmm. But they still do. Give up the domestic-perfection nirvana idea. Yes, you can have the whole house clean and perfect, but then you sit down with a cup of coffee, and you've spoilt it. The cup needs washing!'

'But you *have* achieved domestic nirvana!' said Posy.

'Ha. I don't think so. And try to find something for yourself to enjoy. Taking the children swimming does NOT count.'

'I guess I have to pull myself together. Pull my socks up. Tuck my shirt in. Pick myself up, dust myself down, start all over again.'

'That's not what I meant. I can just see that you aren't that happy. Is there anything specific, anything I can do? Maybe we could do some child-swapping to give each other breaks.'

'That would be good.'

'And take this St John's Wort. I've a spare in the cupboard.'

Posy wondered whether drinking it would turn her into someone who had spare herbal remedies for her friends in the cupboard. She would try. Perhaps it had some Alice in

Wonderland properties too. That would make life more interesting.

Kate put a mug of tea in front of her, and another plate of toast cut into soldiers for Izzie.

'I'll make you some St John's Wort now, it works really quickly. You'll need something else to take the taste away though.'

Posy picked up the box and read it.

'Oh, it says you can't have it if you're breastfeeding. Thanks anyway.'

'I don't suppose it would do any harm, but you never know. Take it for when you've finished.'

'Well she's down to a couple of feeds a day now. I'm sure there must be something else I can do to get myself together. I might stop having baths. I always get depressed in the bath. My aloe vera bath and shower gel looks like intestines when it hits the water . . .' Posy realised that she was droning on.

'Hmm,' said Kate. She saw that Posy's mug was half-empty. Really she could sometimes do with a big kick up the behind.

'If I just have a shower I emerge much zippier,' said Posy, trying to sound zippier.

'Good idea. Just one bath a week from now on.'

'Maybe that was why they were so tough in the olden days.'

'Fancy going into town? We could have coffee at John Lewis. You don't have to buy anything.'

'Well I have got to get a few birthday cards. I could really do with some new underwear.'

Kate was too kind to comment that she had noticed the ancient grey straps that spoilt the look of Posy's actually very pretty shoulders. 'I'm still wearing my horrible old nursing bras.'

'Really? Well there you are then. Let's go shopping!'

When Posy had first met Frank he had seemed very alone, very independent. He lived in a semi-derelict house shared with three second-years, and him a fresher too – when all the other freshers were in halls, getting excited about grilling their frozen pizzas all by themselves under the communal grill. It was a PRANGLE house. She'd never known what that stood for, but it meant that the house had been condemned, along with the rest of pretty little Salisbury Terrace, and was awaiting demolition. It belonged to the University and was destined to be the site of the new School of Physiotherapy and Occupational Therapy. How clumsy that sounded. Frank pictured the therapists of the future massing in their blue slacks, rolling up their sleeves, and climbing into JCBs, ready to pummel his house into dust.

Frank and the second-years made home-brew. This seemed impressive and exotic to Posy as she hadn't come across it before. They were meant to use the talents that they had professed to on the PRANGLE application forms to keep the house habitable, but of course Frank didn't. The maps of damp, the broken sash cords, the leaks and draughts and no heating all seemed romantic to Posy, used as she was to the ideal homes and gardens of Surrey. She even liked the ghostly scratchings of the pigeons (or were they rats?) in the loft. Frank's room was what should have been the sitting room. Sam had the dining room and Al and Rupe had rooms upstairs. It was a long time before she found out that Frank was in the PRANGLE £12 a month house not only through choice and being utterly cool, but because he didn't get a proper grant because Southampton was his home town; not much more distant than the invisible pigeons (or were they rats?) was a trio of Parousellis, who hadn't wanted Frank to leave and were scrabbling and scratching, or so Frank thought, trying to get him back.

The first time Posy met Mrs Parouselli was not very auspicious. She was sitting in Frank's bed at 11 a.m. eating Dutch crisp bakes with margarine and jam, wearing Frank's black jumper. Frank was in the bath.

Now that Posy was at university she was definitely not Posy Fossil from *Ballet Shoes*. At school she had done time as both Amy and Jo from *Little Women* (the world is crammed with them), then Cathy in *Wuthering Heights* and Emma Woodhouse (hard when your Dad is a violent heavy drinker). She was now an aspiring Francoise Sagan heroine, forever 'raising her hand as if to suggest futility', a gesture and persona that was sadly lost on her fellow students. She was meant to be working on her dissertation about the costumes of Queen Marie of Roumania. Her choice of subject hadn't cut much ice in the university's history department. Her tutor thought that 'Threads of Time' was a silly title too, but an improvement on Posy's first suggestion of 'What This Old Thing?: The Historical Significance of the Costumes of Queen Marie of Roumania.' Posy had chosen the subject only so that she could include one of her favourite Dorothy Parker vignettes. She discovered afterwards that this was also the preface to the most important biography of Queen Marie, a book that she had managed to miss in her research.

Posy heard someone banging on the front door. She went to open it wearing only Frank's jumper, which did reach almost to her knees.

'Is Francis in?' It was a cross-looking Mrs Tiggywinkle carrying a blue plastic laundry sack of familiar-looking clothes.

'Francis?' Posy was perplexed, 'There's no Francis here.'

'Francis Parouselli. I'm his mother. Here's his washing.'

Posy stepped back.

'Oh, Frank!' The woman was already in Frank's room, surveying the unmade bed, the copy of *Elle*, Posy's jeans, boots, socks and underwear on the chair beside the bed, the drawn curtains, 400 records out of their sleeves on the floor. The daffodils Posy had bought were in a pickled onion jar, looking, Posy thought, brazen and foolish. The lid was off the cheap red jam, and crumbs were strewn across the bed and the floor.

'I'll just tell him you're here.'

Bending neatly at the knees to retain her modesty as best she could, she scooped up her clothes and fled. She could get dressed in Sam's room if he was out, but he wasn't. Lou Reed was playing, and Louise his girlfriend was probably in there too.

She went on into the kitchen, her feet stuck to the filthy, beer-filmed lino and made a plakky sound as she walked. She was into her knickers and jeans within seconds, but the impostor was behind her. Everything else would have to wait. She darted past the back door where slug trails criss-crossed the carpet tiles, and banged on the bathroom door.

'Frank! Frank! Your mother is here!' She hoped that he detected the urgency in her voice. 'Your Mother is here!'

It would be very like Frank to claim to have fallen asleep or to have been underwater for half an hour and not have heard. He might even climb out the window and leg it off to the bar, but Posy didn't know this about him yet. She heard: 'Shit! Be out in a minute.' There were cascades of water as Frank washed his hair using the huge, heavy glass tankard that Sam had filched from the Oktoberfest.

Mrs Parouselli stood firm behind her, still holding the washing. Why didn't she put it down?

'Let me take that,' Posy said politely. Mrs. Parouselli dumped it in her arms, and Posy became the strumpet who put away Frank's clothes. She thought of all the things she didn't want to be as she plak-plakked her way back across the kitchen floor to Frank's room.

The Parouselli family hadn't always been in brick. A few generations back they had been 'The Family Parouselli', Italian trapeze artistes. A distant branch of the family were still working, some never-heard-from cousins of Frank's toured perpetually with Apollo's Circus.

Frank's great-grandparents had been performers, but his grandparents had settled, opening Fancy Ways, which his parents now ran.

In Fancy Ways there were clowns crying a single sparkly tear, dolls that weren't meant to be played with, musical rocking horses and carousels that looked as though they had been crafted out of icing, lucky black cats, silver plastic keys for twenty-one year-olds to receive from their relatives, balloons, ribbons, christening presents, cards for every occasion. The trapeze artist blood appeared to have thinned by the time it reached Frank. He did have strong, ropey wrists, and he loved to perform, well, to play with the band anyway, but he couldn't do back flips or handsprings, or somersaults in the air. He knew that Posy watched their children, wondering whether they might be throwbacks, throwabouts. She hoped the gifts would be tossed forwards down the generations; perhaps one day James, Poppy, Tom or Isobel would be pulling on the Lycra and spangles, flying away from her, swinging fifty feet above her head and safely, Posy-crossed her fingers, landing in the net and coming back to her.

Frank had tried to distance himself from his family. He never talked about The Family Parouselli. He hated Fancy Ways. It had been the uncoolest place imaginable to grow up. How could he be an existentialist in a card shop? Or a rock star whose day job was selling Engagement, Wedding, New Home, New Baby, 50th, Anniversary, Retirement and Sympathy cards?

'Hell,' he thought, when he saw the people come in and ponder, endlessly, which tawdry greeting with which trite little rhyme to choose, why not get a mixed box, one for every occasion, a box for everyone you know, and post the whole lot at once? Save time and money!' It was a real wrist-slasher working at Fancy Ways.

He had spent too many long dull afternoons, the dead after-school hours there, doing his homework in the back of the shop or behind the till at his parents' behest. He'd look up from his O level revision (Macbeth. Eng Lit. His favourite.) and say to his mum,

' "Tomorrow, and tomorrow, and tomorrow,
Creeps in this petty pace from day to day
To the last syllable of recorded time,
And all our yesterdays have lighted fools
The way to dusty death." '

She'd be working her way through a catalogue of Advent calendars, circling some. 'Looks like penguins and polars are big this year,' she'd tell him.

In the school summer holidays he had sometimes been stuck there for months on end – from the end of July, all of August, into September. At least there were no big celebrations or festivals then, just the usual grim round of birthdays and minor family celebrations. The shop sold many things that many a child would have loved – cake decorations, tissue paper, crêpe paper, Sellotape, brown paper, ribbons, string, tags – but to Frank at sixteen they were the wrappings and trimmings, the trappings of tedium.

Twenty years later he was still there, helping out. They paid him £15 for a day, which for Posy and Frank was not to be sneezed at. The rate had remained the same for twelve years. Oh how could he have let this happen? Why didn't he make his getaway when the going was good? The trouble was that it had never been good enough. The day he'd brought home his UCCA form was the day his Dad had been rushed into hospital with chest pains. A heart condition that, with surgery and medication, had now been brought well under control, and rarely seemed to trouble him. His mum had looked panic-stricken when he'd shown her the form and the prospecti for Durham, Exeter and Bristol. Bristol had been his first choice and it wasn't even that far away. But somehow he had found himself putting Southampton at the top of the list. And then there was the band, and then Posy, and then the children, and now it seemed as though he would be here for ever.

Today he was king of the stocktake. Two stocktakes a year

for as long as he could remember, January and July. Pointless, pointless. He still didn't know why they did stocktakes. What difference could it possibly make how many they have of each stupid item?

'Come friendly bombs' he thought as he piled up the gift boxes of Christmas cards next to him. He lost count. He always did, and just wrote down anything. Dear God. He could not even think about taking stock of his life. That way lay madness.

They were listening to Steve Wright's Sunday Love Songs. Posy had taken the children to The Common. Why couldn't she have done the bloody stocktake while he went to the swings? He could have stayed in bed while the kids watched a video or something. He had driven down there too fast, not wearing his seat belt; she was left strapping the baby into the pushchair and making the endless preparations that she deemed necessary for an hour-long trip to the swings and back. She had used the excuse that she used for everything. 'Isobel might want a feed.' Isobel was nearly one. Surely she didn't need Posy on tap any more.

Frank realised as he revved the engine and pulled out, barely looking, that Posy only ever said 'Drive carefully' if he had the children with him in the car.

People were e-mailing the radio show about the loves of their lives. They had all been through some very traumatic times, messy divorces, everybody dying from cancer, that kind of thing. Frank ground his teeth. But now they had all found somebody who had turned their lives around, brought them sparkle and hope. Frank pictured the loved ones trailing stardust as they went about their work as doctors' receptionists, in offices, wherever. Call after call, e-mail after e-mail was read out. Love, love, love. On this evidence the nation must consist almost entirely of these people, bringing joy, sticking by through thick and thin, always there for each other. It made him want to throw up. How could these people be special if there are so many of them? How can this love, this lurve, be genuine, be worth anything, if it is so commonplace?

'And a special hello and all love and happiness to our friends Cheryl and Mark who are getting married today at the Bluewater Hotel and Country Club.'

Frank thought that talk of love should be reserved for a very few people. It should be profound and rare. Not for the masses, not for these Hallmark card emotions. He didn't know if he and Posy would qualify. He couldn't even think about Melody.

A special mention for my Mum and Dad who are celebrating their fortieth wedding anniversary on Monday. They really are the best Mum and Dad in the world, and we love them to bits and thanks for everything they've done for us.'

He could spit bile.

'Hello to all the staff of the Bracken Ward at Reading Hospital. Thank you for working so hard to save my husband Tony. It's wonderful to know that he's coming home soon, at last after the accident.'

Perhaps he would send in a joint request for Posy and Melody. But how to word it, what to ask for? Tricky. And why, he wondered, did so many dedications include the words 'I love you even if I don't always show it'? More music. Play 'The Lady in Red' Frank willed the radio. Play 'Unchained Melody'. Play 'Wonderful Tonight', play 'Just The Way You Are'. That was a particular favourite of his. 'Don't want clever co-on-versation . . .' How patronising could you get? How low could you aim?

'Yes!' he said out loud. It was Whitney Houston singing 'I Will Always Love You'.

'What Francis?' his Mum asked.

'Oh, just finished these Christmas cards.'

'How many?' She was ready with her pen to write it down. 'How many?'

'Er . . '

'You've forgotten! Do them again.'

Frank's father, Albert was a shadowy figure at the back of the shop. He rarely spoke to customers now, preferring to lurk out of sight, or to disappear for hours on errands. He liked to make price comparisons in Fancy Way's rivals, and to check out the special offers in Somerfield and Safeway.

His favourite shop was Maplins, purveyor of obscure and fiddly little switches and clips, kits and cables. Albert Parouselli was clever with electrical things. He made an extra thermostat for the central heating which could only be turned up or over-ridden by himself with his special code. The family weren't even allowed to turn the heating up for a special treat on Christmas Day, after all, the extra heat generated by the oven would warm them up. The words 'Put On Another Jumper' echoed down the years of Frank's childhood.

When Frank was twelve they had moved out of the flat above Fancy Ways (leaving it at last to his grandparents) to a newish house in Pilchard Avenue, Fair Oak. Frank suspected that his father had chosen the address just to add to his misery and embarrassment. It was the sort of modern house that was plagued by mildew and condensation.

There seemed to be no joy in Albert Parouselli's life. If they had grapes, he would snip off an appropriately-sized bunch for each person. There was to be no picking of the main bunch. Even now, if the grandchildren were coming, Albert would make sure that there was no reckless eating of Pringles. He would use his nail to make a tiny mark on the side of the tube, hardly visible to the naked eye, to indicate where he was going to intervene and stop the eating, he could also then see if his wife had been at them when he wasn't looking. This was unlikely, Mrs Parouselli would never have eaten crisps; they were a young person's food. She did like chocolate though, and she bought quarters of chocolate nougat from the tobacconist across the road, and ate it very secretly behind the counter. If they had a box of chocolates Albert would offer them in such a way that accepting one would appear disgustingly greedy, and having a second, well!

'Granny and Grandpa always have cream cheese and chive Pringles when we go. Yum,' said James. Frank didn't tell him that it was probably the same tube, lasting weeks.

Frank's father sometimes tried to drum some sense into his son. 'There are some good old-fashioned values like "thrift", and, er, "Value" that have been forgotten,' he told him from time to time.

'So why is the stuff you peddle in Fancy Ways such bad value then?' Frank felt like replying, but he never did. He knew that it was pointless. Best just to appear to go along with everything. Albert never told Frank that he hadn't wanted anything to do with Fancy Ways either. It had all just turned out that way.

What nobody seemed to grasp about Frank was that he really did not care about money, about having it, or not having it. He just did not care.

FEBRUARY

THE NEXT TIME FRANK went round with the BettaK-
leen he bravely knocked at Melody's door. The dog was
in and started to bark. It was 2.30 in the afternoon. Grandpa
had limped back to the car. Frank had a carpet protector strip
and a deodorising ashtray to deliver. He figured that if there
was no answer he could leave them behind the wheelie bin and
just shove a note through the door – So Sorry To Miss You –
then leg it. The gods were smiling on him. He knocked again
and the yapping got louder.

As he headed back down the path, between the two lines of
white chain-link fence in easy-clean plastic, (BettaKleen
'Spring Into Your Garden' supplement, 2001) he heard the
door open and the barking grow louder.

'Hey Frank. I am in. I was just having a nap. It's my day
off.' He turned and there was Melody's mum, Anita, in a
shiny, wine-coloured dressing gown with matching slippers.

'Oh, sorry I woke you.'

'That's OK. I had to get up soon anyway. Want to come in?'
Not really, thought Frank.

'Cheers,' he said. 'I'd put your BettaKleen behind the bin.
Can't stay long, my Grandpa's waiting in the car.' Frank knew
that Grandpa would be happy for hours in the car. It was
parked overlooking the water and next to some public lavo-
tories. He had his bag of emergency supplies of biscuits and

Halls, a box of tissues and a copy of the *Echo*. He might even be able to work out how to switch the radio on.

Frank had only been in the house once or twice before when he'd been picking Melody up for gigs. He followed Anita inside. He felt his feet sink into the carpet. No wonder Melody had never left home, it was so thick and soft that any speedy progress across it would be impossible.

'Make yourself comfy,' she said. 'I'm just going to put the kettle on and get dressed.' Phew, thought Frank, The situation was embarrassing enough without Anita being in glamour-wear. He sank down into the sofa. The dog returned snarling to its chair. While he waited he looked at the gallery of photos of Melody and Mark from bonny babies to the present day. There wasn't much space left on the walls. Anita would have to take down some of them, or perhaps her decorative ceramics, to make room for the new baby. All of these studio portraits must have cost a fortune. At least Posy had never considered them necessary, limiting herself to a few framed snaps of the children on top of the piano. Frank would have found it a bit spooky, having them all of these past selves staring down, watching his mundane existence, his every move. Melody and Mark probably wouldn't see it that way. It was lucky that his own mum only had a few photos on display.

'But you were going to be an astronaut,' his five-year-old self would say.

'Not playing for England then?' said the ten-year-old.

'Never been on Top of the Pops?' asked the twelve-year-old.

'Not really that great a musician . . .' commented the seventeen-year-old.

'Didn't do much with the First, did you?' said the gradua-tion shot. And now the 'Outside the Registry Office with Posy' picture. What would that one be saying?

Anita returned in a pair of white jeans, a black v-necked

jumper, and a snakey gold necklace that was never still. Frank realised that she was probably only a few years older than him. She would win any Glamorous Granny Competition hands down, especially if his own Mum was the opposition. She put down the tray.

'Help yourself to sugar.'

'Thanks.' The dog helped itself to a biscuit.

Frank had no idea what to say or where to start. He took a long time putting in the sugar and made quite a performance of the stirring and returning the spoon to the tray. How should he begin? 'Well, sorry that I knocked up your only daughter on a one-night stand, your beautiful, talented daughter. Sorry I'm already married with four kids, one of them a baby. Sorry I've got no money and nothing to offer Melody . . .'

Anita looked at him expectantly.

'I don't really know what to say,' said Frank.

'I can see that. I wanted to know, well, if you've got any plans. She's my only daughter.'

'I'm sorry,' said Frank. 'I didn't mean this to happen.' He could imagine how he'd be feeling if this were Poppy or Izzie.

'Well it does take two . . . and I can't say I'm not pleased about the baby. It'll be lovely to have a baby again. You can't help but wish the circumstances were a bit different though.'

'I know.'

'So what does your wife say?'

'She doesn't know.'

'And how many kids have you got already?'

'Four.' He was ashamed to say it, it sounded excessive, feckless, careless.

'All with your wife?'

'Yes,' said Frank. 'Of course.'

'There's no "of course" about it, is there? So are you going to tell her then?'

'Well, I suppose so.'

'These things always come out in the end. Better she hears it from you.'

'I kind of thought it was better if she never heard it at all. Our youngest isn't even one.'

'Well that's hardly Melody's problem is it?'

'No,' said Frank. He had no idea what his intentions were, or if he could find a set that were honourable.

'I think you've got to get yourself sorted out somehow, haven't you? I know you musicians, all drifters. It's not that I'm threatening you, and nor's Mel . . .'

'Um, no.'

'The thing is, I have to look out for Melody. See that she gets what she deserves.'

'I want to do my best for her,' said Frank. 'Whatever I can.'

'I know what it's like for her. I was on my own when I had her, and things were harder then.' The light flashed off her necklace. Frank wondered if it gave her super powers. She was clearly not to be crossed. She'd probably beat him in any fight.

'I know she deserves the best, better than this,' said Frank. Better than me. He felt like saying that it was all Melody's choice, that she didn't actually have to have the baby, but he didn't. He knew that he wouldn't have been very pleased if Anita and Melody had suggested the same about James, Poppy, Tom or Isobel

'Well. We'll have to find away to make it work,' said Anita.

Frank could see that she wasn't that impressed, that she was waiting for him to make some firm offers or assurances about telling Posy. He should probably be giving money already. The shopping probably hadn't started yet, but it could only be a matter of weeks. Of course he didn't have any on him. He'd have to try to get some extra gigs and not let Posy find out about them.

'They'll be living here at first, but Melody's already got her name down for a place of her own. It will be lovely to have a baby again . . .'

Perhaps, Frank thought, she was wondering if he was going to move in with them. It hadn't occurred to him until now.

'I'd better go,' he said. 'My Grandpa's waiting.' He certainly wasn't going to ask for the money for the BettaKleen. As he trudged back to the car he realised that neither of them had mentioned love.

Al's appearance was deceptive. He had thick straight fair hair that fell across his forehead and gave him a romantic, heroic look, just the sort of look that Flora had once gone for. It had fooled Caroline too. If people's hair reflected their true nature's, then Al should have had unkempt, greasy, chaotic locks that became hobbity as he grew older.

At university in Durham Flora had only ever been out with ex-public school boys. She hadn't made a conscious decision to do this, it had just turned out that way. It hadn't brought her much luck in love. In those days Flora fell quickly but quietly in love with people. (She never let them know how she was feeling.) She thought each time that she had found somebody wonderful, but all too quickly she discovered that they had feet of clay. Then they would start to get on her nerves. She would find herself making too many useful suggestions of ways in which they could run their lives more efficiently or improve themselves, or at least more resemble the person whom she had once thought them to be.

'Have you ever considered changing course from Economics to Law?' she might say; this one, Marcus really would have made a very good-looking barrister.

'Had you ever thought that if you kept most of the tea towels clean, in the drawer, and only ever had two out at a time your kitchen wouldn't be so full of dirty tea towels?'

'You know, if you kept all of your bank statements in a file in chronological order you would be able to see where you were overspending and avoid some of these bank letters and charges that annoy you so much.'

'Perhaps if you planned out your week's meals in advance you wouldn't find yourself spending so much on takeaway food.'

'Have you ever wondered what it would be like if you decided not to drink every night of the week?'

'Why not throw away all of your socks, buy eight identical black pairs, and never have this problem again?'

This wasn't a strategy that made for long-term romance or contentment. As soon as Flora saw that the object of her affections (or best intentions) wasn't going to comply she became annoyed by them, and they by her, and things would fizzle out. It seemed that she would have to find perfection elsewhere. She wrote her dissertation on Christina Rossetti. So it was that she left university unattached, and stayed more or less that way.

When Al met Flora on the Parousellis' doorstep he was at a low ebb. He had just had a twenty-minute phone row with Caroline because she had said that he was meant to have Finn on Sunday, when he could have sworn that the last thing he'd known, it was meant to be Saturday that week. He had met Flora a few times, but he had never really noticed how pretty she was. He'd thought that Posy was the pretty one before, maybe he'd been wrong. There was something about the way that Flora (who was on an errand of mercy, the Parousellis' hoover having packed up) was holding that Dyson: her purple linen trousers exactly matched it, the yellow was picked up by her bright hair. It really tugged at him. It made her look as though she had magical powers. He could feel himself being sucked towards her.

Posy invited them both in. They had met before but had not spoken that much.

Posy made them tea. She told Al that she had no idea where Frank was, but he had a pupil later, and would be back.

'I can wait,' he told Posy, smiling at Flora. 'I thought we were going over a few songs.'

'I thought you were meant to be having Finn today, anyway,' Posy said.

'Well I thought it was tomorrow, Caroline reckoned it was Sunday. Sore point,' he said

'Oh don't you have a regular thing?' Flora asked, sensing something in need of organisation.

'Well it's kinda regular. It is Saturdays, and or Sundays and sometimes in the week if Caroline has extra work on.'

'She's a sign language teacher, and she does interpretation for social services too,' Posy said. She liked to tell people how interesting, useful and impressive her friends were, as though it somehow enhanced her own employment potential and improved her stay-at-home mum status.

'I know,' said Flora.

'As far as she's concerned I got it all wrong. Forgot Finn,' said Al.

'Sounds like you need a diary,' Flora couldn't help interjecting. Posy thought that Al wasn't really the diary type.

'Would you like me to leave the Dyson here, so you have time to do the whole house?' Flora asked.

'I don't know when I last hoovered the children's bedrooms,' Posy said. She had been hoping that Flora might spring into action and do it all for her. Flora, of course, had a cleaner. She had forgotten what domestic drudgery was really like.

'Are you off somewhere?' Posy asked.

'I have a client in half an hour.'

'What do you do?' Al asked.

'Perfect Solutions,' said Flora. 'Here's my card.' She pushed it across the Parousellis' sticky oilcloth at him.

' "Perfect Solutions" ' Al read. ' "Events organised. Clutter cleared. Storage sorted. Problems Solved." I could do with some of that.' He noticed that it ended with Flora's phone number and e-mail address. As if he'd be the sort to e-mail. He

put it into the pocket of his jeans. 'Cheers,' he said. Then
Frank came in.

'Hi everyone. Any tea left, Pose? Whatcha doing then Al?'

'I thought we were having a practice.'

'Tomorrow, mate.'

'Sounds like you need Perfect Solutions,' said Posy.

'We could go through a few now,' said Frank. 'I've got a
pupil in an hour, that's all. You don't need me do you Posy?'

'Isobel's asleep.'

'Ah. OK.' It seemed to Frank that if she didn't need help
with childcare, Posy didn't need him at all.

'Come on then, bring your tea,' he told Al and they headed
for the back door. As he passed the back of Flora's chair Al
caught the scent of lemons, or maybe it was limes, something
bright and clean and sweet and sharp.

Out in Frank's shed they rolled up straight away.

'So, is Flora seeing anyone?'

'Don't think so. Don't really know. Don't think she could
find anyone perfect enough. Don't even think of it, mate.'

'If I hadn't blown it with Caroline and Finn . . . Too late
now though.'

Frank started to play, soft, dark notes. Al took his sax out of
its case. I will always have you, he thought as he brought it to
his lips. It shone gold in the sunlight.

When Frank's pupil arrived, coming through the side gate and
knocking on the window of the summer house, Al left. He
went back through the kitchen, hoping to see Flora. Only the
Dyson remained. Posy was sitting feeding the baby in what he
realised was her typical pose. She had a catalogue of expensive-
looking wooden toys and one of trampolines open in front of
her.

'That looks pretty good,' 'he said' and was immediately
embarrassed. Did she think he meant the breastfeeding? 'I
mean that trampoline,' he quickly added.

But all she did was whisper 'mmm.' She was stroking the baby's hair, and didn't want to distract her by saying anything louder. She didn't know why she was even looking at the catalogues. The children had enough toys and they would never be able to afford a trampoline. She had just finished her book, and she loved reading junk mail, so soothing.

One of the best things about feeding her babies had been the amount of enforced sitting down and reading time. She had learnt how to turn a page in complete silence so as to not disturb the sleepy infant. Strange how long the feeds took. No wonder the Parouselli babies never had bottles. When James was a baby she'd read all of Thomas Hardy (apart from *Jude the Obscure*, of course). She would never choose anything too unpleasant in case it somehow got through the milk. Jane Austen, Barbara Pym and Elizabeth Taylor were ideal. She often hid her book if Frank came in and pretended that she was concentrating on the baby. How self-indulgent it must look, her sitting there, endlessly reading.

Al climbed the stairs to the bedsit that had been home since Caroline booted him out. It was in a block called Stanley Mansions, which, since its elegant beginnings, had been further divided into many small, sad compartments. Caroline wouldn't let Finn visit him here, so either they stayed at Caroline's or hung out on The Common or in cafes or at playgrounds. Finn had been there a few times until Caroline had visited and was appalled (her word) by the squalor (also her word). She said that she didn't want Finn seeing his Daddy somewhere that was so dirty and sad. He could see her point. But now that he was on his own, why bother? There were about two thousand CDs on the floor, these, along with a few towels and one set of sheets, were all that he had taken away from their marriage. He had almost forgotten the wedding with all the presents piled up on a table. Let her have it all.

He kicked aside some cartons that were smeary with the liquor of the take-aways that now were his nightly nutrition. He never got bored because he rang the changes. – curry, kebab, pizza, curry, fish and chips, kebab, and so on, ad infinitum. He rejected Thai, (fancy, foreign, not filling, too healthy). Al thought that he was managing pretty well now. Straight away after the split he would usually pass out before he had managed to eat much, he would wake from the cold at three or four in the morning with the stuff all over his shirt and trousers, the fork often still in his hand. Then he had a phase, when he was trying to get himself together again, where he would buy frozen dinners to microwave, but he often ended up just hacking bits off and sucking them when he got in from the pub as he couldn't be bothered to wait, and wasn't really that hungry. So now, a year on from the split, eating something while it was hot was a major achievement. It was possible that he would turn into a fat guy now. Often he took a short cut through the cemetery on his way home from one of their regular gigs. There were turnstiles instead of gates. He decided that if he got too fat for those cemetery turnstiles, he would cut back, but he still had a way to go.

But he had begun to feel lonely in a different way. Not just desperately missing Finn, but missing being with someone. It was something he hadn't expected. It had been a relief to get away from Caroline's constant disapproval of him. He had just wanted to be his own person, but now he needed a woman in his life. Something made him start piling the takeaway cartons into each other. (So this is why they give babies stacking cups, he thought, this is the skill they need to acquire.) He didn't have any bin bags. He shoved them into some of the takeaway bags and put them by the door, he'd put them out later. He opened the window. He took the sheets off the bed and started to gather all of his clothes. He'd have to take them to the launderette. A service wash would cut out some of the tedium.

When he got back he phoned Flora. He might have guessed that he would get the machine.

'Flora. It's Al. I wondered about some of your perfect solutions for my flat.' He left his number and hung up.

Flora phoned him back that evening, just as he was about to go out. He was glad the call hadn't come later. It might have been hard to sound sincere with a background of pub.

'My rates are £50 for the initial consultation, but that is deductible if you take me on, from the hourly rate of £12.50. Does that sound manageable?' She knew that he had left teaching and was now doing this and that. He thought that she sounded bossy as well as patronising, but still, she was pretty, and he could do with being sorted out, just so Finn might be allowed round again. It was miserable spending every Saturday or Sunday, whichever Caroline insisted it was to be, freezing in Mayflower Park. Maybe he could get a TV and a stack of videos for Finn.

'That's fine,' he said. 'I've got lots of work on, just no time to get sorted. Cash rich, time poor, that's me.' Lying toad, that's me, he smiled to himself.

'I could come round to agree on what needs doing on Monday. Do you have any time in the day? Otherwise, evening is fine.'

'I've work on in the morning. How about two?' Afternoon delight, he thought.

'Two is fine. Give me the address.'

'Flat 11, Stanley Mansions, Lodge Road.'

Al spent Monday morning driving for the scrapstore. He picked up sacks offcuts of wood from pine-furniture makers. Miriam, the scrapstore supremo, said that these could be used for pre-school woodwork activities. He imagined Finn and his buddies let loose with drills and saws. The mind boggled. There was a stack of gold card from the cigarette factory. Nice stuff. He wondered why they weren't using it. A few more stop-offs and the van was loaded with bolts of fabric that had been printed back to front, the usual reams of paper and card, and some lengths of what looked like parachute material. Perhaps, he mused, Southampton's pre-schoolers were going to be making their own aircraft disaster survival kits. The sun was warm and he drove with the window down, radio blaring, enjoying being a van man. This certainly beat teaching. He got back to the scrapstore as quickly as he could. He wanted time to have a shower and tidy up a bit before Flora arrived. He mustn't let her find out what he was really like. He aimed to look appealing, but cool. Not desperate.

He backed the van up to the rear entrance. How he hated that stupid warning beeping it did when he reversed. Council regulations no doubt. No sneaking around in this baby.

He took the first load in. It was a pile of lino offcuts, weighed a ton. He was sweating like a pig.

There was Posy. Shit! What if Flora were there too and saw him like this? He knew he looked a mess. Probably stank too. He did his best to put the stuff down silently. It was tough. He nearly put his back out. He darted back out and hid by the back of the van. Inside he could hear them wittering on.

'This is florists' cellophane,' Miriam was telling them, 'just PVA it around some wire and you can make gorgeous fairy wings.'

'I would never have thought of that.' It wasn't Posy talking, and it didn't sound like Flora.

'I think we should get some of these sequins.' Now that *was* Posy talking. 'And some of these feathers. They're beautiful. And some of these rainbow tissue circles.'

'As treasurer,' said the first voice, 'I think I should point out that we must try to stick to the free stuff.'

'More lentils and cork collages it is then,' said Posy. She sounded really disappointed. 'I suppose some of these fabrics are quite pretty. The fabric scraps are free, aren't they?'

'Remember it's variety and texture that are important in collage activities for pre-schoolers. Pretty isn't what matters. It's the activity, not the outcome that the children benefit from,' Miriam told them. It was part of her job description to offer guidance to the scrapstore's members.

Posy thought that pretty was what mattered. 'I suppose we could take lots of this wholemeal stuff and snip up some of our own tinsel and bits of wrapping paper.'

'We'll have some more gold card in later today,' Miriam told them.

'Great. Crowns again,' said Posy's accomplice enthusiastically.

'Our driver should be back soon,' Miriam told them. 'He sometimes seems to take the scenic route.'

'Huh, thought Al. I'd like to see you humping this stuff around, waiting endlessly at factory gates for some jobsworth who saw you last week to check your ID and get permission from the MD to give you a bag of rubbish. Hell, he was sure it wasn't Flora in there.

'Traffic light today,' he said as he strolled in with a bag of polystyrene bits. 'Hi Posy, what brings you here?'

'St Peter's committee,' said Posy, as if that meant anything to him. 'I wondered if I might see you. Frank told me you work up here.'

'Mostly on the scenic route,' he said, with a wink at Miriam. Who had the grace to blush.

'This is Ursula,' said Posy. 'Ursula, Al.' He looked her up and down. A mummy, a helmet-head, and possibly a Kraut with a name like that. Nothing for him here. He might as well get on with the unloading, then he could get off to make his preparations.

'We'll definitely take some cellophane,' said Posy. 'It's really lovely.'

Miriam made a mental note to suggest that the St Peter's committee members be offered places on the next 'Play Today' course; and she was sure that she'd told Al that they no longer accepted donations of polystyrene chips.

At precisely two o'clock Flora pressed the bell for Flat 11. She was certain that Al had said flat 11, she had it written in her organiser (plus she never forgot things like that, or made a mistake) but the name on the bell was 'Grimley'. She didn't think that was Al's name.

He buzzed her in.

She stepped neatly over the drifts of free papers, menus and leaflets and went up the stairs. The red and black lino was, she speculated, probably fifties, and now collectable. Flora had hated red and black together ever since an art therapist at the day centre where she'd done weekly sixth-former community service had told her that juxtaposing them indicated suicidal tendencies. Flora could not forget the story of the patient who usually drew beautiful and accurate pictures of freshwater fish one day complaining to the therapist that he couldn't get the pike he was working on to look right. The therapist, finding that he had used only red and black, asked for him to have emergency admission to hospital. She was told not to be so silly. When she came in after the weekend she was told that the patient had died after drinking bleach.

There were no windows and it seemed no air. Perhaps Al was the only inhabitant. Flora found number eleven at the top of the second staircase. Al opened the door when he heard her footsteps.

'Flora, come in.'

She thought that Al looked clean, if a little crumpled. She detected a hasty attempt to tidy the place up. This was a good sign. He must mean business. Sometimes her clients were so deeply mired in their clutter that it would appear hopeless to almost anyone but her.

'Coffee?' he asked.

'Yes please.' He had just washed up the mugs. He hoped

she wouldn't want anything to eat. By the time he'd thought of getting biscuits it was too late. He currently had a policy of not keeping any food. If he was hungry, he would get something when he went out. He gave her the smarter of the two mugs.

'Well,' said Flora. 'I usually start by asking people what it is that they think wants fixing, how they want their life to be different. It often seems purely physical at first glance, a clutter problem, needing repairs done, just needing someone to help make an action plan. Once we've agreed on the way forward I can give you a quote and you can let me know if you want to proceed.'

'This is mostly purely physical,' Al said, trying not to smirk. Lewdness, he realised, wouldn't get him very far with Flora. He was going to have to play this very carefully. Watch what he said, not let anything slip about Frank and Melody. Perhaps it would all be too complicated, if anything did happen, but then he couldn't really imagine Flora hanging out with The Wild Years. He would have to conduct the romance elsewhere. 'Yes. Purely physical.'

She arched her already highly arched eyebrows a fraction.

'I often bleed people's radiators whilst we are talking,' she said. 'But I take it you don't have central heating.'

Wow, he thought, complimentary bleeding of radiators. What a woman!

'So?' she said. 'Where shall we start?'

'Well,' said Al. 'I moved in about a year ago, when Caroline and I split.'

'Yes,' Flora nodded, all sympathy. 'I know.' He wondered what else she might know about him; he might be on dodgy territory.

'Well, it's over with Caroline, there's nothing I can do about that. And I don't want to,' he added hastily, 'but I need to make it good for Finn. He's only three.'

Flora knew that Finn's birthday was actually a week before

Tom's and that he was four. She decided that this wasn't the time to correct him.

'Caroline won't let him come here. Says it's too depressing. That he shouldn't see his Dad living like this.'

Flora looked around her. There was a sinister, unpleasant wardrobe. There was a table, ringed by a hundred thousand cold cups of coffee, a white bedside thing, stuffed with books, and the two black vinyl chairs that they were sitting on. These looked hideous and had green foam rubber poking out of gashes in their backs, but were actually very comfortable. There was a Baby Belling with two rings and what Flora took to be an oven. Al had an electric kettle (but she had noticed that it failed to switch itself off) and a miniature fridge. There were no pictures, just a hundred blobs of blu-tack and grey shadowy outlines where pictures had once hung. Above the basin were four mirror tiles. The picture Al would have of himself would be smeared, distorted and dissected. She guessed that the radio and music system were the only things that belonged to him.

'Well it's certainly not a clutter problem. That makes you unusual,' she said.

'Thanks. I'll take that as a compliment,' Al replied.

'None intended.'

'Come on, give it to me straight, Doc. I can take it.'

'Well,' said Flora. 'Have you considered moving out?'

'That bad, huh?'

'Well it's not irredeemable. We could transform this bedsit if you preferred.'

Al didn't want to say that he was strapped for cash, after all he was supposed to be paying her.

'Can we try that? I want quick results. I can always take stuff with me if I move . . .' he realised that he should have said 'when I move', to indicate that his future didn't lie in this bedsit.

'Fine. Mind if I take a look in your cupboards?'

Actually he did mind, he minded a lot.

Flora opened the wardrobe and a binbag of dirty washing lurched out at her.

'Don't worry. I've seen it all before.' There was nothing but books and CDs beside the bed. No food in the cupboard, just coffee, tea and sugar. The smell of the tiny fridge made her give a long, impressed whistle. The bed had no headboard (Flora considered this preferable to having a hideous one) and was covered by duvet in a pale green and brown cover that seemed to be trying for autumn and spring at the same time.

'OK. Here's where we start. The furniture is depressing. I will contact your landlord and arrange to have it moved or disposed of, there's probably an empty room or an attic or something. We'll draw up a list of the minimum you need and I will get it, in consultation with you. My clients don't usually have the time to come with me. We work to a budget. Everything will be new, clean, safe for Finn. We'll get a box of toys for him to keep here, and in consultation with Caroline, something so he can stay over. A pull-out bed that would fit under yours might be best, but something with an air of permanence, nothing makeshift.

'You will have to paint. White or cream would be fine. I often suggest a sunny yellow, but you don't strike me as a very sunny yellow person.'

Al grinned in what he hoped was a cute and appealing way.

'These are just the physical things, the surroundings, the backdrop. If we get these things right, the rest may follow. But you have to start using a diary, for all of your work, gigs, and particularly for Finn. Don't agree to anything unless you've checked it. Write everything down. Insist that Caroline tells you when any school or pre-school or doctor's appointments or whatever for Finn are. Then go to them. Go *instead* of her if she's busy. You have to act like you are responsible. Equal parenting, all that sort of thing.'

'I am responsible,' he said. This was getting quite offensive.

He wondered if she would keep the pace up like this for ever, if this was a 'first visit to a client' persona, or if she was always like this. If she was then he might have made a mistake.

Flora smoothed the golden tendrils away from her forehead. It was quite hot and stuffy in the room. She wondered if the window was painted shut, something else she would fix. She slipped off her jacket which was denim, lined with a Liberty print, and reluctantly hung it on the back of the chair. She got out her notebook, and Al caught a whiff of her alluring clean citrusy scent. How could anyone smell so clean? It filled him with longing.

'There's a pub down the road,' Al said. 'We could adjourn there.'

'Fine. I parked just down the road from it,' said Flora. She really had had enough of his place.

Flora found it astonishing that people were in the pub on a weekday afternoon. Why on earth weren't they all at work? What could they possibly be doing? Perhaps, she surmised, she had stumbled into the shooting of a government ad for benefit fraud snitching.

'What can I get you Al?' she said.

'No, let me.'

'Really, I insist. You are the client.'

'Oh cheers. Pint of Stella.'

'Pint of Stella and a sparkling water,' she said to the barman. 'Bit early in the day for me . . .' she told Al. 'And of course, I am driving.' Al was utterly condemned.

They agreed the plan and an initial number of hours. Flora was to call in a few days later with some catalogues so that he could OK the replacement furniture. Al didn't actually give a damn what it looked like, it was, after all, just somewhere to get his head down, but he thought he wanted to see her again soon, even though he suspected that he was about to waste a lot of money. He said goodbye to Flora outside the pub, and then pretended to go into his block. He stood just inside the front door for a few minutes, until he was sure she would be safely gone. Then he went back to the pub. Drinking just one pint in the afternoon was so unsatisfying, so pointless. He might as well carry on now, the evening was only a few hours away. He sat and thought about Flora. She had looked gorgeous. It was defintely worth a try. He wouldn't let on to Frank yet. What a tangled web, eh, he thought, as he drained his glass.

Flora had twenty-three minutes before her next appointment and a drive that would be fifteen minutes, at most. She sat in the car and looked over her planner for the next week. Then she made sure that her make-up was still perfect. There was a tiny smudge of mascara under her left eye that had to be dealt with. So it was that she saw Al in her rear-view mirror heading purposefully back into the pub. She wondered if his drinking was an issue that he would like her to help him tackle. It wasn't one that she had helped a client with before, or would ever want to. She thought of her father. How not to lead a life.

Flora thought it possible that Al had ulterior motives in hiring her. There was no way that she would get involved with him on anything but a professional basis. Profession, profession Al, she wondered if people made weak jokes about it to him.

If she could make things better for him though, be a means to restoring his relationship with his son, help him get his life back on track, them she would be pleased. She applied some of her favourite rosewater hand lotion. Her hands needed a lot more maintenance now, and she had noticed that they seemed to have taken on a permanent smell of lemon Cif. Her next client wanted help with organising a suprise 50th birthday party for her husband, as well as wardrobe and storage solutions. It was a potentially big job and Flora didn't want to smell like the cleaning lady. That night she would get on with her favourite part of any job, the making of an Ikea list for Al. She would not allow him to come with her.

As she drove off along Lodge Road and then got stuck at

every set of lights in Portswood she was struck by the number of teenaged girls who were wearing kerchiefs and tight brown crimplene trousers and A-line skirts. She remembered Aunt Is saying 'I was brought up to believe that people with large bottoms (and I include myself in that) shouldn't wear tight trousers.'

Judging by the kerchiefs, there must have been a huge influx of Plymouth brethren into the area. Strange that they were all going in and out of New Look and Select Some of them were smoking, others pushing buggies and talking on their mobiles. It was jolly odd. They were more usually spotted choosing dress patterns in John Lewis or fabrics in the Laura Ashley sale. Then she noticed that some of them had ill-advisedly exposed their midriffs or were wearing very short skirts. She realised that these were not Plymouth Brethren at all, but young people. To have become so illiterate when it came to fashion must mean that she was now the wrong side of frumpy, and was accelerating away from the junction towards middle age.

Frank didn't believe in Valentine's Day which meant that Posy would not get a Valentine unless she persuaded the children to make her one. She knew that Frank's feelings came from having grown up in a card shop. He had once explained to her that he preferred to make spontaneous romantic gestures throughout the year, not limit them to the day of the capitalist lurve fest. He hadn't noticed that he had now ceased to make any spontaneous romantic gestures. Posy thought that just a card might have been nice, just so that she could hold her head up at Toddlers if anyone asked. She remembered what it had been like at school.

'How many did you get?'

'Oh just the three . . . sackfuls!' was the standard reply. *Plus ça change*. She wondered how many Flora had got. She usually had some mystery ones from besotted clients, people who might or might not realise that Flora was in a league of her own.

When Flora had been seventeen, and Posy sixteen, they'd had Saturday jobs at Laura Ashley. This was back in the olden days, the age of Lady Di, when jumpers with sheep on and stripy blouses with the collars turned up, and short strings of pearls were desirable. The uniform at their sixth form college had consisted of a brightly coloured Benetton jumper, and a cardigan, also Benetton, knotted around the shoulders in a scarfy, shawl-like arrangement. This was quite useful as the college was always freezing. Flora's wages went mostly on clothes. Posy's clothes were a bit more gothic, Oxfam chic, but even she sometimes wore her Laura Ashley uniform allowance clothes to college, and made use of the staff discount. Nearly twenty years later there were still plenty of flowery skirts lurking in her wardrobe. It had been a Saturday job to warp the tastes (sometimes the girls would find themselves thinking that a lacy sailor-collared blouse was rather nice), but it had given them an invaluable skill – measuring up for curtains. (Height times number of drops plus pattern repeats and seam allowances for each drop.) They could estimate the amount of fabric for kidney-shaped dressing table covers, pelmets and valances, Roman blinds, Austrian blinds with and without flounces, and round tablecloths too. The dithering customers that they sent away with neat little diagrams of what to measure, and plenty of fabric swatches to choose from, always returned.

Flora was clearly management material. The manageress, whose breath smelt of Liebfraumilch, tried to persuade her to stay on full-time after her A levels; but Flora had other plans. When Flora closed her eyes, she pictured was herself alone on a bicycle spinning down some pretty tree-lined street in Oxford or Cambridge or Durham or Exeter. Flora alone, a long way from home in a place without crisis or melodrama.

She would rise on wings like eagle's, make good use of her Young Person's Railcard, and they wouldn't see her for dust. Posy and Mum could visit her if they liked, but she would find some sort of part-time job, perhaps assisting a kindly professor with her research. This job would preclude returning home except for the very shortest of breaks.

Posy was not management material. Sometimes she had an attitude problem. She found the afternoons so long, or the sale days so tiring that she found herself giving the customers alternative names for the designs.

'Oh yes, "St Vitus' Dance" in rose will be perfect for a spare bedroom' or 'I'm afraid that the alopecia colourway is going to be discontinued after the sale, but if you buy all that you need now you should be all right,' or 'That pigeon and peach border tile is also available in the porridge,' The customers never said anything – Posy looked the very essence of a Laura Ashley girl – but they studied their catalogues when they got home. They must have misheard her.

Rufflette tape and curtain-lining estimation had become second nature to them. They would pass the time by calculating how many rolls of wallpaper it would take to do the room they were in, or how many metres of fabric they would need for curtains or blinds, or, say all of the walls were windows, how much would that take? They need never be bored again. A dull evening at the theatre could be spent doing the mental measurements for new curtains for the stage, and was the safety curtain really just a giant roller blind? How much fabric would that take? Would the flame-retardant coating be the same stuff that came in cans with the Laura Ashley kits? They knew the names of all the company's fabrics and wallpapers and which way up the co-ordinating boarders were meant to go. Kate, Mr Jones, Shirt Stripe, Emma, Bloomsbury, Cirque – they could still recognise them all at five hundred paces.

'We'll be in adjacent chairs in the nursing home, muttering with Alzheimer's, 'Rosy Swag in primrose', 'Hey Diddle Diddle border with co-ordinating bed linen and lampshade . . .' said Posy.

' "Bring us the crackle glaze lamp base and the eglantine coolie shade" . . .' said Flora.

' "Cushion pads, no more cushion pads. Cushion pads are extra!" We'll whisper as they stand ready with a pillow to hold over our mouths,' Posy added, making Flora snort. But they both stopped laughing abruptly, remembering their mother's last weeks and days and the search for the right home or hospice. The name of one of them in South London had always stuck in Posy's mind, 'The Home for Incurables'. The building looked beautiful. She had come to think of it as 'The Home for Incurable Romantics'. That was where she should end up.

MARCH

MELODY HAD A PHASE where sometimes she wanted to talk to Frank several times a day. (This was very tricky, he had to sprint for the phone, try to leap subtly across rooms to get there first). Then for a while she couldn't be bothered to talk to him, and if he phoned her, Anita or Mark told him that she was either too busy or too tired to talk. So he gave up phoning for a while.

Frank could hardly bring himself to speak to Posy or Al or anybody. This went on for weeks. He knew that he was behaving badly, that he was a hopeless, useless husband and a failure as a dad. All Daddy jolliness was lost. He knew that he should call Melody again, find out if she was OK, but he couldn't bring himself to do it. Better to do nothing, to let things ride. Meanwhile his self-loathing became like an extra member of the family, some hateful Old Man of the Sea who had moved into the spare room, came silently to mealtimes, sulked at family gatherings, who had to stay in bed late and be taken things on a tray. The Man was someone with bad legs who had to be waited on, who left piles of dirty Kleenex Mansize balled-up around his chair, who was tiptoed around, but must be invited to everything, and whose fussy appetites had to be satisfied. Frank knew all this, but there seemed to be nothing he could do about it.

His whole life now was like something foisted on him. It

was a mangy old black Labrador with one eye whited out.

'Promise me you'll look after Mutty,' The Old Man of the Sea had said, clawing and grabbing at Frank's wrist.

'Of course, of course,' Frank had replied. He'd promised and now he was stuck.

Mutty had been MOTed at the vet's, his coat deburred, inoculations brought up to date, injections given for arthritis. The vet said that all being well, Mutty was good for many more years yet.

Mutty came with a dog bag. He liked to lurk in it after walks. It was meant to dry his coat, but only served to mat his fur and seal in the mud and river water. If anyone tried to take it out of his sight he howled and howled. One day it was seized and put in the washing machine. It clogged the filters and caused a flood. Mutty whined and whimpered throughout the proceedings and snarled during the mopping up. The dog bag didn't come out any cleaner.

Ah, Frank thought, the black dog.

If he wasn't playing his bass then all he ever seemed to do was look after the children or get quietly drunk or stoned on his own. The only thing he and Posy did together was eat their dinner in front of the TV. They couldn't even be bothered to sit at the table now. There was never anything they wanted to watch, but still they felt compelled to have it on.

Posy liked *Gardener's World*, and Frank liked Rachel de Thame; but it always seemed to be Alan Titchmarsh. Here he was now making an Alpine Garden in a series of square planters made from black planks. Frank couldn't fathom why Posy was finding it so interesting, just those planks and the gravel would be beyond the Parousells' means, let alone any silly little plants.

'Pull back some of the surface gravel . . .' Alan Titchmarsh told them. 'They need topping up. Use a mixture of John Innes Number One and some sharp grit.'

'Ah. Sharp grit,' Frank said, finishing off his second vegeburger, putting a handful of crinkle-cut oven chips into another Somerfield sesame seed bun. 'Sharp grit. That's what I need. Sharp grit. You don't hear about that much nowadays, do you? Sharp grit.' He took a slurp of red wine, put a noisy squirt of American mustard on to the chips. 'Don't hear about it at all really, do you?'

'It's all pea shingle now, isn't it' said Posy. 'Maybe B & Q would have some.'

Frank was really too full for this final bap, but he struggled through it. Ah, they were back to Rachel de Thame; he exhaled expansively and forgot about the grit.

A show with Will Self kept them sat there for another hour, apologising to each other for laughing out loud at the TV. So why didn't I get Will Self's life, Frank wondered. I'm tall enough, aren't I?

APRIL

APRIL 2ND WAS FRANK'S birthday. He couldn't believe what an escape he'd had. Thank goodness his mother had laboured for those extra few hours. He had been born at 3 a.m. Only just not an April Fool. He often wondered if he was really an April Fool, and they had falsified the documentation out of kindness. An April Fool growing up in a card shop. It would have been just his luck to have that as a birthday. But it pleased him to be near one of the few festival-type things that didn't have any associated greetings card.

Frank tried to insist on his birthday being a low-key event. No cards by request. But the children still made him some, and he got them from his family, and Posy, and something at once tasteful, ironic and amusing from Flora. The Wild Years never sent birthday cards. All they would do was raise an extra glass, and that suited Frank just fine. His presents were the usual things, T-shirts, pants and socks from Posy and the children, the sort of things that she thought he needed and that he would never buy himself, her twice yearly attempt to smarten him up.

Melody sent him a card. He hadn't known that she knew when his birthday was. He had no idea when hers was. He had doubtless missed it and offended her at some point, or else he soon would. Nobody was paying much attention to him opening his cards. Posy deemed it necessary to buy the children each a little present on his birthday and they were all too interested in those. He felt quite sick. He quickly put the card in the pile with the others. He made no comment. Posy didn't even notice. Perhaps, he thought, he should break with tradition and arrange the cards on top of the piano himself, but that might be more suspicious. The smart thing to do would be to abandon them all in a heap on the bed as usual.

They didn't do much in the day. He had a couple of pupils. There were thundery showers. It was what Mrs Parouselli senior would have called 'a monkey's wedding', and Mrs Parouselli junior was now calling 'a gorilla's birthday: rain and sunshine at the same time. Frank went to get the children from school. A double rainbow was pinned out in front of him, making him feel absurdly happy as he approached the playground. He couldn't help singing.

' "You won't be seeing rainbows anymore" ' he told Karim's grandfather who held the school gate open for him.

' "You'll see lonely sunsets, after all" ' he told Mrs Fleance as she marshalled the children who were going to the after-school club. He did a capering little dance when Poppy and James came out. Poppy ran into his arms, and bashed him on the legs with her Barbie lunch bag.

' "It's over, it's over it's over . . . It's over" ' he told them.

When they got home Posy and the children made him a cake, with lemon icing and hundreds and thousands. He just had a tiny slice; he always said that he wasn't that keen on sweet things.

'Apart from tea of course,' said Posy. He did take three sugars. Sometimes it seemed that she even wanted to undermine him when it came to what he did and didn't like to eat. He didn't point this out, better to keep the peace.

'I thought I'd cook you a special dinner,' Posy said. 'Anything you like.' She meant anything within vegetarian reason of course.

'Thanks, Pose,' he said. 'Maybe another night. Didn't I tell you we had a gig?'

'No. OK then,' she sounded a bit hurt. 'Or I thought we might ask Flora to babysit and go out to dinner or something.'

'You should have said before. Well you could always come to the gig . . .' He knew that she wouldn't. She would have nobody to talk to while they were playing, and anyway Tom had a bit of a cough, she probably shouldn't leave him. Maybe they'd try to go out together another night.

He had quite a good time with the band. They would have gone down better with a few songs from Melody, but she hardly ever showed up now. Al said that he had seen her in town with her Mum. He said that she had been looking a bit porky. Frank nearly punched him.

Coming back from the pub he thought, 'I'll just have another slice of that birthday cake.' He looked in the tin but it was all gone. They had scoffed the lot already. There was nothing left but a few crumbs, some smears of yellow icing, and the plastic candle holders all clogged up. That year Posy had got him a trick candle that wouldn't blow out. Ah well, he told himself, you can't have your cake and eat it. He made himself some crisp sandwiches instead.

There was a constant parade of celebration cakes through the house at the moment. They'd just had Izzie's first birthday. Flora had made her a pink rabbit-shaped cake. Then it had been Easter, and Posy had made her traditional cake decorated with fluffy yellow chicks from Fancy Ways. She had even taken the children to church. James's best friend George had come to play on Easter Monday.

'Did you have a nice Easter, George?' Posy had asked.

'Not really Mrs Parouselli. It was very disappointing,' he had said politely. 'I only got two boxes of Miniature Heroes and three "Premier League" eggs. And two of them were Gary Southgate.'

'Oh dear. Is that bad?' said Posy. 'It sounds like plenty of chocolate to me.'

'We're going skiing in Switzerland next week,' said George, brightening, 'so I should get some more then.'

Posy loved her garden, but she didn't believe in gardening in the conventional, hard work way. She liked buying seeds and putting in slugproof bedding plants, but anything that required special treatment, such as thinning or watering, might as well forget it. Plants should be able to manage, to fend for themselves. She would water her tomato plants and her strawberries, but that was it. Flora had given them a pair of standard bay trees as their wedding present. The pots were now cracked and weathered. Every autumn Posy thought about buying some of that special gauzy stuff to protect them, but somehow she couldn't be bothered. One year she moved them into Frank's shed, but he quickly moved them out again, saying that there wasn't enough room. Posy pushed them up against the side of the house; they would just have to take their chances.

The bay trees' leaves were burnt black by the frost and were falling off prematurely. Eventually so many of the leaves were gone that Posy asked Frank to saw the trees off a few inches above the soil. There were new twigs and leaves sprouting around the bottoms. At least she could have some new bay bushes if the standard trees were gone. She dreaded Flora seeing them. Flora would never have allowed them to get into that state. Flora always labelled the pots of her indoor hyacinths with the correct colour so that she wouldn't give away the wrong ones or place them in an inappropriate room and have to waste time moving them. Posy wondered if she should see the bay trees trees as symbols of her marriage.

She was in the garden, tidying up, when really she should have been in the house tidying up. The next day was James's party. There was too much to do. She felt compelled to clear up the garden as there was a chance that the children would play outside for part of the time, and even more importantly, that some of the parents would make inspections of it when they came to collect their offspring at half past five. She had spent many hours negotiating the guest list with James. They had eventually managed to get it down to nineteen. Posy had thought she could count on at least a few no shows. No such luck. They were all coming. Thank goodness she had booked a magician.

'And how much is that?' Frank had asked. They really were on skid row, financially.

'Only forty pounds to pay for a forty-five minute show.'

'I suppose that's quite good,' said Frank. He certainly wouldn't want to be responsible for keeping them all entertained. Posy declined to mention the £25 deposit she had already paid and the fifty pence for each balloon animal that would comprise the major part of each child's party bag. She had been thinking of making a stand against party bags, but had crumpled under the pressure as the great day approached. She knew that each child winning a prize would say: 'Please would you put it in my party bag, Mrs Parouselli.'

To reply: 'You have no party bag. Put it in your pocket' was quite beyond her.

She wiped the slide with some kitchen roll and picked up all the buckets, balls, spades, and tractors and chucked them on to the lid of the sand pit. It was not picturesque. Would it be possible to cut the grass before tomorrow afternoon? Probably not, it was so damp and long and tangled and muddy. Better to concentrate on the indoors.

Linus the Magician arrived during teatime.

'I am very pleased to see you,' Posy said as she let him in. Her duties were now almost complete, and the baton of keeping the party happy but under control was about to be passed on. 'I thought we'd do the show in the front room. Would you like a cup of tea? Some birthday cake?'

'Tea would be delightful' he said with a small bow. 'I shall take about fifteen minutes to set up. There is rather a lot to bring in from the car.'

'Pity you can't just wave your wand,' said Posy. 'Oh, I suppose everyone says that.'

'You are the first.'

She wished she could stay to watch him set up.

'I suppose I'd better get back to the party.' She could hear the decibel level rising. Frank and Flora might be struggling with all of those boys. How wonderful, she thought, as she headed back to the kitchen, to wear a tuxedo every day. She wondered how old he might be, forty, maybe even fifty. He was balding and really quite fat. She thought of the lines in 'The Night before Christmas.

'He had a broad face and a little round belly
That shook when he laughed like a bowl full of jelly.'

Actually the belly wasn't that little, and she hadn't seen him laugh yet.

'He was chubby and plump – a right jolly old elf,
And I laughed when I saw him, in spite of myself.
A wink of his eye and a twist of his head,
Soon gave me to know I had nothing to dread.'

Back in the kitchen Frank was jiggling Isobel about; she was finding the party a bit overwhelming. The guests seemed to have had enough to eat and looked as though they might start throwing things. Flora was mopping up spilt juice. Poppy, inspired by her red, sequinned, very sparkly shoes, was singing 'Over The Rainbow' very loudly in an attempt to impress her big brother's friends.

'Who needs to go to the loo before they see our special visitor?' Posy yelled. A few hands went up, and an orderly queue was formed. The rest of the children started to charge towards the front room.

'Not yet, he's not ready yet!' she bellowed. She headed them off into the dining room. A sheep dog would have been handy. 'Right. We'll play musical bumps while we wait.' James had chosen their Elvis double CD as his party music. 'Jailhouse Rock' seemed appropriate.

Before Posy had eliminated many of the contestants the magician appeared.

'Mrs Parouselli, are you ready?'

'More than,' said Posy, and switched off the music, which was now 'A Fool Such As !'. She marched them all into the front room. Frank said, 'I think I'll take Izzy in the garden. It's too noisy for her.'

'Shall I cut up some cake for their goody bags?' Flora asked.

'Yes please,' said Posy. 'I'd better stay in here in case they get out of control.' For Posy it was an act of supreme selfishness. She wouldn't miss the show for anything.

'Hello boys and girl!' Linus bellowed. Posy knew from his leaflet that there were several doves and a rabbit hidden somewhere about his person. He had strings of silk handkerchiefs, enough to dry all the tears in Hampshire, bendy wands, feather flowers, puppets, magic boxes, newspapers to tear, springy snakes that leapt out of tins, rope that could not be cut, everything that anyone could possibly want.

Parents started to arrive as the show was finishing. He let the children stroke the rabbit.

'Mrs Parouselli, it has been a pleasure,' he said when she gave him the envelope with the money in. He had noticed that she'd been the most attentive member of the audience, the loudest clapper; he had considered choosing her to help him with some of the tricks, but tradition dictated that he called up the birthday child, not their pretty mother.

'I loved the show . . .'

'I think you've missed your vocation. You should have been a boxjumper. It has been an honour to appear at James's party.

142

I only wish you had parties every day. Here take some of my cards.'

Posy thought that he was about to do one last trick (pick a card, any card) but he gave her a few of his promotional postcards. One side was about him:

Linus the Magician
Children's Party Entertainer
Magic, Balloon Creations, Real Rabbits and
Doves, Jokes, Audience Participation.
Guaranteed Laughter!
Available for small and large bookings.
Ages 4–11 years.
Member of the Wessex Association of Wizards.

Then his phone number and address. She saw that he lived in Winchester, not far from Flora. Magic must be quite lucrative then. On the other side was the ad for 'Stella's Puppets and Magic,' suitable for ages three to eight. Same address and phone number. Married then.

'Come back soon!' Poppy yelled after him. He gave a small bow and was gone. Poppy and Posy stared after him.

'I know, Pops. Let's have him at your party!' said Posy.

'Yeah!'

'It's only six weeks till your birthday,' said Posy, 'It'll fly by.'

When all of the children had gone Frank came back in with Isobel.

'I had to keep her away from all the noise,' he said. They had been sitting in his shed, sort of looking at lift-the-flap books, whilst all the time Frank had been wondering about Melody. He wished that she would find a boyfriend of her own. These twenty-two-year-olds, he thought, maybe they bounce back. Maybe they don't feel things the way a grown-up would. Maybe this was no big deal to her. Young people were so casual about things, spending all their time texting each other on their mobiles.

'The magician was great,' Posy said and showed him the card. 'And it was lovely seeing James confidently go up to help him, knowing that he would be all right.'

'Linus isn't a very jolly name, is it?' Frank said, and grimly handed it back.

'Isn't it? I thought it was quite sweet, friendly, like in Snoopy, and something to do with music.'

Oh, how could she be so ignorant?

'He was taken out into the forest and left to be devoured by dogs,' said Frank.

'Oh.'

He was surprised that she didn't know that, the amount of time she must have spent reading baby-name books.

A week later Posy telephoned the magician.

'Hello. It's Mrs Parouselli. You did my son James's party.'

'I remember.'

'Could I book you for my daughter's party in a few week's time? We were thinking of May 15th or 16th.'

'May is very busy. I'll just have a look in the book.' She could hear some fumbling and a some pages turning. 'Sixteenth you say? I'm sorry, I'm fully booked that day. Or fifteenth? No. Three school fêtes Would half past five be too late?'

'Oh.' Posy was very disappointed. 'I think they might have boiled over by then.' She felt strangely close to tears.

'How about "Stella's Puppets and Magic"? She seems to be free on the fifteenth after two. How old is the birthday girl?'

'Poppy. She'll be six.'

'Stella has a magic princess's hat, doves and a white and a brown rabbit.'

'She sounds perfect,' said Posy. 'Can I book her instead?'

'Certainly.'

'Can we say the fifteenth at four o'clock?'

'We certainly can. Would you post us a cheque for the deposit, twenty-five pounds, and Stella will send a confirmation. She also does balloon animals too if you want them.'

'Thank you. Thank you.' Posy knew that the mention of a magic princess's hat would be enough to convince Poppy that Stella was superior to Linus in every way. She must book Flora to help with the party too. Doing a girls' party was much more appealing. Now where was that Partyworks catalogue? Should they go for a ballet theme, or maybe flower fairies, or princesses, strawberries, or maybe jungle? And what should Poppy wear? My paper cup runneth over, Posy told herself, but she was still a bit miffed about Linus not being able to make it. Perhaps for Tom's birthday, although that wasn't until October.

Flora had practically finished the work for Al. He had been very co-operative and done almost exactly as she told him, painting where and when it was needed, keeping the place cleaner, and paying for the Ikea things in advance as requested. The landlord had been tricky. First of all Flora found him hard to track down, then he was obstinate about moving the furniture. When she told him that it had woodworm and a evidence of a possible beetle infestation he became more helpful. She had started mentioning licences and the Council. After the fifth phone call he had judged it easier just to go along with her.

Now she was taking round the final few pieces, some tasteful toys, child-sized cutlery and a storage unit that Al had agreed to over the phone. She would take it back if he didn't want it. When she had started working with him he'd offered to get a key cut for her, but she had declined, saying that she thought he'd find that making duplicate keys for a rented property was contrary to his contract. It had turned out that he hadn't seen as much of her as he'd expected to. She seemed to get a lot of things done during the short sharp shocks of her visits. When she wasn't there he wondered why he had bothered with the whole business.

Flora rang the bell and when he buzzed her in she carried her first load upstairs. She would get him to help her with the storage unit.

'So,' she said. 'How's it all going?'

'Great,' said Al. 'I got Caroline and Finn to come and see it last week and she was *pretty impressed*. I didn't mention you. It wouldn't have had the same impact.'

'That's absolutely fine,' said Flora. 'Discretion assured. I haven't even mentioned to Posy that I've been working for you. Caroline need never know.'

'They'll be the last to know,' said Al. 'And she agreed to Finn staying over. She was amazed by the furniture. Actually I think she was a bit narked.'

'Maybe she does smell a rat,' said Flora.

'I think it was more to do with how come I had the money for it, and how come I'd never wanted to go to Ikea with her. I told her I hadn't wanted to go now, but getting myself and the place together was just so I could see more of Finn.' He nearly added, 'And she fell for that one too.'

'Good,' said Flora. She was starting to run out of time for this job. She had her invoice ready in her bag. 'So do you want to come down and see the toy storage unit before we try getting it up the stairs?'

'OK.' Al realised that he was going to have to act fast. His guaranteed time with Flora was running out.

She had the back seat of her car down to accommodate the monstrosity of pale wood and brightly-coloured plastic boxes that was to make his life complete.

'I'm not sure,' Al said. 'How much did you say it was?'

'£49.95. No carriage charge,' said Flora.

'Why don't we decide over dinner?' said Al. She looked stunned. 'Flora,' he went on 'I really appreciate all you've done.'

'Prompt payment and a thank you are all that's necessary.'
She pulled the invoice out of her bag. 'Here.' He caught hold
of her hand and kissed it. It was very soft and lemony clean.

'Shall I take it you don't want the storage unit?'

'It's you that I want.'

'You have quite the wrong idea,' said Flora. 'And I'm quite
sure that it's not me that you want.'

'Flora . . .'

'Al, I'm really flattered.'

She glimpsed a whole possible future for the two of them. She
might even have a baby, maybe two. She blinked it all away.

'It would never work.'

'Try. Just dinner.'

'I think I'd better go,' she said. She got into the car, the
invoice still in her hand. She chucked it onto the passenger seat
in an un-Flora-ish gesture of abandon. She would waste the
price of a stamp to be away quickly. Al just stood there and
watched as she plugged in her seatbelt and slid her sunglasses
down from their resting position on the top of her head.

What could he have been thinking? What folly! He hated
people who wore their sunglasses on top of their heads. Lord,
what fools these mortals be! She drove away. Back he went, up
the stairs and into his tidy, tasteful, clean, stupid room. But
what good was sitting alone in his room? He might as well go
to the pub.

On the way home from school Poppy announced the theme of
her party.

'Mermaids. And I will need a mermaid costume, and all my
friends can be mermaids, and you can be a mermummy too.'

'Yuck' said James.

'I don't think I should dress up,' Posy replied. The idea of
herself in a mermaid costume was too awful to contemplate. 'I
wouldn't mind wearing a mermaid's crown, but I think I'll
just wear a normal mortal's dress.'

'But you will make me a mermaid costume, won't you Mummy?'

'Of course. I wasn't a Saturday girl at Laura Ashley for nothing.'

'What?'

'Nothing.'

'And we should go to the beach and find lots of shells and pearls and seaweed to decorate things with.'

'Of course,' said Posy. What was she getting herself into now? She could cut up crêpe paper to make frondy seaweedy decorations. They could have shells on the table, a cake in the shape of a shell (by Aunty Flora), sealife-themed prizes, hunt the starfish, pin the tail on the dolphin or the seahorse . . .

'We'll have a whale of a time!' she said.

She remembered that Frank had a great line in fish jokes, although they would probably be wasted on the young.

In a terraced house in Winchester Linus the Magician sat staring at his diary. He wondered if there was any way he could re-jig the bookings to accommodate Mrs Parouselli. He would have liked to see her again. Perhaps he could move one of the school bookings forwards, but no. He didn't want to seem unprofessional, and the thought of phoning up some Parents' Association secretary, re-opening negotiations, having to wait for the committee to consider it and get back to him . . . he had better leave the Parouselli party to Stella. He went back to his current project. He was making a magic box. The cleverly-angled mirrors meant that things, even quite large things, could disappear inside it. There was a particularly lovely Chopin Nocturne on the radio. Once he finished assembling the box he would clean out the rabbits. Stella was planning a new set of puppets, a nuclear family of meerkats. He was also working on designs for their set, a lookout, which was to have a number of exits for them (or some pretty impressive special effects) to pop out of. He heard

Stella's key in the lock. She was back from a playgroup booking. He went to help her unload.

Stella's method of organising her props was the toast of the Wessex Association of Wizards. She had even given talks at the monthly meetings on the subject 'Magic of Organisation – Organisation of Magic'. So many magicians just hurled everything into a trunk and wasted hours sorting and setting up and looking for things that they had mislaid. They now supplied boxes and many-pocketed canvas bags, designed by Stella and made by Linus to wizards from all over Wessex. Some of them were beyond helping though, irredeemably messy and disorganised.

'You can't teach an old dog new tricks,' Linus had quipped when he saw Stella shake her head in disbelief at some of the members' chaotic ways. She disagreed.

Stella went to change out of her outfit, some denim dungarees trimmed with red spangles, a drapey jacket and pink DMs. It had echoes of her post-punk, 'Come On Eileen' teenage tastes. Neither of them was working that night, and she had been planning a meal around the things that she had bought at the farmers' market that morning.

'I saw you fixed that ridge tile, thanks!' she called down the stairs.

'Cleaned out the gutters too,' he told her. 'I think I'll repaint the weatherboards. I haven't done them for a few years. The rest of the roof looked fine.' He made twice yearly checks from the bottom of the garden with the binoculars, as well as keeping the gutters in tip-top condition.

MAY

FRANK HAD ONLY HAD a few hours sleep, but that was normal for him. He fell asleep easily enough (one bottle of red wine, a bottle of Kingfisher lager) but for some reason he had snapped awake around 4 a.m. He had lain there worrying about everything. Even his usual trick of trying to remember the words of all the songs he most hated had failed to get him back to sleep. He put them in ascending order of awfulness, and then lay there fiddling about with the positions.

1. True by Spandau Ballet.
2. Rio by Duran Duran.
3. Shout/Everybody Wants To Rule The World by Tears for Fears.
4. The Diana 'Candle in the Wind'.

But who would he choose if it was a matter of so-called style? Perhaps The Thompson Twins. They had been really something. Then he began to choose the music for his funeral. He would have to leave clear instructions. Posy would be bound to get it wrong. Perhaps he should entrust it to Al, assuming Al lasted longer than him. Flora would be the one to get it perfectly organised. She wouldn't be fazed. That would be if she could fit it into her busy schedule. Eventually, with amusing, mean thoughts about his sister-in-law, he fell back to sleep.

Poppy flung herself on to her parents bed at quarter past six. Her sharp little knees and elbows made further sleep impossible. Posy pulled her closer and breathed in the chocolate Nesquik smell of her hair.

'Mummy. You haven't forgotten it's nearly my birthday have you?'

'Your birthday will be cancelled if I don't get back to sleep,' said Frank.

'No! No! You can't cancel birthdays, they just come!' Poppy was almost sobbing. Posy hugged her tighter.

'Daddy's only joking. Of course you can't cancel birthdays.'

'Well,' said Poppy. 'We need to get all the things for the party. And don't forget to make my costume and buy me some presents and a card.'

'Don't worry, Poppy. I've got it all planned. Today we are going to get some shells for decorations.'

'Are we?' said Frank.

'We can just go to Netley. It has good shells,' Posy said, placatingly.

'Huh.'

'We'd better bring a bag. If I find a starfish can I bring it home for a pet, or a seagull, or an oyster with a pearl in?' Poppy asked.

'Or a puffin,' Posy added. 'Or a penguin, or a pelican, or a cormorant. You sometimes see cormorants at Netley, but they might be a bit tricky to catch.'

'Can we take a picnic?' Poppy asked.

'Of sorts.'

'I can never decide if Netley is a profoundly sad and depressing place, or a beautiful and uplifting one,' Posy said as they pulled into the car park. She looked up at the Victorian tower and chapel, all that remained of the military hospital, then down towards the shore. 'You can't park here, on this side.'

'Bloody disabled,' said Frank. 'They get all the best spots, all the best views.' He backed the car into another space. 'Right. You take them to the beach, and I'll sit in here and listen to the radio.'

'Ha ha. Not likely.'

'Don't you want to come, Daddy?'

'He's only joking. He wouldn't miss it for anything.'

'Many a true word spoken in jest,' said Frank, but he remained seated and started to roll a cigarette.

'I don't know why you have to smoke in places of outstanding natural beauty,' Posy said.

He couldn't be bothered to reply. He might have said: 'Because we have just driven past where Melody lives. Because I may have ruined her life, and maybe yours, and maybe mine. Because I am trapped. Because the last time I was near here I was screwing her in the vari,' but fortunately he didn't. He knew that Melody only had a few more weeks to go. He should ring her to see how she was.

They were soon plonking about on the beach. Pathetic little waves washed over the toes of their wellies. Tom was almost overcome by joy when a container ship went by. They could see speedboats involved in some sort of racing event, or perhaps just showing off, and Red Funnel ferries on their way to the Isle of Wight. There were rich pickings of shells, and pieces of old rope and driftwood. The children wanted to bring dead crabs home for party decorations, but Posy said no. She was pleased that they were all having a wonderful time. Then Frank said.

'So, do I really have to come to this mermaid party?'

'What do you think?' Posy replied. Don't let Poppy hear you talk like that. Anyone would think you didn't want her to have a birthday.

'I was only joking. You know mermaids aren't my kind of thing.' Well, only 22-year-old blonde mermaids from Weston who sing, he added bitterly to himself. Perhaps she might come walking by with her mum's foul little dog. He kind of hoped so.

'What's that story about the mermaid who gets legs?' he asked.

'Oh,' said Posy. ' "The Little Mermaid". She falls in love and becomes human, but every step she takes is like walking on sharks' fins, something like that. I can't remember what happens.'

'She probably tops herself,' said Frank.

'Or tops and tails herself. Do you want me to take Isobel for a bit? Your arm must be falling off.'

Posy headed back up the beach with the baby and spread out her mac for them to sit on. Isobel could amuse herself by picking up stones and shells and trying to get them into her mouth before Posy stopped her. One day, Posy thought, we will be the sort of family with a blanket lined with a groundsheet that we keep in the car. One that folds up and has cute little handles. She had some packets of white chocolate buttons in her bag, what her Aunt Bea would have referred to as 'iron rations'. She called the children to come and join them. Frank came too, rolling another cigarette. Tom had let the sea get over the tops of his wellies, and the brine was wicking up the legs of his jeans. Posy knew that the tender skin on the insides of his legs would soon be chafed red. She wondered if mutated algae and viruses, warm from the Fawley oil refinery across the water, were now trying to breach his defences. Definitely an early bath for Tom. Perhaps Matey would act like Dettox on him. She ate most of Isobel's bag of buttons, bad for a baby to have sweeties anyway . . .

'It would be nice to live out here,' she said. Posy always said this when they came to Netley. She looked longingly at the Victorian villas, and the pretty terraces, the boats and the deluxe duck-pond that they passed on the way.

It didn't occur to Frank that they might live in one of those big posh houses. He imagined himself living in a solitary beach hut. Ah, that would be the life . . . the simplicity of it all. He would sleep under an army blanket on the hut's narrow bench. No need to wash, just have a swim. No cooking, just go to a café. Imagine no possessions, he thought, just his bass, hardly any clothes, one pair of shoes, a camping gas stove, one tin mug, one spoon, one knife. He would brew coffee that blew his mind, and sit in the dark, drinking whisky, soothed by the warm onshore breezes. It would be like van Gogh's room, just him and his boots. No decorations, no videos of Fireman Sam, no rabbits, no BettaKleen. If Posy had the same hut she would make it into a colossal changing bag. She would fill it with bottles of purple spray-on SPF 30 suncream, plastic sandwich boxes, wet wipes, first-aid kits, and brightly coloured beach games from the Early Learning Centre. He shuddered.

'Are you cold, Frank? We'd better get going or the kids will start getting cold too. I wonder what the Netley school is like,' she said. 'I suppose the proximity to Weston would be a bad aspect.'

'Spoken like a true Surrey girl,' Frank replied. 'You don't even know anyone from Weston.'

'Nor do you.'

'Poppy's bag was full of shells. Posy tipped them out on to one of the beach steps and checked for any that were still occupied. Poppy put these ones back near the water's edge.

Time to go home.

In the pub that night Frank could hardly muster the enthusiasm to play. The music didn't go well. Rich and Ron were being snappy with each other. They'd had a row about ELO. Rich hated them and all their works, Ron was insisting that they had huge merit, whatever the sound was like, and that technically Jeff Lyne was something else.

Melody was there for a while and Frank saw that her transformation from mermaid to manatee was nearly complete. She wasn't in the mood for singing. All she wanted to know was, Had He Told His Wife Yet? The answer was, of course, still no. He couldn't think of anything to say to her. She rang her brother for a lift, and soon she was gone.

Frank realised that he would have to be the one to top himself. There was no way forward that made any sense. During their break he couldn't bring himself to speak. Al noticed that Frank had turned into a sad old polar bear alone in the zoo.

'All right mate?' Al asked.

Frank slowly shook his head and stared into his pint.

'I am in blood
Stepp'd in so far that, should I wade no more,
Returning were as tedious as going on. Or something like that,' he said.

'Get your point. If there's anything I can do . . .' said Al. 'Fancy another?'

Frank nodded. Al rested his hand on Frank's shoulder on the way to the bar. He'd get a couple of whisky chasers too. Poor bloody Frank, he thought. Poor sod. What a mess.

Aunty Flora came up trumps with the birthday cake.

'I didn't even know that there was silver icing,' Posy said. 'It is *so* beautiful. I don't know if the girls will be able to bear to see it cut.'

'It's just a "Little Mermaid" tin that I hired from "The Cake Lady". Easy peasy.' said Flora. Coming up with amazing cakes was all part of her day's work.

'I'm glad she looks so demure,' said Posy. 'Are those real shells?'

'Chocolate. But not suitable for nut allergy sufferers. The rest is fine, of course.' Poppy came in.

'Quick! Quick! Cover her up!' shouted Posy.

'Oh please can I see, Mummy, Aunty Flora? Please!'

'Oh she might as well, Posy,' said Flora, was quite a soft touch with her niece.

'Go on then . . .'

'Oh Aunty Flora, it's beautiful. I can't believe it's for me. It's the most beautiful cake in the world!'

'For the most beautiful niece in the world, with love,' said Flora.

'And izzie,' said Poppy.

'Well lzzie is the most beautiful baby niece in the world. And here's your present.' It was wrapped in exquisite lilac-and-pink shimmery paper with copious bows. 'I like being an Aunt,' Flora said.

Poppy carefully unwrapped it. She would save everything for her making things box. Inside was a Flower Fairies flower press, a flowery apron, and a large, glittery, white teddy with wings and a halo.

'I thought you probably needed an extra teddy,' said Flora as Poppy hugged her. 'Especially an angel one.'

'She's beautiful. What's her name?'

'Well that's up to you, isn't it?' said Flora.

'It might be on her label. Animals come ready-named now. Oh yes. Here it is. Angelica Angelbear,' Posy announced.

'Wow,' said Poppy. 'Thanks Aunty Flora.'

'I'm so lucky to have all of these nieces and nephews. It's a real treat coming to your party. I'm sorry I haven't got a mermaid costume.'

'That's all right,' said Poppy. 'Nor's Mum.'

'Now, Poppy. We have to get a move on, they'll be here soon. Either put on your new apron and help us with the party food, or go and change into your costume.'

'Both,' said Poppy.

'You have to see her costume,' said Posy. 'It's a triumph, though I say it myself. When Izzie's a bit older I might go into business making them for girls and their dollies. I'm going to call it 'Mermaid Tails'. Maybe I could have a whole mermaid and fairy-themed shop. Heaven.'

It was lovely to see Posy looking so happy, having a plan,

being enthusiastic about something. Flora didn't say that if she wanted to make the business a success she'd have to hurry up before the mermaid bubble burst.

Two hours later, fifteen little mermaids and fairies were cavorting in the garden watched by Frank and Isobel. James and Tom were inside still eating. Posy hadn't expected the birthday tea to go so quickly; there was an unplanned-for pause before Stella's Puppets and Magic show was due to start. Stella arrived fourteen minutes before she was due to start.

'Mrs Parouselli? Sorry I'm late. Football traffic,' she said to Flora who let her in. Flora glanced at her watch. An apology for one minute late. Impressive.

'No, I'm the birthday girl's aunt, Flora. Would you like a hand with your stuff?'

'I'm fine thanks. I'm sure you must have lots to do.' Also she had it so perfectly organised that she didn't like other people to have the opportunity to mess it up.

'Mermaid cake? A cup of tea?'

'That would be lovely. With lemon if possible.'

'Very possible,' said Flora.

She soon returned with the tea in one of Posy's Cornish stoneware mugs and the cake on what she considered to be Posy's best plate, the prettiest of a set of four Cath Kidston ones that she had given her.

'Beautiful plate,' said Stella. 'I've seen them in one of my favourite shops. I was very tempted, and by the pink straw-berry oilcloth, but I don't think Linus would stand for it. Too girlie.'

Flora watched enrapt whilst Stella unpacked the show. There were many pocketed canvas rolls full of tricks and puppets, boxes that turned into tables, the magic princess's hat container became a drum, and the rabbits travelled in style in a pink wooden crate with velvet and rope handles. She went back into the kitchen to report to Posy.

'Nearly ready. I think we're kindred spirits.'

'Well, her husband was really nice,' said Posy, tipping what was left of the Iced Gems into the bin.

'The modern child has no qualms about just eating the tops. And they're now enriched with vitamins and iron. Iced Gems! Talk about decadent.'

'Irrelevant if it's the biscuit bit they enrich. You should find out. There might be people relying on that for their children's nutrition.'

'Serve them right,' said Frank, coming in from the garden. 'I can't stand it out there any longer.'

'You're meant to be supervising,' said Posy.

'Ready when you are,' called Stella.

'Phew!' said Posy. 'I'll just line them all up for the loo.'

'You missed your vocation. Should have been a teacher,' said Frank.

'More likely a dinner lady.' Posy pictured herself dolloping out scoops of mashed potato to an endless line of upturned little faces. Large please, and extra gravy. 'Oh I forgot to give them the ice cream. Well, they could eat it while they watched the show.'

'Bad idea, Posy. There's bound to be lots of audience participation. They'd only spill it all over their costumes,' said Flora.

'Never mind. We'll get through it,' said Frank, meaning the ice cream, not the show. 'Why don't you two watch the show and I'll carry on out here?'

'OK, fine, if you don't mind missing it.'

'I don't.'

'You'll have to let the parents in when they start arriving,' Posy warned him.

'Maybe James can do that bit.'

Posy and Flora were entranced by the show. 'I wish we'd had parties like this when we were little,' said Posy.

'Stella's a stunner,' said Flora.

The birthday girl was called up to assist and Stella formed some of the more compliant-looking mermaids into a percussion band. The magic princess's hat was full of flowers and silk hankies, and finally doves and the rabbits.

The parents arrived as it all ended, and Flora helped Posy to give out the party bags. As soon as the children were all gone she hurried back to see if she could help Stella. Too late. Stella was packing her last box.

'Lovely show,' said Flora. 'That's quite a box you've got there.'

'Speed and efficiency are all in the storage and packing. It's all organisation. I can fit in twice as many shows a day as some magicians because I've got this part down to a fine art.'

'Very impressive,' said Flora. 'I'm in the organisation business too, but a different kind of magical transformation.' She gave Stella one of her cards. 'Not that you look as though you need any solutions.'

'I might know someone who does,' said Stella.

'I organise parties and events for people too. If you'd like to give me one of your cards, I'm sure I'll want you soon . . .'

Stella found one of the promotional postcards straight away, Linus one side, herself on the other.

'Thank you,' said Flora. Posy came in with the money in an envelope.

'Thank you. Poppy loved it, we all did. Hope we'll see you again soon.' 'Me too,' said Stella. Flora helped her carry her things to the car.

JUNE

KATE AND HER FAMILY were going to the Longleat Centre Parcs for half-term.

'Huh,' said Frank when Posy told him. 'What kind of a holiday would that be? You might as well go to the school playground at 3.15. What kind of getting away is that? Scoop them all up and take them in a giant dumper. I'd bloody hate it.'

'It's not their holiday. They're going to France in August too. Anyway, it sounds nice' said Posy, feebly.

'Huh. I hope the Lions of Longleat raid the place.'

'There are acres of forest, and cycle paths,' said Posy who wasn't listening to him at all. 'And a health spa. Kate's got all these treatments booked. Oh well, I don't suppose we'll ever be able to afford it.'

'Posy, what's happened to you? How could you want to go there? A holiday to being an ideal family?'

'I could stand it,' said Posy.

He put his head in his hands. 'Posy, it isn't even a real place. How can you go on holiday to somewhere that isn't a real place?'

'You wouldn't be so snobby about people going to Butlins. Just 'cos we can't afford to go.'

'Huh.'

'At the age of thirty-seven,' Posy sang, 'She realised she'd never ride to Centre Parcs In a space wagon With the air-conditioned air in her hair.'

It doesn't even scan,' said Frank. 'And I thought you were thirty-five still.' What he really wanted to say was that he hated her singing; she was always off key, starting out soprano, finishing up as practically a bass. He couldn't believe that he had signed up to spend his whole life with someone who couldn't even carry a tune. They had nothing more to say for a while. Frank left for his shed, Posy carried on with the washing-up. But they both were remembering the last time they'd been abroad, it was nearly ten years ago now, two weeks in Greece. That was the sort of holiday they should really be having now, all sparkling sea, honey, yoghurt and nectarines.

Posy remembered how they'd marvelled at the stars; no wonder the Ancient Greeks had hung their stories on them. It had been total bliss, well, apart from the walk to the beach past a pair of tethered farm dogs. The dogs had looked vicious, had barked and leapt at them every time. Once Posy and Frank had passed, the dogs turned their aggression on each other, throwing themselves again and again the length of their chains, but always finding each other out of reach. Posy expected that the dogs or their descendants were still there, chained, snarling and frustrated.

Posy and the children were spending half-term at the Bee Centre. Frank wasn't going with them. He waved them off, feeling waves of relief that he wasn't with them in that overloaded car, and worry that Posy might be so distracted by the squabbling that they'd all meet their doom somewhere on the A303. The forecast was for thundery showers. He could see Poppy and James starting to argue about who had the least space before Posy had even turned the corner. Her extra-long pause at the junction indicated that she was already reaching for a story tape. If she was really lucky she'd manage it in less than five hours.

The sky was peculiar. There were anvil clouds over St Catherine's Hill. If this was Kansas, Flora thought, there would be a tornado; but it was Hampshire in June; Hampshire, where hurricanes hardly ever happened. The first big splashes of rain hit the windscreen as she turned off the motorway. The unmistakeable lurching and thumping of a puncture began halfway down the hill outside St Cross. It was a stupid time and place for this. She was seeing a new client in forty-five minutes. She rang the AA to ask for assistance. When she finally got through she learnt that there were flash floods throughout the area, they'd be a quick as they could, but she might have a long wait. There was nothing for it but to change the tyre herself.

She stepped out of the car and into the ankle-deep torrent of rainwater. This was crazy but she'd never yet cancelled seeing a client, never. She had to get to Arlesford, on the other side of Winchester. She got her linen mac out of the boot. Putting it on to cover her grey dress seemed rather pointless, but she did anyway. Within moments she was soaked through. Cars sped by, each one spending another wave over her.

Flora knew what she was doing. She had the jack out and the car cranked up, now for the struggle with the bolts. Her fair hair, which that day she'd left loose, was turned dark and plastered to her head, water flowed down her neck and out of her sleeves, and oh, the state of her shoes! Her hands and the spanner were so wet that they kept slipping, but she knew that if she worked fast she'd have time to run in and change and only be a few moments late. The river was now up to her calves. A lesser mortal might have been swept away. She just couldn't get the last bolt off. A car pulled up behind her.

Just what I need, Flora thought, help from some patronising tough guy. She made another attempt at the bolt.

'Can I help?'

It was a woman's voice. The pink DMs were underwater, but the red spangles on the dungerees were unmistakeable. Stella's Puppets and Magic, thought Flora, standing up.

'I can't get this last bolt off,' said Flora. 'Hands are too wet.'

Stella pulled out a blue silk handkerchief, and then another, and another. 'I'll try with these,' she said. As if by magic, the bolt was off.

'Oh thank you!' Flora gushed. She was close to tears. Together they had the wheel off and the new one on. The rain was stopping and the sun was breaking through the clouds. She could still be on time. 'Thank you. You're drenched too now. It was so kind of you to stop. I hope your costume's not ruined.'

'I've finished for the day. Anyway, it has a twin.'

'You're Stella, aren't you? We've met,' said Flora. 'You came to my niece's party, Poppy Parouselli, mostly mermaids, in Southampton.'

'Oh,' said Stella, 'I didn't recognize you.'

'I don't usually look like this,' said Flora. There was water running out of her shoes.

'You look exactly like the princess at the door at beginning of "The Princess and the Pea" ' said Stella.

Flora laughed. 'I know the one. Thanks so much for helping. I have to go and get changed, I've got a client to see. I'm so grateful. Thank you.'

They returned to their cars. Stella waved one of the handkerchiefs. The rain had stopped. Flora pulled away into the traffic and was gone.

There were downpours and flash floods in Wiltshire and Dorset too. It took Posy six and a half hours to get to Cornwall.

'I feel like this is where I belong,' she said. She was stiff after the long drive. The aunts were there to greet them. Isobel was now asleep in the car, having managed to stay awake and moaning for almost the whole journey. 'Thank goodness we're here.' It was all just as it should be. She looked about her, stretched her arms wide and inhaled deeply the healing Cornish air. The sun was shining, the sky was blue. The children climbed out of the car, scattering crisp crumbs and raisins. Poppy and Tom hugged the Aunts. James stood stiff as a petrol pump whilst he allowed himself to be kissed on the top of the head. He'd soon be holding hands with Is as they gazed into rock pools, and sitting on Bea's knee eating honey toffee.

The North Cornwall Bee Centre wasn't much more than some fields with a garden and some hens. The Aunts' house was the Bee Centre, or Bee Museum as people often mistakenly called it. In the grounds were the hives, a meadow and orchard where the donkeys, Barney, Billy and Betsy lived. There were bikes in various sizes and a go cart, and the huge wooden play pen that had once been Flora and Posy's. Upstairs in the Bee Centre were the exhibition rooms and a café of sorts. Visitors who pushed the 'PRIVATE – STAFF ONLY', door (and many did) would find themselves stumbling into the Aunts' bedrooms.

It was the dustiest, most cluttered attraction ever to appear in the guidebooks, but even so they were doing slightly better than their rivals at the Paperweight Museum down the road. Is and Bea were as busy as bees. They had 400,000 of them. The Cornish gorse and heather, and their garden with its beds and beds of lavender and roses and herbs, and the yellow tree peonies beside their door, made, they said, the sweetest honey in England. Posy and Flora agreed that it tasted of the blue sky.

Is was tall for her generation, and her grey curls had once been as dark and wild as Posy's. If she was a queen bee, then Bea was a bumble. It was Bea who made the brown and yellow striped jumpers that sold in the shop, and the lines of knitted bees in black felt wellies and sometimes waistcoats and hats appropriate to their occupations. Gardener Bee held a rake and a trug, Professor Bee had a black-felt mortar board, Doctor Bee had a white coat and a stethoscope, King and Queen Bee had plush purple cloaks and gold paper crowns. Flora and

Posy's favourite was Bee-Keeping Bee with her bellows and veiled hat, made from some gauzy stuff that Bea found in the Centre's first-aid kit. As she grew older the bees' jobs became more absurd, Fishmonger Bee and Fisherman Bee, Javelin and Shotputter Bees, Photocopier Engineer Bee (this one was hard to identify) James Bond Bee . . .

If you costed the time spent making the bees and the jumpers, the profits would have been negative; but Aunt Bea never did. Anyway she had plenty of time, sitting behind the till in the shop or by the urn in the café, which was sometimes quiet.

'If I had a penny for every smart alec tourist dad who quips "Not exactly yer tourist honey pot, is it love?" . . .' Bea grumbled.

'Or a pound coin,' said Is, pushing a cup of tea towards her. 'Biscuit?'

'Actually, I've been thinking about a new line. Donkeys. I think they're just as popular with the visitors as the bees.'

'Probably more.'

'Knitted grey bodies, black PVC-coated fabric hooves, little hats with flowers . . .'

The Parousellis did their best to help in the Centre, but mostly played in the grounds and spent hours and hours on the beach. This was how Posy wanted her children to be: tanned and healthy in shorts, jumpers and canvas shoes that were bleached by the sun and turned crunchy by the salt and sand. When they closed their eyes each night they saw pebbles and shells and seaweed and rock pools behind their lids.

If The Wild Years hadn't been playing at the Gosport Festival, which paid well, Frank would have been in Cornwall too. As soon as he'd calculated that there was no danger of Posy and the children returning, he phoned Melody. The baby was overdue.

Melody answered after two rings.

'Whoever you are, before you ask,' she said, 'I'm still bloody here.'

'I wasn't going to ask,' said Frank. 'I was wondering how you were.'

'How do you think I bloody am?'

'I thought I might come over and see you.'

'Got some time on your hands, have you? Where's your wife and kids then?'

'Cornwall. Or nearly in Cornwall by now.'

'Hang on,' said Melody. He heard. Anita's voice in the background. 'Mum says, have you got the shoe rack and the telescopic duster?'

'Might have,' said Frank, laughing.

'S'pose you can come over then.'

'Be about half an hour,' said Frank. He often felt like calling her sweetheart.

It was Anita who opened the door.

'Oh hello Frank, it's you is it?'

'Seems to be.'

'Well, you might as well come in.' Frank saw her brighten at the sight of the BettaKleen bags. He realised that if Posy had been in this situation she would have brought flowers or biscuits or something for the hospital.

'How much is that then?'

'Er,' Frank looked down at the receipt stapled to one of the bags. '£13.89.'

Anita raised her eyebrows.

'Oh, on the house . . . he said.

'Well, thanks.' He decided not to point out that it was the least he could do.

'Where's Melody then?'

'She's putting her feet up. She nodded towards the front room door. Frank took this as an invitation to go on through.

There was something about the room that made him want to lounge. It was all so comfy and warm – ash trays, the oversized sofa which had footrest bits that pulled out – you could check out any time you liked, but it would be hard to leave. The dog was asleep and gave only a muffled growl to indicate that it knew and disapproved of Frank's intrusion.

'What're you watching?' he asked.

'Oh, I don't know. There's nothing on,' said Melody. 'It's all bloody lifestyle shows. As if anyone with a lifestyle would be watching this crap. I'm so bored just waiting for something to happen.'

'Not long till "Countdown".'

'What? Oh, that "Countdown". You would say that. I suppose all you Parousellis sit around competing at *Countdown* everyday. Want a biscuit?' Melody asked, pointing at the tin with her very pink toes.

Frank shook his head. 'Got your bag packed then?'

'Mum did it weeks ago.'

'Anything you need?'

'Few million pounds. My body back.'

'Melody, you look beautiful.'

Of course Anita chose that moment to come in. Frank suspected that she listened at doors. 'That's what I keep telling her,' she said. 'You soon get your figure back, after the first one anyway.'

'I've got my flat,' said Melody. 'Two bedrooms in Canberra Towers. It'll be really nice when I've painted. I can get the keys on Monday, assuming I'm here.'

'Which floor?'

'Seventh. Everyone says the same thing . . .'

'Lucky!' said Frank. 'Is there a view over the water?'

'It's really nice. We'll be watching all the ships go by.'

'If you want any help . . .'

'My brother's doing it. But maybe. You haven't told her yet have you?'

'What, Posy? Well, no, not yet. She's away with the kids for half-term. It just hasn't been right.'

'She'll find out somehow,' said Anita. 'These things always come out in the end.'

'Mmm. Or maybe there are lots that don't come out, that nobody ever knows about,' said Frank.

'What?' asked Melody.

'If the time's right I'll tell her,' he said.

'Huh,' said Anita. 'I won't be holding my breath.' She picked up the telescopic duster and left the room.

'And when might the time be right?' said Melody.

'Look, what good will knowing do her, or the children?' said Frank. He felt like adding 'And it's not as though you want me anyway is it?'

'I just kind of think that she has a right to know. People always want to know things don't they? Nobody wants to be the last to know.' He couldn't understand why they were so bothered about Posy, what relevance it had to them.

They didn't even want him at the birth. Anita was going to be the one. Frank wasn't sure whether or not he was pleased about this. And Melody hadn't even been to her ParentCraft classes. (When he thought of everything that Posy had dragged him to before Jimmy was born . . . the NCT and the Active Birth partners' evenings . . . She had made him go to so-called 'Refresher nights' for the other three too, despite the fact that when push came to shove she just hissed at his offers to massage her back. Melody seemed to have the right idea. She said she would take everything on offer when it came to the pain.

Three days later Melody's mum rang him from the hospital. It was a girl. Born after a relatively easy for a first time labour.

'I'll be there in ten minutes' he said, and started to cry.

Melody was sitting up in bed looking pretty and pink. Her hair was up in a ponytail. He put the huge bunch of pink roses down on the bed and kissed her cheek.

'There she is,' she said, beaming, tilting her head towards the perspex tank beside her.

'Hang on. Don't pick her up yet or an alarm goes off.' Melody turned the key that meant he could hold the baby.

'She is beautiful. Oh, she's wonderful.' How could he have been so stupid not to realise that he would feel like this when he held her. She didn't wake up.

'Her eyes are very pale blue,' said Melody. 'She's already done three dirty nappies.'

'Oh, that's good, that's very good,' Frank whispered. 'I love her already.'

'Well I'm the one who gets to take her home,' said Melody.

'She's gorgeous.'

'I've settled on a name,' Melody announced. Frank was too busy stroking the baby's cheek to look up.

'Oh yeah?'

'Francesca Sapphire.'

He gulped. 'Are you sure?'

'Don't you like it?'

'Of course I do,' he said. 'It's beautiful.'

Whenever Flora felt in need of spiritual cleaning or grounding she bought herself some wonderful new soap or bath stuff, usually from 'Michaelmas Daisy's', her favourite shop in Winchester. If she were to run a shop, it would be like this. There were great clothes upstairs where few buggies could venture, and she liked to pick up little treats for Posy (goodness knows, she needed them) and things for the children. It was her main source of presents, as well as the Mexican decorations and Christmas things that she sometimes badly needed for clients. She thought that Daisy, the proprietor, was stunningly beautiful. Flora was a favoured customer.

As soon as she stepped through the door her breathing slowed. In Daisy's shop, in Winchester, there's peace and holy quiet there, she misquoted to herself.

Today she couldn't decide between a cocoa butter soap and a thyme one.

She weighed a bar in each hand, sniffing them alternately.

'Take them both,' said a voice beside her. She turned and smiled, but didn't recognise the the woman with a cloud of dark hair rather like Posy's, soft, very laundered-looking jeans and the sort of classic, white linen shirt that magazines are always exhorting people to invest in. She was Flora's idea of perfect and neat, like an off-duty weather woman.

'Stella,' said the woman. 'I don't suppose you recognise me out of my puppeteer's garb.'

'I do now,' said Flora, 'and you're right. I'll take them both. I need some of those new mugs as well. As much as anyone can need Cath Kidston mugs that is.'

'Oh I think one can. Cath Kidston without the kids is what I'm aiming at.'

'They're for a client, for a present.'

'I wish people employed you to shop for presents for me. I was just going to get something to eat. Would you like to come?' Stella asked.

The wonderful thing about women friends, about women, is that you can just say things, Flora thought. How nice to have met Stella in Michaelmas Daisy's. How nice to be invited for lunch.

'That would be lovely. I have a client this afternoon, so I'm afraid it'll have to be quick.'

'Why don't we buy some sandwiches and eat them in the Watermeadows?'

'Mmm,' said Flora. 'But lunch is on me, to thank you for helping me with that tyre. I wasn't even late for my appointment. The Watermeadows are sort of on my way home.'

'Mine too.'

Half an hour later they were sitting beneath some poplars. 'I love it here,' said Flora. 'Home of my heart.'

'And mine.'

'I used to come here all the time with Posy and my Aunts when I was little.'

'And where Keats wrote *Endymion*,' said Stella.

'Mmm.' Of course Flora knew that.

'I might have been reading this incorrectly,' said Stella, 'but . . .' She picked up Flora's hand.

It smelt of the soaps she had been choosing. She kissed it.

Flora smiled, 'I hadn't thought about it, but I think you are right.' She kissed Stella's hand, which smelt of apple. 'I thought you were married,' she said.

'Lots of people make that mistake. Linus is my brother.'

'Hell's Flaming Teeth!' said Posy looking at the Oxfam family planner, a title that always made her snigger, 'I had completely forgotten that Mrs Fleance is coming today.' She had written it in Tom's column, not her's and Izzie's, and somehow it had slipped her mind. Normally this visit would be something to give her several days' angst.

Posy never swore in front of the children. This at the breakfast table meant that she was truly agitated. 'Frank, you have to help me. Can you take the children to school, and take Izzie? Tom has to stay here to meet her. I have to blitz this place. Oh how could I possibly have forgotten? It's even in my diary too. She slammed it down on the table, sending a tsunami of Cocopops onto James's spelling book.

'Mum!'

'Sorry. Oh sorry. Sorry for everything in advance.'

'Kids,' said Frank, 'Mum needs our help. It's all hands on deck. Mrs Fleance is coming.'

Posy didn't point out that it was of course, all Frank's fault that she had overslept and forgotten about Mrs Fleance. The night before Frank had gone out early for a gig. Posy had put the children to bed and then spent her evening cleaning mud off the school shoes, sorting out washing, picking up toys etc., etc. ad infinitum, ad tedium. She hadn't stopped until eleven, when after a few bowls of Special K Red Berries, she had finally gone to bed. Frank had got in soon after, waking Isobel, and filling the house with *the stench of his kebab*. It had taken Posy a very long time and many trips up and down the passageway, to get Isobel back to sleep. Frank had passed out on the sofa with his half-eaten kebab on his legs. He had woken up, freezing, at three, wondering what he had been watching. He stumbled up to bed, and woke Posy again by loudly and inconsiderately stubbing his toe on the bed.

Posy knew that it was not in her best interests to bring this up yet. She could save it for after Mrs Fleance had gone. She needed Frank's help.

'If I was Kate the smell of this morning's bread would be wafting around the kitchen. She'd have some cookies in the oven by now,' Posy, said.

'Pity you're so woefully inadequate then isn't it,' Frank said, kissing her hair.

'Posy remembered Delia's wise words on gingernuts: '. . . like most biscuits, extremely simple to make at home and you'll wonder why you ever bought them!'

She was relieved that Frank was being so amenable. A gig the night before usually meant a hangover and a bad mood the next morning. Today he seemed very jolly. Perhaps he hadn't drunk that much or perhaps he was still a bit drunk. Posy opened the kitchen window and lit a lavender candle. There was quite a smell of kebab coming from the bin and Frank's unwashed plate. She didn't comment on it, she couldn't afford to lose his goodwill at this crucial point.

'I'll supervise them getting washed and dressed. Frank, can you tidy up the front room? I might have time to hoover.' Might Mrs Fleance go upstairs? Tom might want to show her something in his bedroom if they hit it off. She would have to check what sort of a state that was in too.

'Come on kids, lets go and get dressed. Tom, Mrs Fleance, who is going to be one of your teachers next year, is coming to

visit. She's very kind. You could do a drawing for her if you
wanted.' That would impress her. Tom was a great artist.
'Let's find you something nice to wear, Tom.' (Some nice
middle-class clothes, she might have added. Kids' Stuff tartan
trousers with a co-ordinating T-shirt, or perhaps the lamby
fleece that Flora had bought him.)

Posy tidied like a mad thing, a whirling dervish. By ten to
ten she had turned into a will-o-the-wisp, but everything was
more or less done. Frank seemed to have made quite a good
job of the front room, and Tom had been very good, and was
now playing quietly in his room. Mrs Fleance arrived five
minutes early.

'Don't you live nice and near the school,' she said.

'Do come in. Excuse the mess. Would you like some coffee,
or a cup of tea? I'll just go and get Tom, and put the kettle on.'
She meant Mrs Fleance to go into the front room, but she
followed her into the kitchen.

'Mrs Parouselli leaves burning candles unattended,' Mrs
Fleance wrote in her invisible notebook. 'Is Mr Parouselli at
work?'

'Oh he doesn't work,' Posy blurted out. 'Well, he does, but
he's a musician, so it's odd hours. Surely Mrs Fleance would
know that from teaching Poppy, and James before her? Surely
it had been put on countless school forms? Could it possibly be
that the Parousellis didn't figure as large in Mrs Fleance's life
as she did in theirs?

'Would you like a biscuit? I'm sorry they aren't very
exciting.' She offered the tin of digestives. 'I don't know
where Tom has got to. Why don't you go on through to
the front room and I'll round him up.'

'Thank you.'

Don't follow me upstairs, don't follow me upstairs, Posy
willed her. It worked. In his bedroom Tom had pulled out all
of the dressing-up things and taken off all of his clothes, apart
from his Bob the Builder pants. So much for looking middle-

class. He had drawn red and black lines all over his face and chest. Posy sank down on the bed. She picked up Tom's blankety, a mistake. Underneath were damp comics, an apple core, a banana skin, Action Man in his spacesuit, and Poppy's fairy wand which had snapped.

'Tom! How could you!'

'Do you know where my headress is? I can't find it. I don't want to be Batman.'

'Tom, how could you? You know Mrs Fleance is here.'

'I'm going to kill her with an arrow.'

'If I find you your headress will you promise not to kill her, or even shoot at her? We have to be friendly. She's nice, and she's come to visit you, to make friends ready for next year.' White mum speak with forked tongue, Posy told herself. 'Do we have a deal?'

'OK.'

'Your feathers are in the animal box.' Poppy had counted them as a parrot, and tidied them accordingly.

'Thanks Mum.'

'Come on. And lets put these trousers and this T-shirt on you. Indian's never reveal their Bob the Builder pants.'

'Only trousers,' he said darkly.

'OK. But come on.'

Mrs Fleance would have had time to go through all of their belongings by now.

They found Mrs Fleance reading the spines of the books.

'Hello Tom,' she said in a special 'I am talking to a child' voice. She squatted down to be at his level. 'Have you been dressing up?'

'No,' said Tom.

'Oh he always looks like that,' said Posy. 'Especially the felt pen.'

'I'm sure it will come off in the bath.'

'There was a dead slug in our bath,' said Tom.

'Oh. Do you like animals?'

'Woodlice,' said Tom.

'We have some fish at school. And some ants in a special tank so you can see what they are doing. And some worms. Last spring we had some chicks.'

'I know. Poppy cried when they were all dead.'

'He does have a very good memory,' said Posy.

'What sort of things do you like to do, Tom?'

No answer. Tom looked blankly at her. He is actually very bright and very charming, Posy felt like saying. He could write his name before he started pre-school. But she knew that it was pointless, it would count as nought, availeth nothing, signify nothing.

'Tom, why don't you go and get some paper and pens?' she said.

'Can I watch a video?'

'Not now darling. You know we don't watch videos in the morning or when we have visitors.'

'Yes we do.'

'So you like Indians do you?' asked Mrs Fleance, trying to be tactful. 'I suppose "First Americans" would be more accurate.'

'I like their horses and their weapons,' said Tom, who had suddenly decided to be friendly. 'And they always had picnics. I like picnics.'

'What do you think they ate?' Mrs Fleance asked.

'Baked beans and, and, and . . .' He couldn't think of anything else.

'I have got to ask you to fill out this form, Mrs Parouselli. Now where did I put that pen?' Her bag had slipped sideways, spewing some of its contents onto the sofa. 'Maybe it went down here,' she said. Posy watched in horror as Mrs Fleance slipped her hand down the side of the cushion, and then withdrew it holding something brown and dried. It could only be a piece of Frank's midnight kebab.

'Oh.'

'They ate pemmican,' said Tom.

'Well your vocabulary really is very good,' said Mrs Fleance.

'Let me take that,' said Posy. She held out her hand and Mrs Fleance let it fall into her palm. 'I am very, very sorry. Let me put that in the bin.' She tried to walk casually out of the room.

'I'll just be in the kitchen slashing my wrists!' she felt like calling back.

At quarter to eleven when Mrs Fleance had gone, Posy called Flora for a chat. The phone rang and rang. Flora must be out with a client, but she would never forget to put the machine on. This was worrying. Then it was answered, but not by Flora.

'Oh hello. That's not Flora is it? Sorry. I must have dialled wrong Sorry.' She was about to hang up when the voice said,

'She's just in the shower. Shall I ask her to call you?'

'Yes please, it's her sister.' She felt like adding 'And who might you be?' Perhaps someone was keeping Flora prisoner in her own house.

'Oh. Hello. This is Stella. I did your daughter's party. How are you?'

'Er, fine.' And rather taken aback.

'When's the next birthday?'

'Flora's actually. August 11th.'

'Oh, thanks. Here she comes now.'

Flora came into the bedroom in her white waffle-cotton kimono. She was planning to buy another now for Stella.

'I hope you don't mind me picking it up. It kept ringing. I thought that you wouldn't want to miss a job. It's your sister,' Stella told her.

'Thank you,' said Flora. 'Shower's all yours.' She kissed Stella's bare shoulder, a shoulder that certainly passed muster.

'I can't remember why I rang now,' said Posy. 'Are you all right? Not ill?' Flora taking a shower this late in the morning, her phone being answered by somebody else, it was unprecedented.

'No I'm fine. More than fine. Stella's here, the magic person.'

'That's lovely,' said Posy.

'Mmm,' said Flora, taking a sip from the cup of tea that Stella had made her. 'Why don't you bring the children over for tea one afternoon this week? Or we could all go for a picnic in the Watermeadows.'

Stella was nodding enthusiastically.

'Would Stella bring the doves?'

'Posy says "Would you bring the doves?" '

Stella just laughed.

'I was just going to tell you about the awful time I've just had with a visiting teacher,' said Posy. 'But we'll catch up later.'

'I'll call you tonight,' said Flora. And she would just have time to do this while Stella threw together a nasturtium and walnut salad and picked a few extra flowers to decorate the lavender sorbet.

It was a Father's Day card to stop the heart. Frank couldn't believe Melody had sent it. She must be planning to force the issue. He smiled grimly at his own pun. Of all the cards in all the world, Melody had picked out this one, a rabbit with an oversized head saying 'Hi Daddy on Daddy's Day,' When he opened it he saw that there was an ulterior motive.

Dear Frank,
Happy Father's Day from Francesca. She's doing great, but wonders why she hasn't seen her Daddy for a week or so.

Also there are some things I need some help with and I don't just mean money. She's nearly too big for her Moses basket. Her cot's arrived but needs putting up. I thought

you might decorate her room too. We've moved in now.
Call me.
Luv,
Melody.

PS It says you need a phillips alan key.

He screwed up the card and put it in his pocket. He was
screwed. He still couldn't believe this. How could all this have
happened to him? How could it? He wondered if he might be
able to ignore them for ever. For ever until the blood hounds of
the Child Support Agency sniffed out his non-existent income.
Did they take credit card debts into account, he wondered,
offset them against the putative father's putative income?
They didn't actually have any disposable income. Or should
he be thinking *he* didn't now? But when he thought about the
baby he felt love for her sparking and flickering inside him.
    He had no idea what Posy would do if she ever found out.
With any luck she'd just kill him. She'd probably get off with
probation. Dear God. He could hear them all coming in now,
the bump of the pushchair up the step, her key in the door, the
children shouting,
    'Daddy! Are you in? We're home!'
    Posy struggling as usual with the straps on the pushchair,
saying,
    'Let's get your sun hat off, Come on baby . . .'
    He couldn't bear it. Silently he slipped out of the back door
and legged it for his shed.

The next day Caroline and Finn were coming for tea. If Frank
had been the sort of person who didn't leave his clothes in a
heap on the floor by his side of the bed, if Posy had been the
sort of person who stuck to her guns and really did refuse to
pick up and sort out her husband's dirty washing, and if she
hadn't been bothered about how untidy the whole house was,

even their bedroom which Caroline would never have gone into anyway, then she might not have found the card as she emptied Frank's pockets, intending to wash his greasy two-months-at-least-since-they-had-been-washed jeans.

'I cannot think of this. I cannot think of this. I cannot think of this. I will freeze my mind. I will not think of this until they are gone. Inject the brain and soul with Botox.'

She carried on with the cleaning.

When Caroline and Finn had gone she pinned the card and letter up on the noticeboard above the sink. It obliterated the school newsletter, Isobel's vaccination appointment, the virgin-white terry bib that Flora had bought for Tom in New York which Posy used as a cheer-up decoration ('Mom You Are Gorgeous' it said), the leaflet about the Pilates class that she had yet to attend, the expired coupons for nappies and baby wipes.

When Frank returned she did not look at him. She was never going to look at him ever again. Her tears were scalding.

They did not speak until the children were asleep.

'Posy, I'm sorry. What do you want me to do?'

'To never have existed. And don't you ask me what you should do. How about drinking bleach? But not anywhere that I have to clean up the mess.'

Frank left the room. A few minutes later she heard the front door being quietly shut. How considerate of him, she thought. She ran after him.

'Coward!' she yelled. She would have been even angrier if she'd known that he took this as a suggestion and went for a few pints at The Cowherds on The Common.

It is a fact universally unacknowledged nowadays, Posy told herself, that children sleep better when their daddy is in the house. All I ever wanted to do was to have a sensible family, to be able to get through bank holidays without a scene of some sort, to have my children growing up in an atmosphere of love, of security, where they can rely on their parents not to do anything awful. I know I didn't mean to get married and have children when I was a teenager. I shouldn't have. I should have turned out like Flora and turned into Aunt is. I should never have let things turn out messy. My ambition was to Not Get Divorced.

She could hardly think about it. It was like acid thrown in her face. And how could she bear to tell anyone? She wouldn't. She'd say that if they wanted to know the reason for the Parousellis falling apart, they would have to ask Frank. Perhaps if she completely ignored it, didn't speak of it, it would all go away. And what was she going to say to the children? And Flora? And Kate? And the Aunts?

Posy wondered what she would have to do to get someone to take over. Sit down in the school playground and cry? She would probably just be given a cup of tea and a talking to in the school office. Not turn up to collect them? Climb out of the bathroom window and run away? But of course she couldn't. She walked around with her fists so tightly clenched that by the evening her fingers and wrists ached, and there were little pink crescents in her palms where she had dug her nails in.

By day it was as though it had not happened, as though she had been pricked by a poisoned needle and had fallen asleep, but nobody had happened to notice. Life continued. The children were taken to and from school and pre-school. Isobel was got up and fed and played with and put down for naps and got up again and fed and played with. Life was as normal apart from Posy not looking at or speaking to or even acknowledging Frank's existence. This lasted for four days. She felt so lonely and miserable that she kept wanting to call The Samaritans, but whenever she went to pick up the phone she was interrupted.

'Mum, my wand is broken. Can you fix it with sellotape or glitter glue?' Poppy held the two halves out, her eyes full of tears. 'And the Prittstick's all dried up. And the tinsel's all coming off.'

'I know, I know, I'll try.'

'Mum, can I have a plaster on my knee?'

'It isn't cut.'

'But I want one to stroke.'

'Can I have one too? I want one to sniff.'

Why bother having feelings, Posy thought. Surely it was an evolutionary dead end? No time for feelings. Better to be a robot.

'No you can't have plasters, just for nothing, if you don't need them.' ('Keep your arms soft, but your lower body hard like steel,' she told herself.)

'Muuum, oh Muuum . . .'

'Go and play outside.' 'I am hard like steel, I am hard like steel,' she told herself.)

And of course Tom fell over and grazed both knees and needed two plasters, and Poppy managed to find a tiny cut that merited a plaster too. And by the time this was done Isobel had woken up from her nap, so that was it. No more time to herself for another six hours. When the children were asleep Posy took very long showers or baths and cried. She found that as soon as the water started running she could start crying. When she finally got out she could make herself stop. Then she would go to bed and cry some more until she heard Frank coming up the stairs. This would make her freeze, and stay frozen until her next shower.

Then one evening he said,

'Can't you just talk to me? I don't know what I am meant to be doing.'

'Are you expecting me to help you?' she said, her voice flat, cold and hard. Her face an icy pond. 'You are not worthy of my thoughts, you are beneath contempt. I cannot even think about you, contemplate what you have done. I regret every moment I have spent thinking about you, ever. I can only hope that none of the children will turn out anything like you.' She was about to leave the room when she heard Isobel's sudden anguished cry. She was up the stairs in the most dignified scurry that she could manage.

Isobel had a temperature. She was pulling at the hair behind her ear. Definitely an ear infection.

Frank loomed like a huge stupid sheep in the doorway of Isobel's room.

'Want some help?'

She was rocking Isobel, singing softly into her hair, wondering if the Calpol was in the upstairs or downstairs bathroom cabinet, or perhaps in the kitchen cupboard, what about that baby Nurofen? Was it all right to give her both or, or might some Olbas Oil clear the blocked tubes, and would she be able to get an early appointment at the doctors?

She turned her back on him.

'Perhaps you have forfeited the right ever to hold her again,' she said.

'Posy. I only did it once. I just made one mistake.'

She felt like screaming obscenities at him. She turned her back so that he wouldn't see the hot tears that were now running on to the downy dark swirls of Isobel's hair. She heard Frank retreating down the stairs, and then the familiar squirt of the wine-box tap. He hadn't told her what that one mistake had been; now he thought about it, his one mistake had been staying in Southampton. If only, if only . . . saddest words in the English language.

'Self-indulgent shit head,' she thought, but didn't say. She was determined that she wouldn't do anything wrong, that she would get to hold on to every scrap of the moral highground.

He might at least get the bloody Calpol. It didn't take much imagination to fetch that and Isobel's Tigger beaker with some water in it.

But Isobel had fallen asleep again. She put her back in the cot and stood there for a few minutes watching her breathe. In the bottom of the airing cupboard was a rolled-up futon. She hauled it out and silently spread it out beside the cot. She found the spare quilt. It was the one she had owned as a girl, had brought to university with her. She still had the yellow and white stripy cover that her mum had bought for her. It was washed and faded almost to transparency. It was the first one she could find in the dark heap of towels and tablecloths and dinosaur-themed bedlinen. She was pleased. If only she could slip back in time, not meet Frank, but then of course no children . . . She was soon asleep, even though it was only half past nine.

Isobel woke and cried again several times in the night. So did Posy. In the morning she woke with her fists clenched, her teeth gritted, ready to fight. To be angry before she was even awake, that was pretty impressive. She was crammed full of anger, hatred, and resentment. She was a stuffed date. Thick marzipan anger rolled around a walnut, hard and nubby, insoluble hatred, stuffed into her split self.

They got an appointment with Dr Patrick for 9.40. That, at least, was good.

The doctor was Posy's favourite. Usually you had to wait weeks for an appointment with her, or try your luck at the Monday Wait and See surgery which started at 12.30 and lasted all afternoon. People started queuing for it at 11 a.m. Dr Patrick did most of the surgery's antenatal work. That was how Posy knew her. Dr Patrick had two children of her own and a husband who went pot-holing at weekends.

Isobel's name was called at 10.15. This was prompt for Dr Patrick. She was too kind. She listened to her patients and took too long. Posy had often wondered whether doctors kept their patients waiting in order to wear them down. It seemed to be a successful method of reducing people to a state of tearful anxiety where they would reveal their true feelings quickly, and spill the beans about what was really wrong. It got her every time. And so it was that when Dr Patrick said:

'And what's the trouble?'

The whole story, Frank, Melody, the baby, came pouring out. Blood and guts on the consulting room floor.

'Well,' said Dr Patrick. 'I'm afraid I really don't know how to make that one better.'

'But Isobel has an ear infection. That's why I'm here. I didn't mean to say any of that. You must think I'm mad. A crazy fantasist. But it all seems to be true.'

'Let's have a look at these ears . . . mmm. This one is quite inflamed. You'd better have some Amoxycillin. That will sort it out.'

'Thank you,' sniffed Posy. 'It's probably Frank's fault. He still smokes. I told you he didn't when I was pregnant, but he does. Only in the garden and in his shed. It's his fault. A psychic connection.'

'Undoubtedly. Now about you . . .'

'I haven't been right since Isobel came along . . . I just always seem to be struggling. I feel as though I've got my boots on the wrong feet all the time, or my trousers on back to front or something. That I'm forever scrambling up a shingle bank and slipping back down with my shoes full of stones. It all seems to be stormy weather, heavy weather, I don't know which one I mean.'

'Perhaps you've had some post-natal depression.'

Posy nodded silently, crying again.

'I'm sorry to make a fuss.'

'Have you tried St John's Wort? It's very unpleasant, the tea, but very, very good. I don't want to give you Prozac straight away unless you want me to. You are quite right to be depressed. There would be something wrong with you if you weren't very, very unhappy at the moment. You need to work through this. Somehow you will. You will. I know it doesn't seem like it, but you will.'

'I haven't any choice. The children,' said Posy, with a vague wave of her hand, indicating the invisible presence of James,

Poppy and Tom. 'I feel as though I can't exist as a real person. I have to just keep going through the motions, keep functioning until I can react. I don't know what to do. There isn't any solution.'

'You have to think about what you want.'

Posy nodded, but found herself thinking, 'What I really want is a flat stomach.' She was amazed that she could be so frivolous and cold and so alone all at the same time.

'Could anyone help you, your sister? A friend?'

'I haven't told anyone. I can't have them all thinking and pitying me. Everything is ruined for ever.'

'Then don't tell anyone yet. It's amazing how little people notice about those closest to them.'

Posy nodded. Reached for yet another tissue.

'Or you could make him tell them all.' The doctor said this with a sly smile. 'But I am going to refer you for Therapeutic Therapy. It's something we are doing a trial study on. It's an experimental pilot scheme, usually only available privately, and there's even a crèche.' Dr Patrick opened her desk drawer and found a pink stripy folder, much prettier than the sort of thing medical professionals usually use. She took out a card with an address and a design of primroses on the front. Inside were columns for dates and treatments.

'Pitty pitty Mummy,' said Isobel reaching up for the card. Posy smiled.

'She's never said "pretty" before.'

'Your mummy is pretty,' The doctor told her. 'And this will make her look even prettier. Now Posy, don't whatever you do mention this to Frank. And we'd be grateful if you kept it as quiet as possible. Places are very limited and if word gets out we'll have a real clamour. Private pleasures are often the sweetest. Remember that you deserve this. Don't go for the flotation tank until you feel much better, they usually make people cry. Unless you want to have a good cry, of course.

'Give them a ring. They're open till late. You have to make

your own bookings. You have ten sessions to be used over the next ten months, quicker if you want. Make the most of it while it's free. They'll give you a diary. It would be very helpful if you could keep a record of how helpful or otherwise it is. To help us get future funding if it's effective. And I'd better see you again soon. We'll try Prozac in a couple of weeks if you need it.'

'Thank you, thank you.' Posy scooped up Isobel and their huge bag of changing stuff, breadsticks, books, boxes of raisins, spare clothes. The people in the waiting room glared at them. Dr Patrick was now running forty minutes late.

Posy strapped Isobel into the pushchair and headed for the chemist. While she waited for the antibiotics she read the list of treatments. What should she choose? Aromatherapy Massage? Deluxe Jessica Pedicure [with hot wax bootees]? Vital Eyes Treatment? Aromatherm Perfect Legs? The list went on and on. She smiled. She would ring them as soon as she got back. There was still nearly a month to go before the end of term. Perhaps she could fit in two visits before then, perhaps three . . . and then maybe in the holidays she could leave the children with Flora or Kate and still go. Oh, the Doctor had said there was a crèche. It said complimentary refreshments too. What bliss, what luck.

She walked back up the hill and home. At the top of the road she could see lorries with fairground rides, huge trailers bringing marquees, men putting up signs to direct the balloonists, exhibitors and visitors to various parts of The Common. It was the Balloon and Flower Festival at the weekend.

Frank was out, doubtless hiding from her. Good. Pitty pitty Mummy, thought Posy. Pity Mummy. Pretty Mummy. Pity Mummy.

She made a booking for the following week. Aromatherapy facial with back, neck and shoulders massage. That sounded rather good.

The post had been. Yet another Mini Boden catalogue and a

letter that, with the wonky typing and second class stamp, could only be from her Aunt.

> Dear Posy,
> We hope you are all keeping well. Bea has had a rather nasty fall in Morwenstow church and has broken her wrist (fortunately her left one), whilst I have gashed my leg on Barney's gate. It is taking its time to heal, and the district nurse is coming every few days to replace the dressing. Between times we are putting honey on it, but my rather poor circulation is making it all rather slow and tiresome.
>
> I wondered whether you and or Flora might be able to come and spend the hols with us. We don't have many parties booked, but there will be the usual trippers I suppose.
>
> It would be delightful to see you and your brood, and we would be jolly glad of an extra pair of hands or two, even though yours are already so full.
> With best love,
> Your Aunt Is.

She wiped Izzie's sticky hands and face, changed her nappy, and put her up for a nap. She made herself a cup of tea and sat down to phone the Aunts.

'Aunt Is?' said Posy.

'Yes,' she barked.

'It's Posy. Thanks for your letter. I was so sorry to hear about the leg. How is it now?'

'Oh, still very tiresome.'

Posy knew that Aunt is would never admit to anything of her own being painful. She also admired the Aunts' telephone style. They would say only what needed saying and then hang up. No endless chit-chat. Posy knew that she had to state her business quickly.

'We'd love to come,' she said. 'As soon as the summer holidays start. That's on the 23rd.'

'Jolly good,' said Aunt is.

'We'll stay as long as possible,' Posy went on, 'maybe for the whole summer. Frank and I weren't planning on going away anywhere, so this will be a lovely holiday for the children. We'll have to bring the rabbit, but she can go in with the hens, can't she? I haven't asked Flora yet, but I expect she'll come down when she can get away. She's very busy with work, as usual. I don't think Frank will be coming.'

'Not at all?'

'I don't know. We've been having some problems.' Posy could feel her lip tremble. She felt like blubbing. She hoped that this wasn't detectable.

'Oh dear,' said Aunt Is, 'Sorry to hear that.'

Posy couldn't think of anything to say. There was a long pause, the sort that would usually signal the end of a phone conversation with her Aunt. She could hear Aunt Bea in the background shouting 'Get down demon dog!' and then a metallic sort of quiet thump, the sound of the lid of a cake tin being replaced. She thought she could smell Madeira cake coming down the wires.

'My dear, er, do try not to worry,' Aunt is said. 'These things tend to work themselves out.'

'This is pretty bad,' Posy said. 'I wish I was with you now.'

'All this business about love,' Aunt Is said, 'I do sometimes think its importance is much exaggerated.'

'Maybe,' said Posy. 'But you do have Aunt Bea to keep you company.'

'Ah yes. I suppose I don't really have to think about it much.'

There was a chink of teacups. Really, Posy smiled to herself, they should get jobs doing sound effects for radio plays. Tuck in, she thought, tuck in.

188

It was time she told Flora.

'Flora, it's me. Could you come over? I need to talk to you about something.'

'I'm in John Lewis. In a queue in Toiletries. I've got present buying and wrapping to do. Could you come and join me?'

'Better not. I haven't got long before I pick Tom up. Sorry to sound so feeble as usual.'

'Would you like me to come round? I could be there very soon.'

'Yes please. If you've got time. It's all a bit awful.'

'Nobody's ill or hurt are they?'

'Not really.'

'Why not just tell me now and get it over with.'

'Um. It's pretty awful.'

'You aren't pregnant again? Oh Posy, no more!'

'Not me. This 22-year-old. Melody.' She spat the name.

'What do you mean?'

'Well, she's not pregnant any more. She's had the baby. I found out through a Fathers' Day card Frank had left in his pocket. Apparently he and Melody . . .'

'Posy, no!'

'Yes.'

'That is disgusting. How could he?'

'Er. I don't know. He says they only did it once.'

'What? Well that's hardly the point.'

'No. It seems that it is a girl. Called Francesca.'

'Oh my God. I just can't believe this. I mean, I know things haven't always been great between you two . . .'

'Well I thought they were more or less OK. I thought we were just tired and struggling a bit.'

'What are you going to do?'

'I don't know.' Posy was crying now. 'What am I meant to do? Send an "It's a Girl" card? Pass on the baby clothes? There is no solution. Look, I know you have to go.'

'I don't.'

'Come round later. I can't face saying anymore about it now.'

'OK. I just can't believe this.'

'Nor could I.'

'And it's all so tacky,' Posy said between sobs.

'I love you. I'll see you later.'

Flora arrived with very many John Lewis bags. She hugged Posy for a long time. Posy started to cry. Flora kissed her hair. Smoothed it back from her teary face. Posy wiped her nose and eyes on a bit of kitchen roll.

'You look about twelve.'

'I feel about twelve. Or a hundred and twelve. I wish I didn't have any feelings. I haven't told anyone else. I feel so ashamed.'

'Posy! You aren't the one to feel ashamed! You haven't done anything.'

'I've let it all go wrong.'

'Absolutely not.'

'How do I hold my head up in the playground? What are the children going to feel like?'

'You can't be the first person this has happened to.'

'The first one that I know.'

'You don't have to tell anyone anything. Just say nothing. Or say you split up and can't talk about it.'

'We haven't actually split up yet.'

'Can you forgive him?'

'No.'

'Live with it and make it work?'

'I can't think. I don't know what I want, except for it never to have happened.'

'Mmm,' Flora nodded.

'My main feeling towards him at the moment is murderousness. You could take out a contract on him for me. That would be a perfect solution. If I could go back in time and vaporise him when we were students . . . but the kids. What am I meant to do? It's their so-called Daddy. I can't decide on the extent to which I should poison their love for him.'

'Mmm.'

'I look at the boys and I think, I hope you don't turn out anything like him.'

'Oh I just can't believe this. It's awful.'

'So awful.'

'I'm glad the house is all yours. Maybe you should throw all of his stuff out of the windows.'

'He doesn't even have any decent clothes for me to slash. He probably wouldn't even notice. And he's hardly got any stuff. He just doesn't have much. Only what students have, records, books and his instruments. Everything else seems like mine or the kids. I can't bear to tell them. What do I say? "Oh Daddy thought you weren't good enough so he is starting another family with another new baby and a person called Melody?" '

'Oh Posy!'

'Well, at least Francesca will grow up in a Sure Start Area . . . In a way it bloody serves him right. He hates the newborn phase. Or perhaps he's missed that. I don't know what he's doing. I don't know how often he sees them. I don't think he's faced up to any of this. He doesn't know what to do. I think he wants me to make some sort of decision so he doesn't have to.'

'Typical.'

'But I don't see why I should give him that luxury. I don't know what's best anyway. Except for none of this to have happened.'

'I don't think I can ever talk to him again. Oh Posy, how could he? He had everything.'

'I think he thought it was nothing.'

'Look, I'll make us some tea.'

'I'll sit here and sniff.'

Flora was soon back with the teapot and some mugs on a tray. Posy had tried to pull herself together and was standing looking out of the window at The Common.

'And what does Frank say?' Flora asked.

'Nothing.'

'A car crash is the best idea. A freak accident with the amp. Or push him off a cliff. The balcony of a Weston tower block.'

'I don't know if they have balconies. A baby in Weston with no garden.'

'Don't start feeling sorry for them.'

'It is awful for everyone.'

'But mostly for you.'

'Does Frank love her? Is he in love?'

'I think he's incapable.'

'Had he been seeing her for a long time?'

'He said it only happened once. I really don't know what has been going on or what to believe. My life wasn't meant to turn out like this.'

'It hasn't turned out yet. Anyway, stupid messy things happen even in Jane Austen.'

'I really don't think anything good can come of this.' It wasn't something that she could blink into non-existence or rationalise away

'No,' said Flora.

'Well a baby has. Does that make it somehow good?'

'Posy, your judgement about babies is really warped.'

'Umm. I just can't think of this baby being related to mine. It's unthinkable. She even has a nice name.'

'Calling her Francesca was a low shot. Blackmail. This Melody must really want him.'

'Maybe she can have him. If it wasn't for the children . . . I don't know what's best for them. I don't even know what Frank wants, if anything. Posy, Melody – what's the difference? Two stupid names. I almost don't care.' She was crying again. 'All of our slipping-down flakiness is revealed. We can't pretend to be a proper family anymore.'

'Come here. Sit down,' Flora led her to the sofa. 'You might

as well cry. Oh how could he do this to you? Beautiful Posy.
Kind Posy. Precious Posy.'

'Stupid Posy, blind Posy, ineffectual Posy, duped Posy,' said
Posy.

Flora's arms were around her. Her fair curls and Posy's
dark ones mingled.

'You have yourself, and the children, and me. Look, our
hands and arms are the same. Together we're strong. We're
one of those Indian goodesses.'

Posy smiled and tried to wave one of her arms gracefully.

'I think we look more tragic pre-Raphaelite,' she said.

'Are you saying I have a thick neck?' Flora laughed.

'No! And your skin is still lovely. Mine's not,' said Posy.

'Look. I brought you some things.' Flora started to unpack.
'I know this doesn't make any difference, but it might help a
tiny bit. You should have nice things.' There were bottles and
jars and tubs and tubes of wonderful potions. Things that Posy
would never in a million years have bought for herself.

'Flora, this is too extravagant!'

'I wanted to. I could make it tax deductible if I wanted, but I
don't. And there's some stuff from Waitrose that I left in the
car. I'll just go and get it. Put some of that Origins "Calm
Down" cream on.'

'Here you are,' said Flora, coming back in with three
bulging carriers.

'Flora, you really didn't have to. Sadly I haven't lost my
appetite.'

'But I wanted to. I hope it's all stuff Frank hates. He doesn't
like fruit much, does he?'

'Only nectarines.'

'Good. I got peaches instead. Come through and I'll
unpack it.'

In the kitchen Flora started to unload it onto the table.'

'It all looks beautiful,' Posy said. 'Thank you.'

'How does it go?

"Citrons and dates,
Grapes for the asking,
Pears red with basking
Out in the sun,
Plums on their twigs;
Pluck them and suck them,
Pomegranates, figs . . ." '

'And lovely bread,' Posy added. 'And lovely coffee. I'll make some proper coffee in a while.'

'Also chocolate, but only a smallish bar. You know the saying: "Get mad, get thin, get even,' said Flora.

'And you know the saying,' Posy told her,

' "For there is no friend like a sister
In calm or stormy weather" . . .'

They heard Frank's key in the door.

'Oh no, it's him!' Posy looked horrified. 'I don't want to see him at the moment.' Flora slammed the kitchen door shut, but not before she had given Frank a look of loathing and disdain.

'Where are the children, anyway? Their Aunty has to give them a cuddle.'

'Oh no! I completely forgot. Tom's out in the garden. I'd better check on him. He's probably playing with snails.'

He was fine. Just playing with the sand. His chin and T-shirt were stained pink from raspberries.

'Tom,' Posy called, 'Aunty Flora's here! I didn't know we had all those raspberries in the garden. I don't suppose you've any room for some of the lovely fruit Aunty Flora brought?'

'I might. If it's strawberries or plums.'

'Come in then. We'll have to go and get James and Poppy soon. Do you want to come with me to school, or stay with Daddy, if he's here?'

'He waved at me out of the window,' said Tom. 'Can I watch "Thomas"?'

'If you give me a kiss.'

'If you give me a strawberry.'

'I love it when their breath smells of strawberries or raspberries,' Posy told Flora. 'Izzie's asleep. I expect you guessed that. There was something else I wanted to talk to you about.'

'There surely can't be more, or worse,' said Flora, rolling her eyes.

'Kind of. Aunt Is has gashed her leg and even honey poultices aren't working. Aunt Bea has broken her wrist in Morwenstow church.'

'Oh no' said Flora. 'Are they all right?'

'She says it's all very tiresome,' said Posy. 'She wants us to go down and help if we can in the summer.'

'Oh Posy, I will between bookings. I've got a couple of weddings, all the usual stuff. I'm sure I could get down a few times for long weekends. I wonder if Stella might like to come too. She's very useful. And I would like her to meet them. Maybe we could come down for my birthday.'

Posy raised her eyebrows very slightly. 'Well that would be good. Actually, I did tell Aunt Is that you'd come down when you could. I was thinking of taking Lettice and the children and going for the whole holidays. I don't know what to do about Frank. I don't like the idea of him being here all by himself. Or not, she added darkly. "But someone will have to feed the cat, and I don't want to be with him at all.' She offered Flora a piece of chocolate and then went on. 'I really don't know what use Aunt Is thinks I'll be with all the children there, but we'd certainly have a nice time. In her day babies and toddlers spent their time asleep outdoors in their prams, or playing in their playpens.'

'They have still got our playpen in one of the barns. It might be worth trying, you never know,' said Flora.

'It really would be such bliss to get away. I've always wanted to take the children on holiday to Cornwall for the whole summer. And if people knew I was going for six weeks without Frank they'd start to speculate, and maybe I wouldn't have to say anything to anyone. I suppose the children would miss him.'

'But they'd have such a good time. You never know, things might get better.'

'Unlikely, unless he gets a time machine. Or I do. I keep wondering if it's all somehow my fault, that I wasn't paying enough attention.'

'Posy! Don't be ridiculous. He's the one who did it. Write out a thousand times "It isn't my fault. I am in the right." '

Flora thought that in a way Posy might have a point, but she wasn't going to say so. She thought that Posy had never, ever, seemed to pay enough attention to anything.

JULY

'I'M TAKING THE CHILDREN to the Balloon and Flower Festival,' Posy announced to Frank while the children were eating their breakfast.

'Daddy come too! Daddy come too!' Poppy chanted, and he kissed the top of her head.

'Yeah Dad, come,' said James. 'There's rides. It'll be cool.'

'Can I ride my bike?' Tom asked.

'It's much too crowded for bikes. There wouldn't be anywhere to leave it if you were going on things, we'd never get it through the marquees.'

'We never take our bikes to The Common anymore,' Tom grumbled.

'Oh that's not true,' said Posy. 'We certainly took them at, um, Easter. Anyway, your father's in charge of bike-riding so ask him why.'

'We can't take them to the Balloon and Flower Festival, but we'll try and take them out soon,' said Frank.

'And I want my other stabiliser off,' said Tom.

'OK, OK, as soon as I get time,' Frank sighed. Tom had been riding very well and very fast with just one stabiliser since the last summer.

'Time between smoking in the shed, not cutting the grass, going to the pub and doing other unmentionable things,' muttered Posy.

'Mummy, please can I bring Lettice? I want her to see all the flowers.'

Isobel started to pelt the table with pieces of her toast and circles of banana.

'Izzie! No throwing toast!' As Posy bent to start wiping the debris of breakfast from the floor, Izzie scored a direct hit between her shoulder blades.

'I really don't know why I wear black T-shirts. I should wear yellow and brown smear-patterned ones,' she said. 'We might as well try and go early, before it gets too crowded.'

She hadn't planned on doing anything with Frank, but seeing as it was Saturday and everyone was at home, seeing as the children wanted him to come, seeing as taking all four of them to the Balloon and Flower Festival by herself would be a complete nightmare . . .

'Daddy can I bring my bike? Please? Please?' Tom implored.

'OK, Tom. But you won't be able to go on any rides or buy anything or go in any of the tents, or have a go at anything . . .' Frank said. Posy conceded to herself that he could be quite useful with the children sometimes. She decided to just act as though he were coming, as though it weren't an issue. She was determined not to do any arguing in front of the children. Then she had a bright idea.

'Why don't you just take them? I'll stay here and get some chores done.'

'Oh Mum,' said James. 'You have to come. We always all go to the Balloon and Flower Festival together.' Posy realised that he must have sensed that something was wrong.

'Well go and get dressed then. OK, we'll all go.'

Honestly, Frank thought, all this fuss and deliberation about something so simple. It would be at least another hour before everyone was ready to go.

Finally, finally, the children were ready. Posy was packing a bag with drinks of water, nappies, wipes, boxes of raisins, little tubs of strawberries and grapes, kitchen roll, tissues, a bib for Izzie, plasters, antihistamine cream. Frank couldn't stop an audible groan from escaping.

'I think I'll just see if Izzie wants a feed before we go . . .' she said.

'Posy, she seems fine. She is past one . . .' He immediately wished he hadn't said it. He was no longer allowed to make suggestions, or say anything that might be construed as criticism. Now Posy would be in an even fouler mood with him, if that were possible.

'Well you're the expert on babies. Just don't blame me if I have to stop to feed her. Now where's Poppy gone? Oh, honestly.'

'I think she went outside, Mum,' said James, trying to be helpful.

'Poppy!' she yelled, even though Poppy would have no chance of hearing her if she was in the garden, 'Hurry up! We're going! James, go and get her. Be quick.'

Frank didn't know what the hurry was. The bloody show would be open all day for two days. All they had to do was cross a road and walk down a path to get there. Only Posy would behave as though it were one of the Wonders of the World, The World's Fair come to Southampton, a visiting land at the top of The Magic Faraway Tree, soon to move off on its cloud and never be seen again.

That morning they had all been woken by the hisses and roars of the hot air balloons launched for the 6 a.m. mass take-off. There would be another one tonight, more tomorrow, and now they would see some of the balloons tethered in a field at the top of The Common. Frank had got back to sleep, but the children had been up and rampaging since then.

At last James and Poppy returned sniggering from the garden. Poppy had her Miffy rucksack bulging with what Posy supposed were dolls and other unnecessary things to bring. She felt too weak and defeated to protest. She knew that she would end up cramming it all into the pushchair basket or carrying it herself.

As they set off down the road Posy thought 'What a nice picture of a happy family out for the day we must make.' The children were all wearing shorts and stripy tops, Frank was looking as close as he got to smart in some relatively unscathed khaki trousers and a shirt that Flora had given him for his birthday. It remained smart because he hated it and wore it only when nothing else was remotely clean. Posy thought that she herself was the one rather letting the side down in her summer uniform of faded flowery skirt, black T-shirt and dreadful M & S mummy sandals.

Tom was holding onto the handle of the pushchair, telling her all about the things he might ride on, Frank was holding hands with Poppy whilst he simultaneously played plantain 'soldiers' with James. They love him so much, she thought, and he they. Now where had she packed the tissues?

Karim's grandfather was dozing in his front garden on a dining room chair, his baseball cap pulled down over his eyes. He woke up as they passed.

'Mrs Parouselli! Please wait.' The party came to a halt. He went into the house and reappeared holding an envelope. 'Family are all in Pakistan. Please take this. I am too old to go.'

Posy saw that it was one of the raffle prize envelopes from the school fête.

'Oh thank you. That's really kind of you.' She opened it. 'Wow! A hot air balloon flight! Thank you! Oh it's for today. That's so lucky. Thank you. Look Frank! I wonder how many it's for.' She turned the leaflet over. 'Oh, it says "family", that's great. Thank you.'

'It is for you,' he said solemnly.

'Thank you,' said Posy.

'Cheers,' said Frank.

Karim's Grandfather nodded at them and returned to his chair.

'We'll wave as we go over,' Posy called. 'Thanks.'

As soon as they were out of earshot she started to worry. 'Do you think they have crash helmets? Perhaps we should go back and get the cycle helmets. Do you think there are baby-sized ones? Do you think babies are allowed to go? Perhaps Izzie and I will just watch while you all go . . .'

'She is a toggler,' said Poppy. 'Are we really going in a balloon?'

'Maybe,' said Poppy.

'If Mummy thinks that the crash helmets arrangements are sufficiently impressive,' said Frank. 'If the parachutes come with belts and braces.'

At that moment Posy wished that he was dead. She felt as though venom must be squirting out of her eyes at him. She could push him out, or win a real life balloon debate on who was the most at fault.

'Wow, are we really going in a balloon?' James couldn't believe it.

'We'll see,' said Posy.

They went to the so called 'community marquee' first because each year their favourite thing was the Southampton Geological Society's lucky dip. For just twenty-five pence you got a small labelled rock – often rose quartz (Poppy's favourite), or smoky quartz or strawberry quartz or iron pyrite. Elsewhere there were rides and hook the duck, and some of the hot air balloons tethered next to the arena. The children had their faces painted – James as Spiderman, Poppy as a butterfly, Tom as a ladybird. As they wondered what to do next they spotted a small purple and yellow striped tent, like the ones that knights have at jousts.

'Hey kids. It's Linus the Magician! And Stella. They must be doing a show. Let's go and say hello.' Posy's heart was gladdened by the sight of them, but as she approached Linus disappeared into the little tent that was to provide the backdrop for the shows. Her face fell, and Stella noticed.

'Hi Posy! Hi kids!' she said. Frank hung back and Posy noticed that Stella didn't acknowledge him. Posy knew that Flora had been out with Stella the night before, and she thought that Flora would have told her about Frank and the baby – she hadn't asked her not to. 'Linus is just getting changed,' said Stella. 'He doesn't like the audience to see him in his civvies.'

'Pay No Attention To The Man Behind The Curtain!' Linus yelled. 'Mrs Parouselli, I will be right out.' He reappeared in his costume, a dinner jacket with a purple silk lining, a fez, his huge trousers (surely a clown size) held up by green braces. His bow tie was purple, spotty and askew.

'For you,' he said, and presented her with a feather bouquet. Frank looked disgusted and walked off to the next stall to examine a display about Hearing Dogs for the Deaf.

'May I keep it?' she asked.

'Of course,' he said.

'You can't guess what I have in my bag,' said Poppy, doing a twirl to show him her Miffy rucksack.

'And you can't guess what I have in my bag,' he replied, taking off his fez and pulling a black velvet bag out of it. 'Now, James first.' He gave the bag a shake, it acquired some angular bulges. He offered it to James. James pulled out a turquoise calculator with buttons like Smarties. 'It will help you to find the answers,' he said. 'Now Poppy.' This time the bag contained a silver and pink sequinned heart-shaped purse.

'Wow' said Poppy. 'Is it magic?'

'You will always be rich in love,' he said.

'Now Tom.' Tom got a bendy plastic sword. 'To help win all of your battles.'

Isobel was asleep in the pushchair. 'Come back for the show and I'll make her a balloon animal,' he said.

'What about Mummy?' asked Poppy.

'Oh, I don't think there's anything in that black bag for me,' said Posy. Behind them a band struck up. 'We have to go,' said

Posy. 'It was lovely to see you. Thanks for all the presents. We've been given a balloon flight ticket, somebody else's raffle prize.'

Linus raised his impressive eyebrows. 'Well Bon Voyage. Are you all going?'

'Probably,' said Posy. 'I don't really know what's meant to be happening.'

'A common feeling,' said Linus.

'Come on then kids, let's go and find our balloon. Where's your Dad got to?'

'Bye everyone,' I said Stella. 'Flora said she'd come and see us later.'

Frank was now watching the brass band that was marching around the arena. Why was it that marching music always filled his eyes with tears? How he loved those upright xylophones.

The band were dressed in fake-fur tiger costumes. They must be bloody hot in those, he thought, hard to play and march in them, pretty clever. He wondered if they had any vacancies; perhaps that was where his future lay. He could recall seeing them before when they had been bears. Or perhaps that had been their rivals. In which case he wondered who would win in a pitched battle? What would they be like zipped out of their suits? Much camaraderie in the pub or on the coach home afterwards he supposed; or perhaps that very tall one with the trombone was a bully. He was wondering whether to approach them afterwards when he sensed Posy and the children standing next to him.

'Daddy, look what the magician gave us!' said Tom.

'He's not a real magician,' said Frank sourly. 'He's a party entertainer.' Posy looked at him with thin eyes.

'Are those tigers meant to be scary?' Poppy asked. 'Because they are.'

'I think menacing, or sinister might be the words you want, Pops.'

'Do you have to spoil even a marching tiger band?' Posy asked. 'They are meant to be fun, friendly, Poppy,' she said. But Posy could see that Poppy might have a point. 'Come on, let's go and find out about this balloon flight.'

'Can we get an ice cream on the way?'

'I think that might be a good idea.'

Izzie woke up, as if by magic, in the queue for the ice creams. Posy got her a strawberry Mini Milk, a mistake. She would want a Ninety-Nine like everyone else, so of course Posy swapped.

'I wonder how many Mini Milks are actually eaten by children,' Posy mused. The children's chins, hands and fore-arms were soon streaked with ice cream.

'Well I hope we wont be too sticky to be allowed in the balloon,' Posy said when they had all finished, She set to work with the wipes whilst Frank queued at the balloon flight Portacabin window. He returned smiling.

'We can all go. We can either go soon or come back tomorrow, but then the weather might not be right.'

'Go now! Go now!' shouted the children.

'I suppose we'd better go today,' said Posy.

How could she be so downcast about a balloon ride? All the joy really had gone out of her. She wasn't even pleased about this. Was it really just another thing to worry about, to be organised and got through? Then he remembered that, of course, everything was his fault.

'The man said that it's not really a balloon flight, it's just going up for a bit, then coming down again. You stay tethered,' said Frank.

'Well that sounds like a balloon flight as far as we're concerned,' said Posy.

'We have to wait in there, about half an hour,' said Frank.

'Well that will give me time to change Izzie and take everyone to the loo,' said Posy.

If Posy had been a bit quicker with the wipes she might

have met Melody and Melody's mum in the loos. She might have met Francesca. As it was they had disappeared into the tea tent by the time she got to the front of the queue.

Melody waited with Francesca while Anita came wobbling back with a tray of tea, scones and a jug of hot water to warm up the baby's bottle. Melody had reserved a few of the white plastic garden chairs, enough for them to put their feet up and put all their stuff on. The matching table was ringed and smeary from many previous cups of tea and coffee and cakes. The smell of the hot canvas marquee, the trodden grass and the nearby sweet pea displays was quite soporific. Anita always liked to look at the horticultural displays, the hanging basket and fuchsia competitions, the cacti and bonsai exhibits, the roses and begonias. It all seemed a bit pointless to Melody, but she plodded round without complaining. Francesca looked almost insignificant inside her vast Burberryish checked conveyance. It was a pram that was also a car seat and a buggy. Frank had paid for half of it, five gigs that Posy had never known about. It had cost more than The Wild Year's van was worth. Isobel's Silver Cross pushchair, state of the art when Flora had bought it for James, looked scruffy and ancient in comparison, even to Frank. The matching changing bag that Melody had chosen was loaded with more stuff than even Posy could have thought to bring. Posy had missed out on all the paraphernalia and extra baggage of bottle-feeding.

'Oh Mum,' said Melody, 'I wanted a Diet Coke as well.'

'They'd sold out. You'll have to get one outside.'

'Warm her bottle up Mum. That doughnut van'll have some.'

Caroline would have, as she put it, gone ballistic, if she'd seen Finn and Al tucking into their bag of ten doughnuts. If she'd seen the flagon of squash that Al had bought Finn, there would have been hell to pay. If she'd known then about Frank and Melody, and seen Finn being introduced to Melody by the doughnut van, sitting on Anita lap while he ate his fourth doughnut, consorting with the enemy . . . but she was at home, having some time to herself, and would never find out, at least about the doughnut and the squash. The doughnut van was also out of Diet Coke. Melody bought herself a raspberry Slushpuppy.

'She's really cute,' Al told Melody as Francesca drained her bottle. ('An empty bottle is a reproach – Penelope Leach' is what Posy would have said.)

'Look at those blue eyes!' Francesca's eyes were beautifully, impossibly blue, exactly like Frank's. Al realised that might not have been the best thing to notice, 'And that golden hair,' he added quickly, 'just like her Mum's.'

'Her middle name's Sapphire' said Melody. 'Want a cuddle?'

'Sure, said Al, though nothing had been further from his thoughts. 'Pass her over.'

Francesca Sapphire was dressed in a lilac and white outfit of many ruffles. Al thought that it didn't look very comfortable for a baby. Anita spent many hours ironing little Frankie's things.

Al had completely forgotten what babies felt like, but it all came rushing back, the weight of them in your arms, the heavy, heavy head.

'She is gorgeous,' he said. He found that he had to do some hefty sniffing, 'Hey she smiled at me! Look Finn! She wants to be friends with us.'

Finn looked up from the little square tub of jam that Anita had given him.

'What can she do then?' he asked.

'Just smiling, pooing and crying,' said Melody.

'Soon she'll be laughing and sitting up, rolling over, crawling . . . you'll have to get your flat all baby-proof,' said Al, concerned. Melody did seem very young to be in charge of a baby.

'Hey, I am her Mum,' said Melody, taking a big swig of her

SlushPuppy. She rattled the ice against her teeth. Instant headache.

'If you want any help Melody. You know I'd love to . . .'

'Cheers,' said Melody.

'That's an offer you can't refuse,' said Anita.

'You could come back for a cup of tea, on your way home, if you wanted. I could give you a lift in the van . . .' He had biscuits, those new white mugs, he even had a litre of fresh milk in his very clean fridge. He could picture the baby kicking on the soft cotton rug that Flora had chosen for him. Melody would be pretty impressed with that box of toys. He'd get a changing mat, anything she wanted. He had new sheets, a new quit, even a spare cover.

'I dunno,' said Melody.

'It's only down the road,' said Al.

'We've got Mum's car,' said Melody. 'Bloody miles away, in the car park.'

'Maybe one day next week then, maybe go overflew songs. We've missed you. It's ages since you sang with us.'

'I've had my hands a bit full, haven't I?' said Melody.

'I've done my place up,' said Al. 'Painted, all new and clean. It's really nice.'

'Dad got me my own bed, and a pop-up tent with balls. You could put your baby in the tent,' said Finn. Melody offered him some of her SlushPuppy.

'How about Wednesday then?'

'Don't you work?' asked Anita.

'He does a lot of work for charity,' said Melody

'Paid,' Al put in. 'And the band of course. I'm going back to teaching next term too.'

'You're a teacher are you?' This looked promising.

'Yup.'

'I didn't know you were a teacher, Dad,' said Finn.

'I took some time out from it while you were a baby,' said Al.

'Oh. My mum's a teacher too,' said Finn.

Al decided it was time to go.

'Come round on Wednesday.' He wrote his number on a napkin. 'Great seeing you. Look, she's fallen asleep.' He carefully passed Francesca back. Melody deftly strapped her into the pushchair. She wasn't someone who would be fazed by harnesses, correct adjustment of car seats, and the workings of microwave steam sterilisers.

'Quite a machine you've got there,' he said.

'Pardon,' said Anita.

'Nice pushchair. Great to see you. Come on Finn, let's go and find the bouncy castles.'

'He looks like a great dad,' Anita said, as soon as they were out of earshot.

'Mmm,' said Melody. 'And he's already divorced.'

There were no crash helmets to fit the most junior balloonist, but the Parousellis decided to risk it anyway. It was just going up whilst remaining tethered and then coming down again, but thrilling none the less. The enclosure where they-waited was next to the entrance to the main flower show marquee. Posy closed her eyes and breathed in roses, popcorn, candy-floss, lavender, doughnuts, the strawberries the children were eating, all her favourite smells of summer. A display of police dog antics was now taking place in the main arena, the children were entranced and clapped at appropriate moments. Isobel shouted 'Woofman! Woofman!' whenever a dog trotted by. Frank stared away from the festival towards the trees. They didn't speak.

'Parouselli family,' called the balloon-ride organiser.

'It's us, it's us!' shouted Posy. 'Come on.' She frantically loaded everything that they wouldn't be taking into the tray of the pushchair. 'Come on kids, dump all your stuff,' she said.

'I need to bring this,' said Poppy. She had taken off her Miffy rucksack and was clutching it.

'Really Pops,' said Frank, 'your dollies wont mind staying here. They'll be quite safe.'

James gave a huge snort.

'What's so funny, Jimmy?'

'Come on, time to get in,' said Posy. How typical of us, she thought, to have been waiting for half an hour and then not be ready when our names are called.

The balloonist helped them into the basket, he was firing up the gas, casting off.

'We are going to have such a lovely view of everything,' said Posy. 'This is so exciting.'

'I can't believe we're really going in a balloon,' said James. 'This is the best day of our lives.'

'And Lettice's,' said Poppy. She opened her rucksack with a flourish. 'Abracadabra!'

Lettice peeked out of the top.

'Poppy! How could you! You can't take rabbits up in hot air balloons.'

'You didn't say she couldn't bring her,' said James.

'James you knew! You were in on this! You should have known better!' Posy was too astonished to appear very cross.

'Aiding and abetting the bringing of a rabbit to the Balloon and Flower Festival,' said Frank. 'That's pretty serious, Jimmy.'

'Is that a rabbit you've got there?' asked the balloonist. 'I can't be responsible for a rabbit.'

'Mightn't she be able to cope with the altitude?' Posy asked.

'What if she jumps out?' said the balloonist. 'I don't have bunnychutes.'

'She won't jump out,' said Poppy. 'She'll be very good.'

'She is a very well-behaved rabbit,' said Posy.

'It's "no dogs except guide dogs" ' said the balloonist.

'But she's not a dog,' said James.

'She will be good,' Poppy pleaded, stroking Lettice's velvety ears. 'Please.'

It was then that Lettice caught a whiff of the horticultural exhibits. The lure of the vegetables was too much. She leapt out of Poppy's arms, over the rim of the basket and into the crowd. Posy, still holding Isobel, was after her, neatly scissor-jumping over the side in a way she hadn't known was still possible. Poppy, James and Tom scrambled after them.

'There she goes!' yelled Posy, seeing a white tail bob beneath a tent flap. They apprehended her in front of the Southampton Allotments Association display. James stole a carrot for her.

'Let's get back to the balloon now,' said Poppy. 'I'll keep her in my bag.'

'I'm holding on to her for now,' said Posy. Managing with Izzie and Lettice was tricky but possible.

But they were too late. The balloon was taking off. They didn't see the flash of purple silk and a bobbing Fez as Linus untied the ropes and disappeared back towards his tent, because, of course, the show must go on

The children were waving and half crying. Posy stood with Isobel on her hip, The rabbit under her other arm. Her hands were too full to wave goodbye, her mouth hung open, an empty balloon. Above the children's heads the speech bubbles floated up but popped before they could reach Frank.

'Come back Daddy! You're leaving us behind!'

'Bye Daddy!'

'Bye Daddy!'

The roar of the gas drowned their voices. All he could do was yell 'Sorry!' and spread his hands, pantomiming helplessness.

'Isobel was whimpering. Posy had to act fast or they'd all be sobbing. James helped her to cram Lettice back into the rucksack. She wrestled Isobel back into the pushchair.

'Let's all go and ride on the biggest carousel. I'm sure we'll all get to ride in a balloon another time,' she said. 'And how would you like to go to Cornwall for the whole summer and look after the donkeys and hens and be-ice-cream people in the cafe?'

'Yeah, Mum, yeah!'

'Come on then, kids, let's go.'

They all looked up and saw their Daddy's balloon drifting away over the trees, heading east.

'Dad can find his own way,' she told them.

'What by balloon?' asked Poppy.

'By baboon,' said James. They all laughed.

'It was an accident,' said Posy. 'He didn't mean to leave us behind. But never mind.'

They passed a bin overflowing with ice-cream wrappers, cans, popcorn boxes and the sticky polythene bags that had held candyfloss. Wasps buzzed around it. Posy pushed off her bendy M & S sandals and chucked them in.

'Mum! Your shoes!' Poppy was horrified.

'I'm getting new ones,' Posy explained.

The shoes of the future were dancing towards her: sun-bleached sandy canvas deck shoes, a pair of sparkly jellies for the rock pools, some ankle-length wellies like the ones her aunts favoured, some red velvet ballet pumps that somehow she really would buy. Here they came, dancing towards her over the shards of all her broken dreams.

A NOTE ON THE AUTHOR

Rebecca Smith is the author of one other novel, *The Bluebird Café*. Born in London 1966, she lives in Southampton.

A NOTE ON THE TYPE

This old style face is named after the Frenchman
Robert Granjon, a sixteenth-century letter cutter
whose italic types have often been used with the
romans of Claude Garamond. The origins of this
face, like those of Garamond, lie in the late
fifteenth-century types used by Aldus Manutius
in Italy. A good face for setting text in books,
magazines and periodicals.